FOOL'S ERRAND

ALSO BY JEFFREY S. STEPHENS

Rogue Mission
Targets of Revenge
Targets of Opportunity
Targets of Deception

Crimes and Passion (A Robbie Whyte Mystery)

FOOL'S ERRAND

JEFFREY S. STEPHENS

Post Hill
PRESS

A POST HILL PRESS BOOK

Fool's Errand
© 2020 by Jeffrey S. Stephens
All Rights Reserved

ISBN: 978-1-64293-738-1
ISBN (eBook): 978-1-64293-739-8

Cover art by Cody Corcoran
Interior design and composition by Greg Johnson, Textbook Perfect

Post Hill Press
New York • Nashville
posthillpress.com

Published in the United States of America

"Every good deed a man does is to please his father."

—*Maxwell Perkins*

For Blackjack…Now we're even.

CHAPTER ONE

It was September of 1979, and my father had been dead more than six years when I discovered his letter. I can still imagine him sitting down to write it, enjoying the prospect of carrying his secret to the grave, leaving behind a mysterious legacy, creating a puzzle for me to solve, all of that. I don't believe he intended to cause me the trouble he did, but he had to realize that once I found the note I would have no choice—I would have to chase after the clues he provided, fumbling for answers no one was willing to give, tracking down an international theft that happened decades before.

By then I had a successful career in advertising, my life was on a decent course and—to the great relief of my mother—I had navigated the dangers his life posed for me. When his letter surfaced, all of that was turned upside down.

But I'm getting ahead of myself. I should begin, I suppose, by explaining the ruckus at my cousin Lena's wedding.

It was a wintry Saturday afternoon in March, a couple of years before my father died. The day was cold and, although my cousin Lena had her heart set on an outdoor wedding, she was already well into the third term of her pregnancy, so waiting for warmer weather was out of the question.

As my father was so fond of saying, timing is everything.

Lena lived with her parents in Rockland County, which is on the other side of the Hudson River from New York City. My Uncle

1

Vincent and Aunt Mary were proud of their home, even if it looked like all the other homes on their street. It was a modest split-level covered with aluminum siding, set on a half-acre of lawn and trees in the midst of a quickly growing suburban sprawl, but, compared to our cramped apartment in the southwest corner of the Bronx, it seemed like a palace in the wilderness.

A distinction not lost on anyone in my family. Especially my father.

The morning of Lena's wedding, my father, mother, sisters and I prepared for the day, vying for time in our one bathroom, as it became increasingly steamy with each shower. We dressed in our Sunday clothes, which was all sorts of fun for my sisters, but an awful inconvenience for me. I was in from college for the wedding and, although I remembered to bring my sport coat and a clean shirt, I forgot a tie, which meant I had to wear one of my father's. This was an issue, not only because our taste in clothing was far from the same, but because he was finicky about his wardrobe. He went on about the stains, burns or other havoc I might inflict on his precious silk, eventually handing me some dark blue relic that widened to about eight inches at the bottom and probably last hung around his neck when he saw Sinatra at the Paramount.

Finally, when everyone was ready, we trudged down three flights of stairs single file, piled into my father's big, blue-green Oldsmobile 98, and headed off to join the festivities.

* * *

ARRIVING AT THE SMALL CHURCH, we found it was already packed and the opening sermon had begun. Unlike the rest of my father's relatives, my immediate family was never religious. My mother is not Catholic—she's not even Italian—so it was never a big part of our lives. All the same, Uncle Vincent saved us a space in the first pew, from which we had a good look at the priest, an elderly gentleman with a pleasant smile who seemed intent on moving the service along as swiftly as possible. Perhaps, given the size of Lena's midriff, he feared she might give birth right there in front of God and the entire congregation.

The sacred formalities complete, we made our way back to Uncle Vincent's, where everyone poured into the house, jamming the place to the rafters.

Lena's wedding reception was a family affair, with no caterers, waiters, bartenders or other hired help. Mismatched dishes, serving plates and glasses were borrowed from various relatives, which was fine, because it was the food that mattered, and the food was wonderful. It was presented in a huge buffet, featuring lasagna with marinara sauce set beside a large bowl of meatballs, and a huge tray of sausages and peppers that sent the aroma of garlic and sautéed onions floating through the house like a sweet mist. Baskets of large, crusty Italian breads were everywhere, accompanied by condiments, such as black olive spread, caponata and other dark concoctions I found inedible throughout my childhood. Thick discs of spicy red pepperoni were alternated with small, milky white slabs of provolone in a pattern that spiraled around a large platter like fallen dominoes. There were wooden boards featuring prosciutto, salami and crumbly chunks of parmigiana and Romano cheeses. And, as I say, there was bread everywhere.

Chianti flowed freely from large jugs as the adults in the group got themselves pleasantly *ubriaco*. As they moved from one noisy conversation to the next, they left half-finished glasses of wine sitting on tables and credenzas and shelves, finding clean goblets and filling them again. The younger kids were having a good time sneaking sips from the abandoned glasses, and I wondered how many of them would wind up doubled over in the backyard by the end of the night.

Grandparents, great-aunts and great-uncles took their rightful places on the comfortable couches and chairs in the living room, while aunts, uncles, cousins and assorted others roamed about. The Serious Men, such as my father, Uncle Vincent and my older cousins, took over the dining room, where they showed their real mettle by hitting the scotch bottle as soon as we all settled in.

Serious Men, as my father explained to me innumerable times, are distinct from other men, who were not to be considered serious. It had nothing to do with a somber affect or an underdeveloped sense of humor, although that was often part of the profile. It had to do with an attitude toward life and career choices. Corporate workers, for instance, could never be considered Serious Men or, for that matter, Action Guys, another important designation. Corporate types were tied to their desks and did not enjoy the freedom of time and movement essential to being a Serious Man. Civil servants, the oxymoronic title given government employees, similarly could not be Serious Men, unless they were on the take.

Serious Men and Action Guys could hold jobs, just not the nine to five variety. That was the domain of Working Stiffs, who aren't available to meet for espresso at eleven in the morning, or to sit through weekday lunches that last three hours, starting with whisky, moving to red wine and finishing up with anisette and coffee. These gatherings, built around discussions of Big Deals, necessarily exclude the Working Stiffs, not only because they have to be back at the office in an hour, but also because Working Stiffs are, by definition, small thinkers.

From what I've seen over the years, Serious Men rarely get anything serious done and Action Guys seldom swing into action. Serious Men certainly discuss serious matters quite a lot, and once in a while an Action Guy will engage in some violent endeavor, but mostly they just talk, scheme, argue, eat and drink. They really ought to be called Get-Together Guys, because that's what my father and his cohorts would do, get together. From time to time he would bring me to lunches where I heard talk of a lot of big plans and great ideas, most of which were big and many of which indeed sounded great. Unfortunately, I never heard of a single plan or idea at any of those lunches that came to anything. As you'll come to see, the brawl at Lena's wedding was caused in part by the discussion of a Big Deal my father mentioned, which turned out to be the same Big Deal he wrote me about in the letter I found all those years later.

Sorry if that sounds confusing. In my family, as in so many others, we really needed to pay attention.

The fact that my father never told me about his Big Deal before he died, choosing instead to leave me a letter I would have to figure out for myself, was the sort of contradiction that defined him. If he wanted me to do something about the stolen money, you might think he would have mentioned it to me somewhere along the line. He did not. He was a mass of paradoxes.

I'm not bragging, for example, if I say he was possessed of a surprisingly agile intellect, since he was also capable of revolting ignorance. On the one hand he could be warm and generous, but on the other, was such a racist that he judged almost everyone first by ethnic makeup, usually with some negative connotation. We had more than one argument where I accused him of bigotry, but he insisted he treated every group pretty much the same. He was just as likely to call an Italian a wop as he was to insult a black man, Jew or Puerto Rican, which in his mind meant he was fair.

Go figure.

He adored reading Yeats and Shelley and Keats, yet he sometimes earned his living by breaking a stranger's arm for not paying a gambling debt or smacking someone around for falling behind on the payment of usurious interest charges they owed to his boss.

That said, he couldn't bear it if someone didn't like him.

When I was ten or eleven, there was a mentally challenged man who used to round up shopping carts at the local supermarket and roll them back inside, two or three at a time. As far as I could tell, that was the guy's entire job. Every time my father and I went to that store, to pick up milk or bread or whatever, he would give this man a big, smiley greeting. The man never responded, never changed his facial expression—he had serious issues, for God's sake—but it really bothered my father that the man was not friendly toward him. As far as Blackie was concerned, the man shouldn't allow a slight case of Down's Syndrome to interfere with their relationship.

To each his or her own contradictions.

* * *

MY FATHER WAS THE YOUNGEST of the three Rinaldi children, Uncle Vincent the oldest, my Aunt Anna in between. His given name was John but most people called him Blackie, or sometimes Blackjack, owing in part to his love of gambling but mostly because of his appearance. He had a dark complexion and eyes that seemed to be made of polished ebony, shining with an intense quality that made it clear he was not someone you wanted to cross. He wasn't as tall as he claimed, at least three or four inches under six feet, but he was broad shouldered and powerful. He had a large nose, small mouth, a cleft chin and straight, jet black hair, those last two features convincing his mother he looked like an Italian Cary Grant. As the baby of the family he was his mother's *adorato,* for whom she chose *Santo* as his confirmation name, which ought to tell you something.

I have to say, I never saw any particular resemblance to the actor, but he did have the cleft chin, and he always got the hair right.

The afternoon of Lena's wedding, as others occupied the rest of the house, Uncle Vincent was holding court in the dining room, seated at the head of the table. My father was to his left and their father, known to everyone as Pop, was to his right. My grandmother had died years before, and Pop was almost ninety by then. The rest of us seated around Uncle Vincent's oversized dining room table were all men, young and old, talking and laughing and passing around bottles of booze and wine and beer, all one big happy family.

Happy, that is, until my cousin Frank slapped my father across the face.

The dining area was not large to begin with and, with all the extension leaves inserted in the table, the chairs were pushed to the outer limits of the room. The walls were adorned in an ornate floral print of dark reds and golds, and a brass ceiling fixture with a dozen small lights hung low over the center of the table, all of which made things seem even closer. Anyone wanting to leave his seat would need the cooperation of at least three other people, unless he was prepared to climb over them.

The table was covered with a white linen cloth that seemed big enough to do service as a circus tent. By the time everyone had eaten, it was soiled with spots of wine, coffee and various tomato sauce drippings, littered with ashtrays, wine and liquor bottles and covered with broken walnut shells, torn orange peels, espresso cups and every imaginable type of drinking glass. Conversation flew back and forth in this direction and that, interrupted only by calls for the bottles that were in constant motion as they were handed around. Some of the men were smoking cigarettes, the noxious fumes forming a gray-brown cloud that hovered over the table, feeling thick enough to threaten rain.

My father and uncle were drinking Johnnie Walker Black Label, the scotch of choice for special occasions in the Rinaldi clan. Pop was sipping Chianti and repeatedly announcing, to anyone who would listen, that he never indulged in hard liquor, not like his *sciocco* sons.

Given the quantity of liquor being consumed, the cast of characters in attendance and the cramped room, it was obvious to me, long before the slap occurred, that there was simply no way the evening was going to end quietly. There were forces at work that only a fool would call chance. Even Joe Btfsplk could have made book on the outcome.

"You're the best friggin brother in the whole world," my father said for about the nineteenth time in the past hour. He gave the statement special emphasis by gathering Uncle Vincent into an affectionate headlock. "Don't you worry. Don't any of you worry. Blackie's gonna take care of everybody," my father told us. "Benny and I have you covered. You wait and see." Then he gave his brother's head another squeeze.

My father was bigger than my uncle, not in height but in brawn, and with each drink and renewed declaration of fraternal affection, Blackie became increasingly physical.

My uncle disliked roughhousing, particularly since he had a back problem that caused his neck to remain painfully stiff. And, while that suited his personality—when he voiced an opinion, his posture gave the statement a haughty air—it was not helpful to have his brother draped around his shoulders.

None of this was lost on my father.

When he told us again how terrific Vincent was, he made it sound as if you'd have to be an idiot not to realize that my uncle was America's poster boy for Big Brother of the Year. He followed the statement with another bear hug, followed by a little pinch of my uncle's cheek and a series of gentle love smacks.

Blackie was a great button pusher, he really was, but if there was one guy on the planet he could not get to, it was his older brother. When my father let go of my uncle to have a taste of his scotch, Uncle Vincent simply sat back and sipped his own drink.

"I remember when we were kids," my father told the group, "I remember how Vincent took care of me." He moved his head side to side, looking into the distance in that way people do when they're so drunk they've lost their ability to focus. "Took care of me," he said again, followed by yet another headlock and a soft little smack on Vincent's face. "Now I'm gonna take care of him and everybody else in the family. Everybody. Am I right Vincenzo?"

My cousin Frank, Vincent's son, was a year older than I and far better suited to my father's peculiar world than I would ever be. Deciding it was time for him to get in the act, he said something like, "Hey, Uncle Blackie, you're always talking bullshit about your big deals. What the—," but Uncle Vincent cut him off in mid-sentence.

"Mind your business son. If you want to sit with the men, then act like a man."

It was, as they say, too late.

Blackie was already glaring at his nephew, a withering stare that everyone in the room knew was no sort of bluff. Say what you might about my father, his bite was definitely worse than his bark.

"You little snot nose," Blackie hissed across the table. "Who the fuck are you to talk to me that way?" He didn't wait for a reply. "I saw you with shit in your diaper, and as far as I'm concerned you're still not man enough to wipe your own ass."

We'd all had a lot to drink, as I've explained, but when Frank started to get out of his chair I began sobering up fast.

Frank said, "Maybe you should keep your hands off—"

"Siddown," Uncle Vincent hollered at his son. "What's between me and my brother is just that—between brothers." He pointed a finger at Frank. "Don't make me say it again."

I couldn't tell if my uncle was being sincere or if he was just trying to save his son's life, but my cousin heeded the warning. Frank fell back into his chair, between me and our other cousin, Nicky, and things became quiet for the moment. But that was not going to last for long, as my Uncle Vincent and I understood better than the rest.

Blackie loved my cousin Frank, but that wouldn't stop him from caving his head in if he felt it needed to be done. For now, my father was content to grab his brother around the neck again, good and tight this time, and start kissing him on the forehead.

"You see, Pop?" Blackie said to his father. "You see how Vinny always takes care of me?"

My grandfather nodded slightly—you don't get to be ninety by wasting a lot of unnecessary energy. He took a sip of his wine and said, "*Bene*," although I wasn't sure if he was commenting on Uncle Vincent's protective instincts or the taste of the Chianti.

Whatever Pop meant, Blackie took it as license to engage in another full-scale assault on his brother. He grabbed at Vincent's face with both hands, and I had this image of Moe Howard going at one of the other Stooges with a series of rapid-fire slaps.

Then Vincent, from beneath the barrage, said, "All right, John, that'll be enough."

My father drew back slightly, a wounded expression on his dark face. "Vinny," he said. Then he said it again, "Vinny," and his hurt look broke into a drunken smile as he slowly reached out, grabbed another handful of my uncle's face and gave it a good squeeze. "You think this place of yours is a house?" he asked, the smile fading. "I'm gonna have a house where you can put this whole joint in the friggin' garage. You hear me?"

As the anger rose in my father's voice, the room went quiet, the other men turning away or staring down at the table.

"What, you don't believe me?" Blackie asked them. "All I gotta do is snap my fingers and the money is there."

"Enough," my uncle said softly.

Blackie turned back to his brother, as if just remembering he was there. "Vincent," he said, then lunged forward with both arms extended and wrapped my uncle in a vicious headlock.

That was when Frank sprang across the table, screaming, "Get your hands off my father," managing to reach far enough to land a glancing slap alongside my father's head.

It was one of those events when time seems to stand still, all of us frozen in place until my father rose from his seat. The table was too large for him to flip over, especially with Frank still stretched across the width of the thing, but Blackie managed to give it a violent shove.

"You miserable little bastard," he hollered as Nicky and I grabbed Frank's legs and pulled him back just before my father's fist came crashing down where my cousin's head had been.

The liquor bottles and glasses that Frank hadn't already knocked down went tumbling over, some falling to the floor.

The other men in the room began scrambling to their feet, except Pop. He slowly slid back against the wall, out of the line of fire.

Uncle Vincent said something quietly to my father, then extended a hand as if to help Blackie back into his chair. But my father smacked his hand away.

"What the fuck are you talking to me for? Talk to that piece o' shit son of yours, cause after I get my hands on him you won't be talkin' to him for a long fucken time."

Blackie did not curse much, not unless he was very drunk or very angry. That night he was both. He climbed past my uncle and began to make his way to where Nicky and I had taken hold of Frank's ankles. As he came toward us, he stared directly into my eyes.

"Stay the fuck out of this, son, it's not your fight."

Recognizing the look, I decided to take his advice.

Meanwhile, Frank wasn't waiting to see what Nicky and I were going to do next to help his cause. He spun free of our grasp and took off like an Olympic sprinter.

By now the yelling in the dining room brought in the first wave of women to see what was going on. "Blackie, Blackie," my Aunt Anna intoned over the din as she poked her head in the room. "What wrong, Blackie?"

Blackie wasn't in the mood for a chat with his sister. He pushed two of the other men aside as if they were mannequins, providing a clear lane out of the dining room. Hot on the trail of my fleeing cousin, he stomped into the living room, where all conversation abruptly came to a halt.

My Aunt Anna's sons, Richard and Butch, were a couple of strapping young men in their late twenties, and they had the best chance of slowing my father down. They followed him, and were now on his flanks, my Uncle Vincent and I right behind.

My father spun to his left, then his right, searching for his prey. When he saw his brother, he demanded, "Where the hell is he?"

Uncle Vincent calmly said, "Sit down, will you please, John?"

"Sit down? I'll sit on that little fucker's head." Blackie glared at his brother. "You let your kid treat me like that, Vincent? That's how you raised that rat bastard?" He reached up and tenderly touched the side of his face, as if Frank had gashed him with a grappling hook rather than landing the barest of slaps.

Someone hollered out that Frank had left the house, a few of the women were imploring my father to stop the madness, and I think if everyone had just let him alone he might have headed out the front door and walked it off. But a lot of the other men were also drunk, and a couple of my uncles made the mistake of grabbing Blackie's arms and suggesting he take it easy.

Taking it easy was not in my father's repertoire at the moment.

Pulling away from them, Blackie did a neat pirouette and threw a right cross at the biggest guy in the place, Aunt Anna's son Butch.

The yelling and screaming resumed when everyone realized that two of Butch's teeth had gone flying across the room.

"My teeth," the big guy started hollering. "My fucken teeth." And there, in the midst of all this, my cousin Butch, all six foot something of him, dropped to his hands and knees, crawling around the beige broadloom carpet of the living room floor, blood dripping down his chin, looking for his missing teeth.

Blackie had no intention of helping Butch search for his teeth, instead shoving his way forward and turning for the kitchen. I'm not clear why he went into the kitchen, but the crowd followed him, backing him into a corner, which was not a great idea.

I made an effort to edge my way forward, foolishly thinking that I ought to say something. This had gone too far, and I was his son, after all.

As I neared the front of this mob scene, my uncle Fred stopped me. "Better stay outta this, kid," he told me. "Leave it to us."

Realizing how well he knew and loved my father—not to mention my own wealth of experience with Blackie—I backed away to let the elders sort things out.

By now, my father was shouting, "Get the fuck outta here, all o' you," but how many of us can turn away from an approaching train wreck? It was apparent no one was going anywhere, so Blackie reached up to the wall rack and pulled down a butcher knife that looked about two feet long. "I'm telling you," he hollered as he waved it at us, "get the fuck outta here," and the crowd shrunk away just enough to stay out of range of the blade.

That's when my Aunt Mary forced her way past everyone and got right in his face.

She said, "Stop this right now, John. Are you out of your mind?" That was one of my Aunt Mary's favorite expressions, and it was nothing short of remarkable how often she could work it into a conversation. At the moment, it happened to be the perfect fit.

"Stay outta this," Blackie warned her.

But Aunt Mary was not about to stay out of it. This was her kitchen—with its yellow-flowered wallpaper and avocado green appliances, which were quite the rage in those days—her knife, her daughter's wedding and her son that Blackie was looking to slice up. She also had a special relationship with my father. If Vincent was never actually the big brother Blackie pretended he was, Mary had always been one hell of a loyal sister-in-law.

Aunt Mary held out her hand and said, "Give me the knife, John." The room full of drunken people became quiet as everyone watched Blackie standing there, his weight shifting uncertainly from one leg to the other.

"Stay outta this," he told her again, but there was less conviction in his voice this time. Not only did he love Mary, but she was a woman, which meant he couldn't shut her up by dropping the blade and hitting her with a series of left and right combinations.

"I won't stay out of this," she announced firmly. "One of my neighbors called the police. They're going to be here any minute. You hand over that knife, I'll make some fresh coffee and we'll sort this whole thing out."

Fresh coffee? I was surprised my father didn't burst out laughing.

People were jammed into all three doorways to Aunt Mary's kitchen—one leading to the dining room, one to the living room and the third to a short flight of stairs down to the family room. My father jerked his head back and forth, like a cornered grizzly bear, assessing his choices, his husky figure framed by the large bay window behind him.

"Get outta my way, Mary," he growled, although she wasn't exactly in his way and he hadn't actually made a move toward her.

"Don't be ridiculous," she replied with her sweetest smile. "You're not going to knock down your old sister-in-law, are you?"

Uncle Fred stepped up, standing just behind Aunt Mary. "She's right, John. Put the knife down and we'll go inside for a cup of coffee." When he began to move forward, my father slashed the air with the stainless steel blade.

Uncle Fred jumped back.

"Stay away from me," Blackie warned him. "And stop with the fucken coffee."

Brother of the Year, Uncle Vincent, was nowhere to be seen—I've always believed he was the one who called the police—so the next to approach my father was the bridegroom, who managed his way through the crowd until he was alongside his brand new mother-in-law.

"Hey, Uncle Blackie," Ray greeted him as he approached, already three sheets to the wind himself. "Let's go downstairs and have a drink. Somebody really did call the cops, so we better cool it for a while. Whadda ya say?"

My father was still looking at Mary. "Come on," she said softly, holding out her hand again.

But this was no time for my father to gracefully retreat. He'd backed himself into a corner, in fact and in form. What was he supposed do, put down the knife and go inside for espresso and a polite chat?

So, when the doorbell rang out front, he made his move. In one wild motion he threw the knife to the floor, wheeled around and, with his hands over his head, went crashing through the glass of the bay window, onto the back lawn and into the darkness of the night.

Ray, not about to miss this sort of adventure just because it was his wedding night, promptly executed a drunken leap through the jagged glass in pursuit of my father.

I was not about to risk getting cut to shreds, but something told me I had better keep an eye on Blackie, so I shoved my way down the stairs, through the family room and out the back door. What you may or may not find surprising was the identity of the fourth man who joined our little party that night. My cousin Frank had been lurking just outside, waiting to see how the drama played out. When my father came flying through the window, followed closely by Ray, Frank hollered "Wait up," then he and I chased them around to the driveway. As my Aunt Mary would say, we were out of our minds.

Standing in the cold, Frank pulled out a bottle of Johnnie Walker Black Label he had cadged from his father's liquor cabinet as he ran out. We all had a taste, then started talking—and laughing, if you can believe that.

The important point is that it would be years before I learned of my father's letter, but looking back I realized that night was the first time I heard Blackie discuss Benny and the stolen treasure, even if he was short on details.

CHAPTER TWO

At this point, a little background on my parents and how I came into possession of the letter would make sense.

They met in the late 1940s, shortly after the war ended. Blackie had returned from three years overseas, determined to write a personal account of his days in Europe and be hailed as the next Hemingway. Unfortunately, his need to earn a living got in the way, and the best job he could find was as a liquor salesman, logging endless miles in a Ford sedan, traveling from one end of New York State to the other hawking the virtues of second-rate whiskey and cheap gin to thankless bartenders and perpetually cash-strapped restaurant owners.

My mother was several years younger, a wannabe model in Manhattan. She could be found most days behind a counter in Lord & Taylor selling ladies lingerie, spending her off hours posing for artsy snapshots in a West Side photographer's studio. She wore her blond hair long and combed to one side, a peekaboo style fashionable in that era. She longed for the moment when she would be discovered as the next Veronica Lake—when she would become known as Roxy or Cherie or anything other than Harriet—all golden tresses, creamy complexion and a smile that was part virgin, part vamp.

By the time they met, reality had taken a large bite out of their dreams, but love can often fill life's voids. Harriet saw Blackie as worldly and exciting and just a little bit dangerous. Blackie saw Harriet as young and beautiful and smart, that last quality a throwaway bonus.

It was a cold January afternoon when they tied the knot, my father twenty-seven, my mother not old enough to vote. They found a small tenement apartment in the Marble Hill section of the Bronx, where they barely had time to unpack the dishes and arrange their meager belongings before discovering they were going to become parents.

It was May when they learned she was pregnant, a rough adjustment for my mother who, having just turned twenty-one, was still being weaned from her cover girl aspirations. By Christmas she was nursing a colicky infant with a penchant for boils, ear infections and insufferably long crying jags. It didn't leave her much opportunity to negotiate the difficult transition into married life, especially since she was shouldering most of the burden alone.

Be assured, Blackie never changed a single diaper.

As my mother negotiated the difficult transition from aspiring ingénue to housewife, Blackie's career path was taking an unexpected turn.

By all accounts, my father was a good salesman who was simply given a bad choice of products to peddle. Drug addicts generally make bad candidates to run a pharmacy and you never want a sex fiend to oversee your harem. If Blackie had been selling shoes or widgets he might have made a decent show of it. But he was selling liquor, spending his time in the company of barflies and wiseguys, becoming seduced with tales of easy money and good living, all through a haze of companionable drinking. He was introduced to illicit means of supplementing his paltry income—from running numbers to picking up and delivering gambling payoffs. He soon graduated into arranging loans from nameless men who were willing to provide the cash, in exchange for exorbitant interest to be paid by those "broken-downers" that Bankers Trust didn't want as customers.

Blackie was on the road to becoming a Serious Man.

While my mother didn't approve of Blackie's choice of employment, she didn't have much to say about it. Divorce wasn't as popular then as it is now, especially for a young woman whose responsibilities had grown—in the four years since I made my entrance, my two sisters arrived on the scene—and whose husband was now reporting income on his federal tax return of about four hundred and fifty dollars a year. As a Serious Man, Blackie's job as a salesman was long gone, together with any semblance of a regular paycheck. What was Harriet going to do in divorce court? Tell the judge her husband worked for bookies and loan sharks and ask if they could please arrange to have her support payments dropped off?

Added to this was the peculiar fact that my mother really loved him. Some people say that doesn't mean much when you have no real choices in life, but I kind of believe it's just the opposite.

No one in my family was going anywhere, and fast.

As for me, I don't think I was ten years old yet when I realized my father worked for the mob, or whatever it was called in those days, but I'd already seen enough television to put together the bits and pieces I overheard when he was on the telephone or when one of his business associates came to visit. One day, while he was working in his bedroom with one of his confederates, I strolled in and asked them what they were up to.

"Nothing, son. Why don't you go back inside?"

I stood there, looking at the scraps of paper strewn across my parents' bedspread. Blackie and the other man were standing side by side, sorting these fragments of information, my father making notes on a pad. "Are you bookmakers?" I inquired politely.

This was apparently the funniest thing my father's friend had ever heard. Once he started, he couldn't stop laughing at the notion that some little pipsqueak had "made them," as the expression goes.

Blackie looked at me solemnly and asked, "What does that mean to you, son? Bookmaking."

I stared at the bed again and thought it over. I had certainly heard a lot of my father's jargon, but had no idea what it meant. "I'm not sure," I admitted. "Do you make books out of all those pieces of paper?"

Well, if Blackie's pal thought I was funny before, I was now the second coming of Jerry Lewis. He said, "You got some kid there, Blackie," and went on roaring. "We better keep an eye on this one."

God, was I a riot or what?

My father stood up, came over and put his hands on my shoulders. "It's something like that son," he said. Then he turned me around and pointed me toward the door. "Why don't you run along and I'll explain it to you later."

"You promise?"

"I promise."

Blackie was fairly reliable at keeping the promises he made to me when he was sober, so that was good enough for me. After they shut the bedroom door behind me, I could hear the other man still howling.

On Saturday mornings, one of my favorite activities was riding in the car with my father while he made his rounds. I loved that term, "rounds." Made it sound like he was a surgeon or something. In fact, his rounds consisted of picking up money and betting slips and making payoffs all over the Bronx and the northern reaches of Manhattan, areas like Inwood and Washington Heights. I've been on New York City streets I'll bet the police don't even know exist, dark and twisty lanes with warehouses and factories and tenements and bars. Always bars.

I spent countless hours sitting in the car, waiting for him outside those places, wondering what was going on inside, reading my schoolbooks or studying the people on the street, and always worrying about my father. I was not sure why I worried, I supposed it was just instinct. Even so, I would often pass up neighborhood games of baseball or football or stickball, just to spend that time with him.

Over the years, my mother fought hard to keep me away from Blackie's business, and when I graduated high school, sending me away to college was going to be one of the proudest achievements of her life. She not only wanted me to have a good education, but she also needed to provide the ultimate insulation between me and the Serious Men my father associated with—distance.

Blackie had other ideas.

One afternoon, during the summer before I set out for the university that would take me three hundred miles from home, my father asked me to take a ride with him to Tenafly, New Jersey. What he didn't tell me, and had definitely not mentioned to my mother, was that he'd located a dealer with a used XKE convertible for sale.

For the uninitiated, you need to know that the Jaguar XKE was more than a car. It was a passion. It was a work of art. Even now, it occupies a unique place in the Pantheon of the most beautiful cars ever built.

That day, when my father and I drove into the parking lot of the dealership, Blackie had this big, wicked grin on his face. "Come on," he said, "I want you to see something."

We entered the showroom and there it was, sitting in the middle of the floor, its top down, the dark red paint Simonized to a high gloss, glistening in the sunlight that streamed through the large, plate-glass window. The XKE appears to be moving even when it's standing still, and I noticed that the cars on the road outside slowing as they passed, people ogling the sensuous lines of the sexiest car in the world.

My father introduced himself to the salesman, saying something about being the guy who called about the car. The salesman then turned to me.

"Go ahead young man. Get in. See how it feels."

Get in? I couldn't believe he was asking me to get in.

"Go ahead," Blackie said with a little underhand motion intended to propel me forward.

So I walked over and opened the door and it felt great. I mean, this was some kind of door. You could feel how solid it was just by opening it, so I shut it, just to feel the weight and test the perfect fit. Then I opened it again.

"Get in," the salesman said again. "Just eleven thousand miles on this beauty."

I lowered my butt into the seat, which felt about six inches off the ground, swung my long legs under the dash and pulled the door shut. I was at the wheel of an XKE.

When I looked up at my father, he and the salesman were smiling. I opened the door and began to climb out.

"What's the rush?" my father asked. "How does it feel?"

I sat there, half in and half out of the car, staring at my father. "What's this about?"

"You like it?"

"Like it?" He must have been kidding. I turned back to study the burled wood dashboard, the leather seats, the gearshift with the polished walnut knob. Then I looked at him again. "I love it," I said. And I did. I loved it. How is that possible, to love a machine? What is it about cars? "I love it," I said again.

"Good," my father responded simply. Then he turned and said something quietly to the salesman who nodded his understanding. I was still dangling there, neither in nor out of the car, when Blackie said, "Come on, let's take a walk."

We went outside, which is where Serious Men often go to discuss something serious. We were in the parking lot, walking slowly away from the showroom, when he said, "Beautiful car, eh?"

"Beautiful," I agreed.

"That's the car you and your cousins are always talking about."

"That's the one."

He nodded, not speaking for a while. Then he said, "Here's the deal. You stay home and go to city college and I'll buy you the car."

I stopped walking and gaped at him. Even at my impressionable age I knew the tradeoff was absurd. I also knew what this was about. My father was conflicted about my going off to school in Pennsylvania—not because I wouldn't cut it, but because he would miss me—yet being Blackie, he couldn't just come out and say that, it wasn't his style. This was his way of letting me know, his way of asking me to stay.

Not only did I realize the idea ludicrous, but I knew he was failing to factor in my mother's views on the subject. He and I were aware of how determined she was that I go away to college, but that was not something I was going to bring up at the moment.

What I wanted to say was that everything would be all right, that my leaving would not change how we felt about each other, but I was his son and suffered from the same inability to express those emotions directly. It just wasn't the sort of thing I could bring myself to tell him. The best I could come up with was, "I have to think this over."

Which I know was not much.

"What is there to think over?" he asked.

I felt like saying, "Nothing much, just my whole life," but instead I shrugged.

His reaction was a mix of anger and sadness. His dark eyes clouded up and his small mouth tightened, as if he might spit. "Okay," he finally said. "Then we'll *both* just think about it."

I didn't manage another coherent sentence all the way home, and decided not to say anything more about it, to him or my mother.

In September I went off to Penn State, and in the end, Blackie was glad I did. To this day I've never owned a Jaguar.

* * *

YEARS LATER, AFTER I FINISHED COLLEGE and was working in New York City, I received a phone call from my younger sister telling me Blackie had been in a car crash.

She said it was bad, but I had no idea he was going to die.

I hurried from Manhattan up to the medical center in Westchester. He was in a coma, a broken-up mess connected to a thousand wires and tubes in the intensive care unit. He lasted less than two days and never regained consciousness.

I don't think anyone is ever ready for their parents to die, not unless they're about a hundred years old. But Blackie was only fifty, and the idea that I was not going to have him in my life anymore was beyond my comprehension. I never even got to say all those last things we wish we had the chance to say when someone we love has passed on.

As you can imagine, my family was devastated. Not only was my mother alone, but given my father's history, she was left with less than nothing. For all his plotting and dreaming and untold hours chasing the brass ring, Blackie had remained a much more effective spender than an earner. He had a small life insurance policy, but that was barely enough for my mother to pay off his bills. I gave what little assistance I could, helping her make the distinction between the debts she would have to pay and those I assured her could be filed under the category "Tough Luck for Them." When I got all that straightened out, I believe it was the first time my mother had been free of debt since the day they were married. She still had the office job she started right after my younger sister Kelly was old enough to begin school, so she was going to have no problem taking care of herself.

As for me, all I had as a legacy were his watches, each of which was too garish for my taste. They're still in my jewelry box, and none of them work anymore. If there had been any other artifacts of his life, I assumed my mother threw them away, protecting me from Blackie even after he was gone, and so I never pressed the point.

It was therefore more than a little surprising when, six years after Blackie died, she phoned me about the box filled with his papers she had never mentioned before.

My mother lived in a little house on a quiet street in Yonkers she and my father had rented a couple of years before he died. I was already on my own in Manhattan by the time they left the Bronx, but Emily and Kelly each spent some time there. It was a nice place, a small Cape

Cod, with three bedrooms and one bathroom upstairs and everything else, including a second bathroom, on the main level. There was also a large kitchen, where my mother spent most of her time when she was home, cooking and cleaning and talking on the phone.

Blackie's favorite spot was the large recliner in the living room, where he would intermittently watch television and doze off. He was pleased that he had a garage for his car, although he was always coming and going so much that he usually parked in the short driveway beside the walkway that led to the front stairs.

A lot of the furniture was new to me, there were different pictures on the walls and I never did figure out which kitchen cabinet had the glasses or which drawer held the bottle opener. I wonder if that's how it is for everyone, when their parents move out of the place where they grew up.

Anyway, six years after Blackie was gone, my mother was planning to move again. Several of her friends were already down south and she decided it was time to head off to sunny Florida. For the past couple of years she had been dating a very decent guy and, even though she had not said anything about it, my sisters and I figured they were going down there to live together. After all those years with Blackie, she learned to play it pretty close to the vest.

The afternoon she called me at work about the box, she claimed she found it while packing for her move. She said it had some of my father's papers, nothing more. That evening I drove up to the house in Yonkers, parked my Karmann Ghia in the short driveway beside the front walkway and knocked on the door, interested to see what she had.

Sitting in her living room, just the two of us, I found myself remembering our little apartment in the Bronx. I had a look around and recognized the cherrywood coffee table, a couple of matching porcelain lamps painted in a colorful mosaic pattern and some old bric-a-brac. Somehow, all of that made me feel better. Staring at an old silver-plated candy dish, I began to see how much I was going to miss my mother.

Not that I visited her all that much. I was a single guy and figured the real visiting would start after I married and had my own children. I thought that's who my mother would want to see, the grandchildren.

For now, I was consoling myself with the knowledge she was still going to be a phone call away, which is how we did most of our talking anyway. But I was starting to understand how different it was going to be.

"You want something to eat?" she asked.

"No thanks, Mom."

"A soda?"

"No thanks."

She waited, as if she needed to solve the riddle of why I wouldn't want a soda.

I gazed around the room again, trying to sound casual as I said, "I have to admit, I'm curious about this box."

Then I turned back to her, and she just nodded.

The living room was quiet, with no music playing and no television on. My father was never comfortable with silence. He'd walk into a room and switch on the television before he'd turn on a light. My mother was different.

She obviously didn't want to get into the subject of the box yet, so I said, "The place looks good, Mom." I was sitting on the couch. She was on the matching loveseat, facing me. I reached down and ran my hand along the soft, polished cotton, noticing the bright floral pattern as if seeing it for the first time. The whole room looked pretty much as it always did, and I figured if she was packing to move, she was doing all of it upstairs. "These sofas should look nice in Florida."

She stared at me for a moment, then said, "I hope I'm doing the right thing, giving this to you."

I couldn't bear the look of concern in her eyes, so I scanned the room again, as if I was searching for something I'd lost.

"I just hope I'm doing the right thing," she repeated.

"Don't worry, Mom. It'll be fine, whatever it is." Then I smiled at her. "It's not an old pack of betting slips, is it?"

That earned me a serious frown. "Just the kind of nonsense I'd expect from you," she said, but somehow my nonsense seemed to provide something she needed. Perspective, maybe. She stood up and came towards me, so I got to my feet. She put her arms around me, gave me a tight hug, and said, "I love you, son."

"I love you too."

When she let go and turned away from me, she headed toward the stairs. "Give me a minute," she told me over her shoulder.

I began wandering slowly around the small room, looking for some more familiar objects. When I heard her coming back downstairs I resumed my seat, as if I didn't want her to catch me in search of memories. I watched without speaking as she walked toward me with an old cardboard carton sealed with masking tape across the top.

"These are all that's left of your father's papers." She placed the box on the cherrywood cocktail table and sat down, facing me again. "I guess you should have them." The way she said it made it clear she still wasn't too sure.

"Why now?" I was struggling to look right into her eyes, which can be a tough thing to do with your own mother in the tough moments.

"He was your father," she said with a sigh, as if she would have done something about that if she could. "You should have these." As I reached out to touch the box she leaned forward and took my hand. "Your father was a strange man. I don't know how else to say that, but you know it's true."

"I do."

She nodded slowly but didn't let go of me. "He talked about a lot of silly stuff your father. Not your kind of silly stuff," she explained. "Big plans. Big schemes. I was always worried you'd wind up the same way. The same kind of person."

I tried to come up with a reassuring smile, one of those smiles where you don't show any teeth, you just sort of turn the ends of your mouth up to let the other person know that what they've said is all right. "I'm not that kind of person."

"No, you're not..." She released my hand and sat back. "Don't open it here."

"I won't," I said, and I sat back too.

We were quiet for a moment.

"You remember how your father talked about his big secret, the one big deal that was going to make everything all right?"

"Which one?" I asked with a short laugh.

"No, I mean it. Toward the end. Do you remember that?"

"I do, but you have to admit, he said those things quite a lot."

"I know. Sometimes he got himself in trouble for it, too."

I didn't say anything.

"Sometimes your father talked about blood money." She shook her head. "I always hated that expression."

"I know. You hated a lot of his expressions."

My mother nodded. Then she surprised me. She smiled. "I loved your father very much, even if I despised some of the things he would say. Especially that." I watched her amusement evaporate into another look of concern. "When he talked about blood money it always scared me, maybe because of some of the things he did. But I know you're not that way. I do."

"Thank God. I thought you were still worrying I was going to become a hit man or something." She grimaced, and I didn't blame her. "Sorry," I said.

"He was your father, and I know how you felt about him." She was staring at me again. "Be sensible, son. Don't romanticize who he was. He was a very troubled man."

I wanted to say something encouraging, so I said, "I'm twenty-seven years old," which was neither encouraging nor particularly informative to my own mother. Then I said, "I know who I am, Mom," which felt a little better.

"I know you do, son," she agreed. "I know you do."

I offered to stick around and help her with her packing, but it was an empty gesture since she wasn't moving to Florida for several weeks. I asked if she wanted to go to dinner or something, but she tilted her head and gave me a look that said she knew I wanted to get the hell out of there, go home and look at whatever it was that she'd given me.

Mothers are great in ways fathers will never comprehend.

She gave me another hug and told me to drive safely—as she always did—then I took the box and left. In my car, headed south along the Henry Hudson Parkway, my heart was pounding hard enough for me to notice almost every beat. The drive back to the city passed as if I were moving through a dense fog, until there I was, in my apartment on East 55th Street, sitting in my living room, staring at this old carton on my coffee table, waiting as if it would move of its own accord. Or speak to me.

I stayed that way for several minutes, just waiting for something to happen.

Nothing did, so I tore away the masking tape and removed the top.

Most of what I found inside is the type of stuff guys collect when they served in the armed forces. Old letters. Discharge papers. Blackie's service record, which is how I came to know about some of the things he did at the end of the war in the south of France with Benny, which became important once I found the letter.

There were also a lot of photographs. Ribbons. Medals. Several medals. They gave out medals like crazy in World War II, which was the least they could do for that incredible generation of soldiers who fought overseas. I couldn't make heads or tails out of what any of them were for because they don't say anything on them. I supposed you need a book to explain them, and I decided I would buy one first chance I got.

The photographs were interesting, old black and white snapshots of various comrades in arms, all of them looking young and thin and some of them staring at the camera with posed grins that could not do much to hide their fear. There were pictures of different girls from back home with catchy notes on the back. "Hi Blackie. Thinking of you." "This is my friend Janet that I wrote you about. She's cuter in person." "For you, doll." Things like that.

I didn't recognize anyone in the photos except my father, my uncle Vincent and Benny.

There were also a lot of letters Blackie received when he was overseas, many of them from his sister Anna. I wasn't interested in reading them just then.

In a large brown envelope I found poetry and a few short stories my father wrote. I knew they were written when Blackie was in the service because he dated everything. I thumbed through them, brittle old pages that were so delicate to the touch I thought they might crumble in my hands. I remembered Blackie telling me that he wanted to be a writer when he was young, but that he'd given up on that and thrown away everything he wrote long ago. Now here it was, a portrait of the failed artist as a young man. It made me feel like crying, so I slipped the pages back inside the big brown envelope. I decided to read those later too.

There were other things, from after the war. More photos, papers from his days as a liquor salesman, old driver's licenses and so on. And then I saw the white, letter-sized envelope. He had written on it, "For My Son."

That one stopped me cold.

I turned the envelope over in my hands a few times, as if there was some ceremony I should follow before I tore it open. I was only going to get to do this once in my life, open this and read it for the first time, the last words I would ever hear from my father. I studied the thing carefully for what felt like a long time, wondering what it might contain, then began to carefully pull the flap away.

Some of the envelope tore as if came apart, so I worked around the edge in case I might be ripping whatever was inside. Then I took out the letter. It consisted of two pages, with a date on top of the first, just over a month before Blackie died. His handwriting was as familiar to me as my own.

Dear son,

If you're reading this, then I'm probably gone, and since I have no intention of passing on for quite a while, this letter may not come into your hands until many years from today. I mention this, because it could mean that some of what I've got to say won't make any sense by then. I'm sorry to sound mysterious, but I need to be careful. You'll also need to be careful.

Up to now things haven't worked out for me as well as I wanted. I've told you from time to time that I had something really big in the works. The only people who know the truth about it are Benny and an old friend you've never met. And now you.

When Benny and I took the Money in France we knew the risks. We knew it was even possible we might never be able to use it. We've waited a very long time to make our move and Benny tells me he wants no part of it anymore. You know Benny, he's always been my anchor, so I've got to give careful thought to his advice. I'm not making a move until he and I straighten things out.

In the meantime, if anything should happen to me, I want to be sure you have it. In a way you already do. You're my son, and what's mine is yours.

So talk to Benny. If Benny's not around you'll have to figure it out for yourself. Even though I never told you much about my time in France, I know you can pull it all apart and piece it together because you're a smart young man.

Be careful. There could be trouble about this and that's the one thing I don't want for you. Your mother has spent your whole life worrying that I would drag you into my world, but I think you know I never would have allowed it. This is something different. I may not have done everything I wanted for you, but please believe that I did the best I could. Maybe I can make things better with this.

I expect you to do the right thing. I know you will. If you have any doubts, just remember that song you loved as a little boy—things are seldom what they seem.

Dad

I stared at the letter, at his handwriting, at what appeared to be water stains at different places on the pages, little drops that made it look like the paper had been left out in the rain for a few seconds. It left a few of the words blurry, but I could still read them, even if my eyes were getting blurry too.

Looking back, I can't recall every thought that ran through my head that evening, but I know they were all bumping into each other like a bunch of people in a pitch black room, rushing around, looking for a light switch. There were images of my father, of course, impressions of so many moments, good and bad. I tried hard to imagine him writing this to me—when and where and how he looked and felt at the time—but for some reason that made me feel even worse. And then I was hit with the stark truth, the knowledge that this was it. This really was the last thing he would ever say to me.

I had trouble breathing without my chest catching each time it heaved up and down. I read the letter again, slowly. It really did not tell me much, except that I'd have to talk with Benny. Benny, who I hadn't seen since my father's funeral, six years before. Benny, who my father was telling me, didn't want any part of whatever this was about.

I placed the paper down and stared out at nothing at all, my entire focus somewhere inside, stumbling around in that dark room.

Then I thought, *If I show this to Benny, maybe he'll change his mind.*

CHAPTER THREE

My father and Benny hung out in the same crowd when they grew up in the Bronx, but they didn't become really close friends until they went into the service together. As soon as they came of age, which was a couple of years after Pearl Harbor, they enlisted in what used to be called the Army Air Forces, with the hope of becoming fighter pilots.

Blackie told me stories about his fly-boy days over India, but it turns out they were pure invention. When I went through the papers in the box I learned he never earned his wings. Benny filled in some blanks later. Turned out, neither of them even made it through preliminary flight training.

They began in a classification program at a base just outside Nashville, then shipped out to Maxwell Field for air cadet training. When Benny got into a scrape with a couple of infantry grunts at a local tavern, his Commanding Officer politely explained how the Army Air Corps was not looking for some hothead to be jockeying their expensive airplanes over Germany. Then he politely showed him the door. My father had his own problems, finding it a chore to keep up with the tedious classroom work that was far too much like school for his taste. He was more interested in dressing up in his clean, pressed uniform and chasing the local skirts, which led to some miserable scores when exam time rolled around. He received the bad news when the results were posted on the barracks wall. His name was, as Benny explained, below the line.

After washing out of aviation cadet training, they were both assigned to a ground support detail, stationed in India. Shipped off to a place called Chabua, Assam, they reported to a unit known as the India-China Division of the Air Transport Command. Blackie and Benny were not exactly in the thick of the fighting, unless someone can recall Hitler making a big putsch to seize Calcutta.

Blackie never rose above the rank of Private during his tour in India. According to the discharge records I found in the box, the most dangerous assignment he ever pulled was as Radio Operator, a position he applied for when he tired of training as an interpreter. That one really got me, the thought of my father as an interpreter in India. I wondered what he was interpreting and for whom.

Sometime in the summer of 1944, shortly after the D-Day invasion, Benny was sent off to Marseilles. My father was transferred there a few months later, joining his friend in the south of France. According to Blackie's records, his military career took a substantial turn there. He and Benny were attached to a unit investigating sabotage, subversive activities and war crimes. Their specific assignment was to locate and recover valuable artifacts taken by the enemy during the Occupation.

My father never told me much about those last four months, but the one thing he brought back from the war, other than the pocketful of medals and ribbons I found in the box, was an oil painting of the countryside near a town called Gourdes in Provence. It's nothing special, just a landscape that hung in our living room all through my childhood.

I was surprised the picture had any history at all. "I brought this back from France, from when I was in the service," he told me when they were moving to their little house in Yonkers. Up to then, the painting was just one of those things that your parents have that you don't bother to think about, like one of those old lamps I noticed in my mother's living room.

I said, "You never told me about that."

"I guess not," he said. "Anyway, I want you to have it. Just promise you'll never get rid of it."

I promised, took it back to my apartment, and it's been hanging in my bedroom ever since.

As for Benny, I think I mentioned that the last time I saw him was when Blackie died. He came to the wake and sat alone in the back of the funeral parlor, mourning in his private way. Other than my mother and sisters and me, I think he was the saddest person there.

My mother was not as touched about his sorrow as I was, mostly because she believed that Benny and the rest of my father's cronies represented the worst part of Blackie's life. She graciously thanked those who attended the services, but after that was done, she told me she never wanted to see any of them again. And we never did. Benny was the only one of Blackie's friends who came to the church for the Requiem Mass and then to the cemetery, but after that he also disappeared from our lives.

My father had told me more than once that Benny was his best friend. He also said that Benny was a straight shooter, an important distinction according to Blackie. He believed that straight shooters always win in the end, and that they were the only guys you should ever trust. When I read the letter from my father telling me about his last Big Plan, I was glad it was Benny he pointed me to for help.

I remembered hearing that Benny and his wife had moved away a few years back, but Benny was not the kind of guy you were going to find in the phone book. This was before the internet age, where everyone is findable, so my options were limited. I knew my cousin Frank still had contact with Blackie's old crowd, having entered the "life," as they called it. He probably would know where Benny had settled, or at least have a way to find out. Since I had no such contacts, the only problem was the thought I might have to give Frank a call.

* * *

First, I contacted a friend at the phone company. As I feared, she came up empty in her effort to find Benny, as did my second and third attempts to locate him.

It was becoming clear I was going to have to call Frank. I simply did not have another way to get to Benny and, after reading my father's letter for the twentieth time, Benny was the person I had to speak with.

It was not easy to bring myself to ask Frank for anything, even something as simple as a phone number. Over time, he had become more like Blackie, something my father encouraged. Frank was now making his living in the same world Blackie had occupied, which meant our lives had moved further and further apart, until there was nothing left between us but family history. I suppose a therapist could spend ten years trying to convince me I was jealous of the attention and approval he received from my father for becoming a hoodlum, but what the hell would that get me?

Deciding there was no choice, I phoned Frank's place in Florida, listened to the infuriatingly cheerful message on his answering machine, and left my number. I spent the rest of the evening reading through my father's thirty-five-year-old short stories until I finally fell into an uneasy sleep. Very much a creature of habit, I still managed to wake up early and, as I got ready to go to the office, Frank called.

"Hey," he greeted me, "I'm in New York, why the hell did you call me in Lauderdale?"

The better question was, *Why would I have any idea where he was, since we hadn't spoken in a couple of years?* But his tone made it clear I was the moron for wasting a long-distance call down south, so all I could think of to say was, "You're in the city?"

"Yeah, I've been here on business since Friday. Get up here all the time."

I really didn't want any more information than that about what he did, even if I was tempted to ask why I never heard from him if he was in town so often. I said, "I was wondering if you know where I could find Benny these days."

"That's it?" he asked with a forced laugh. "Don't you want to know how I've been? No catching up on the family?"

"Sorry. How've you been?"

He ignored the question. "Benny, huh? Some sort of reunion I haven't been invited to?"

"Not exactly. My mother's moving down your way next month."

"I heard. That'll be great for her."

"I hope so," I said, not bothering to ask how he'd heard about my mother.

"What's that got to do with Benny?" He laughed into the phone. "Your mother's leaving town and you're suddenly lonely for the old crew?"

"Updating my Christmas card list," I said.

"Come on, cuz. What gives?"

I took a deep breath. "My mother was going through some things. Found a note from my father, said I should keep in touch with Benny. Made me feel bad I hadn't talked to him for so long."

Frank uttered a soft whistle. "A note from Blackie? After all these years? No kidding?"

"No kidding."

He told me he'd find out where Benny had gone and get me the info, then asked me to meet him at Benson's Steak House for lunch.

I was too busy wondering why I'd been stupid enough to mention anything about the letter to turn down his invitation.

Relationships can be strange.

After we hung up I stood in front of my bedroom closet, deciding what to wear.

36

I don't normally get dressed up for work, not in the traditional sense of suits and ties. The advertising game is supposed to be a blend of business and art, so it's important to keep one foot in each of those worlds so people know you're into the program. You've got to look chic without appearing seedy. Successful but not corporate.

Today was different. I was going to see my cousin for lunch, and I wanted to look good. I realize that might sound odd, but I assumed Frank was making barrels of dough running whatever scam he was running at the time, and I didn't want him to think I was some broken-down Working Stiff.

I will not get into the bell-bottom pants and colorful shirts we wore in those days, one of those embarrassing memories from the era. Be assured, I chose my best suit, which was a conservative navy blue, a white shirt and a fancy red tie with funny little blue characters on it. I think men look best in a navy blue suit with a white shirt and red tie—not counting tuxedos, of course, but a tuxedo for lunch would have been overkill.

After an uneventful morning in the office—I had no enthusiasm for work that day—I got to Benson's just after one o'clock. I knew that Frank would be late, because that's one of the many affectations of any Serious Guy. They've got to be late to prove they're involved in some big action, something more important than arriving on time to meet you. I bet Frank shows up late for his first appointment of the day.

Back in the seventies, Benson's was a Manhattan rendition of an old-fashioned saloon, with paneled walls and soft lights, the sort of place that's tough to find anymore. I sat on one of the wooden stools at the large, square oak bar, said hello to the bartender and ordered Gibson on the rocks to keep me company. He served the drink in a heavy tumbler with small, crunchy cocktail onions and, by the time Frank breezed through the door, I'd made most of my way through that first cocktail.

On an empty stomach, except for the onions, I was feeling pretty good.

Frank looked all right, although he'd gained a few pounds since I'd last seen him. He and I were always the trim guys in the family, so it surprised me to see him filling out around the middle. He was still handsome, with dark hair and eyes like my father and uncle, but with better features than either of them, including a straight, small-ish nose that he won in the gene pool from his mother's side of the family. He had a deep Florida tan and a big, white-toothed smile that he used quite often, as if he just thought of a punch line to a joke he isn't telling you.

"Hey cuz," he said as I stood to greet him. He wrapped me in a bear hug, then took me by the shoulders and held me at arms length, giving me the once over. "Nice suit," he said "but where'd you get that tie? Looks like you're going to assembly in grade school."

I shook my head slightly. "Good to see you too," I told him as I sat back down on my stool.

He was dressed in a white silk shirt left open at the neck, dark trousers and a pair of expensive loafers that had cost some reptile its life. He had a cotton sweater hanging off his shoulders, just like in *GQ*. "Let's have a drink," he said.

"I'm already working on one."

"You been here long?"

"Nah," I said, looking at the large glass that was empty but for the remaining ice. "I was just thirsty."

Frank smiled again. I don't think I've seen him laugh since he was seventeen or so, but he smiled like crazy.

He ordered a Chivas on the rocks. I sucked the last of the vodka from the ice cubes and asked for another.

"It's really great to see you," he said.

I believed him. I tend to do that a lot in life, believe what people say. It gets me into all kinds of trouble.

"How's your dad?" I asked. Aunt Mary had died a couple of years before and the last time I saw Uncle Vincent was at her funeral. It occurred to me that was the last time I'd seen Frank.

"Good," he told me. "He's good." Our drinks were served, he picked up his scotch and said, "*Salud.*"

We touched glasses and tasted our drinks. Then we spent a while going through the family roster, comparing notes on how our sisters were doing, sharing the gossip we'd heard about various aunts, uncles and cousins, just generally catching up.

An old friend once warned me that "catching up" is the death knell of a relationship. When all you've got to talk about is how other people are doing, it means you have nothing in common anymore. It happens a lot when someone moves away, then tries to keep in touch, and those telephone discussions are the worst. You're each trying to think of things to tell the other, instead of saying what you really feel. Something like "You know Hank, you're not actually a part of my life anymore and I'm not a part of yours. What do you say we eighty-six this crap, and if you're in town some time we'll get together and see a ballgame or get drunk or something, okay?"

"Are you listening to anything I'm saying?" Frank asked me.

"Sure, I'm listening. Just got a little distracted, that's all."

"The letter, eh? Let's see it."

"The letter?" I gave him one of those bobble head doll nods, as if once I started I might not be able to stop. "It was just a note."

"Let's have a look."

"I didn't bring it."

"You didn't bring it?"

Don't you hate it when people repeat what you've just said as a way of expressing their disbelief? It's so demeaning. Especially when you're lying.

"No, I didn't bring it," I said, then stared down at the little ivory colored onions in my glass, as if I should be embarrassed about not having the letter with me.

"I thought you were going to let me read it." He actually managed to sound hurt, although I knew—even well into my second drink—that I never said anything about letting him read it.

"I told you what it said about Benny. Kind of cryptic, actually," although why I added that last bit of information I'll never know. Alcohol can be a sonuvabitch.

"You see. It's cryptic. That's why I've got to read it if I'm going to be able to help."

Another thing I knew I hadn't said, was that I wanted his help. All I wanted was to find Benny. Still, I was the one who had opened the door. "You know how my father sometimes talked about a big deal?" I shrugged, as if it wasn't really important. "Just wondering if he ever said anything to you, about money he stashed away or anything like that?" I know, I know, I should have kept my mouth shut. Mr. Smirnoff and I couldn't help ourselves.

Frank smiled a genuine smile, which was rare for him. I think he ought to try it more often, swap it for that studied grin he favors, the one he probably uses when he's about to sell you a car with the odometer turned back. "Blackie always had something on the back burner. You know that."

I nodded.

"You remember the night of my sister's wedding?"

"When you took that swing at him?"

"Forget that," Frank said as he waved that thought away. "I'm talking about later that night. When we went to Jonesy's."

"Of course I remember."

Frank pushed out his lower lip. "He was talking a big deal that night."

I shrugged. "He did that a lot."

"He did, but that night was different."

"Different how?" I asked.

"Don't you remember, at the end, how Benny kept trying to shut him up?"

I had not remembered that, not until he reminded me, not until he and I relived that night together.

* * *

AFTER THE BRAWL AT LENA'S WEDDING, after my father crashed through the window and the four of us ended up standing in the driveway drinking scotch—my father, Frank, the bridegroom Ray and me—we eventually climbed into Frank's car and drove to Jonesy's Bar.

Jonesy's was a gin mill near Greenwood Lake, without tables, booths, menus or any other pretense about the singular reason for its existence, which was the sale of booze. It consisted of one long, narrow room, dominated by an oak bar with a worn, scarred top and a solid brass rail that runs just a few inches off the floor where you could rest your feet while you sit there getting loaded. There was a row of stools with shiny metal legs and round, red vinyl seats that spin all the way around if you had interest in facing this way or that. Behind the bar were shelves stocked with bottles of liquor. Not fancy cognacs or single barrel scotches like they feature in upscale places nowadays. Just scotch, rye, bourbon, vodka, an assortment of domestic beers. Behind the bottles was a large mirror, nothing etched or ornate, just an old looking glass that left you to stare at yourself, if that was your pleasure.

The room was paneled in dark, rough-hewn wood, the kind that looked like they forgot to plane it down, very Adirondacks, and just the right touch to complement the view through the large windows, where you could see the lake sitting quietly beyond a stand of tall old trees.

The bartender, Gus, was a burly guy who must have been in his mid-forties when I first met him, but who always looked around sixty and likely still does. He was the only bartender I had ever seen at Jonesy's. Gus had a receding hairline, broad shoulders and a large tattoo on his left arm that proclaimed his service with the 102nd Airborne. I think he liked us, my cousins and me, because we enjoyed his stories, and because most of his other customers were older and burned out and never seemed to say much of anything, except "I'll have another, Gus."

By the time we got to Jonesy's that night it was nearly eleven and there were only four other people at the bar. As we came in, Gus greeted my cousin by name.

"Hiya," Frank replied happily, then extended his hand. "Gooda see ya, Gus."

Gus shook his hand.

"Gus, you know my cousin."

He asked how I was doing, and I told him I was fine.

"And you know Ray," Frank said.

"Sure," Gus said. "How are ya?"

"Married," the young bridegroom muttered, followed by a short burp.

"What's that?"

"He's married," Frank interpreted. "Married my sister Lena this afternoon."

"No kidding?"

"No kidding."

Not allowing the obvious to go unspoken, Gus asked, "Shouldn't you be with the bride?"

"Married," Ray croaked.

My father, who had been quiet up to then, stepped forward. "Am I nobody here?"

"Sorry," Frank said. "Gus, this is my favorite uncle. Best guy in the whole world, my Uncle Blackie."

"I thought maybe you forgot me," my father said.

"Blackie?" Gus inquired politely.

"That's right," my father told him. "Blackie." Then, just to be sure there was no mistake about it, he said "Blackie" again, and asked if anyone had a problem with that.

Gus shook his head. "You Vincent's brother?"

"You know my brother Vincent?"

"Sure. Good guy."

"Good guy? Great guy," Blackie said, wringing three syllables out of the word "great," like Tony the Tiger. "Greatest brother in the whole fucken world." He accompanied that proclamation with a sideward thrust of his right hand that caught Ray flush on the side of the head and almost knocked him to the floor. Frank helped his new brother-in-law regain his balance, as my father said, "Sorry, kid. I think you need a cocktail."

Gus could see that none of us needed a cocktail, but he probably figured there was no way we were going to be able to find our way back to the car, let alone drive it. "What'll you have?" he asked.

My father ordered scotch for all of us, Johnnie Walker Black Label of course, then turned to survey the length of bar. The other four men were seated, quietly enjoying their drinks. Blackie called out to them. "You guys know my brother, Vincent Rinaldi?"

The closest of the four looked up from his shot glass. "Sure, I know him."

Blackie pushed away from the bar and strode purposefully toward the man. Standing over him, he said, "Is he the greatest guy in the world or what?"

The man had the look of a pipe-fitter or mason—thick arms, thick neck and a jaw that hadn't seen a razor in a couple of days. He was wearing a heavy, blue flannel shirt and the mottled look of intoxication. If he had been a trifle less inebriated, he might have just agreed with my father and gone on drinking. Instead, he said, "Vincent's a right guy, but the best guy in the world? Come on pal. Gimme a break."

"Give you a break? Is that what you want?" Blackie wasn't in the mood to give him a break. Instead, he pulled a revolver from somewhere inside his sport coat and held it where the man could get a close look at it. "I'll give you a break. I'll break you so many times you'll look like you went through a fucken wood chipper."

As soon as Gus saw the gun he said, "Hey, hey, Blackie, let's put that away. We don't want any trouble here."

My father turned to Gus and told him to keep his hands on the bar. Then he asked, "Why do bartenders always say "I don't want any trouble here?" You look like a smart guy, Gus, but that's a dumb thing to say. Think about it. Where the fuck *do* you want trouble?" Blackie gave everyone a moment to consider that. Then he said, "There's not gonna be any trouble, just everybody take it easy."

Taking it easy was apparently no problem for the three men seated further down the bar, who were so potted they didn't even know there was anything to be troubled about. Ray had passed out by now, face down on the oak countertop. Frank and I were just standing there, watching.

The man seated in front of my father, the one who had the nerve to suggest that my uncle wasn't the greatest guy in the world, was staring at the barrel of the gun. When Blackie waved it closer to his nose, the man began to urinate down his leg, the pale liquid dripping onto the floor for everyone to hear in the momentary silence. "Look buddy," he began to say in a frightened voice, but my father cut him off.

"Shut the fuck up, all right?"

The man nodded.

"You don't think too much of my brother, eh?"

"I, uh, I didn't say that."

"I told you to shut up," my father snapped at him. "Because I'm gonna tell you something about my brother." Brandishing the pistol for emphasis, he began pacing the length of the room. "Lemme tell ya what kinda brother Vincent's been to me, all right?"

Frank tried to say something, but my father cut him off. "You started this, you weasely little fuck. You think I forgot that?"

I had the sense to keep my mouth shut, at least for now.

Working hard to sound as friendly as if two old pals running into each other on the street. Gus said, "Hey, Blackie. Why don't we call

Vincent and get him down here? Before someone gets hurt, all right? How's that for an idea, huh Blackie?"

My father stopped, thought it over and seemed to like the idea. Then his mouth curled into a vicious sneer. "Very good, Gus, you're a smart boy. You figure I'm so stinkin' drunk I'm gonna let you pick up that phone and calla cops, right? Come on, Gus." Blackie started laughing. "I like you, Gus. You're a smart boy." He turned to Frank. "Call your father. Tell him to come over. Alone," he added, snarling the last word for emphasis.

So that's what Frank did. He picked up the bar phone and dialed his father's number, told him the situation and asked him to come over.

There's so much more I could tell you about my Uncle Vincent, but for now it's enough to say that on the night of his daughter's wedding, when he received a call from his son informing him that his brother was striding up and down Jonesy's Bar, waving a pistol and extolling the many virtues of Vincent Rinaldi, the said Vincent Rinaldi did not jump in his car, drive over and take my father home. No, while my father paced up and down the room, regaling the group with tiresome stories of his childhood, his days in the military and all the family history that's never interesting to a stranger unless he's demented, my uncle responded to the call by hanging up and then calling Benny.

You might wonder why Benny wasn't there already, why he wasn't invited to Lena's wedding since he knew the whole family and had been Blackie's best friend dating all the way back to the Second World War. There is no way for me to be sure, but maybe it was tough enough for my Uncle Vincent to retain his brother's title of Best Guy in the World without unnecessary competition.

Whatever reasons he had for not inviting Benny to his daughter's wedding, it didn't stop Uncle Vincent from phoning Benny to say that Blackie was in a jam. And Benny, being Benny, got out of bed, threw some cold water on his face, pulled on his clothes and drove up from the city to get my father before things got any uglier.

By the time Benny and my uncle made their way into Jonesy's, almost an hour later, Blackie had become less a lethal threat than a crashing bore. Everyone in the place was sick of hearing about Vincent and Blackie, so my father turned to the claim that he was sitting on the biggest deal since the building of the Suez Canal.

He and Benny.

"We're gonna have more dough than I'll know what to do with," he proclaimed.

Frank started to say something but, after the earlier dustup I grabbed my cousin by the arm and quietly convinced him to shut the hell up.

While Blackie went on about all the money he was going to have, he ordered round after round of drinks for everyone. Everyone, that is except for Ray, who remained face down on the wooden bar, snoring loudly out of his mouth and into his own nose. The other customers downed the free booze as Blackie continued his sentinel's pace, up and down the length of the narrow room, the revolver a prop now, while Gus the bartender kept a watchful eye to gauge when the soliloquy might wind down enough for him to talk my father into giving up the gun.

When the door to the bar opened, letting in a gust of cold night air, Blackie spun around, not quite leveling the pistol at the intruders, but certainly waving it in their general direction.

"Lower the gun, Blackie," his friend said in a composed but firm voice.

My father took a moment, then said, "Benny! Vinny! Hey everybody, it's my brother and my best pal."

It was a fucking Norman Rockwell homecoming.

The faces of the four strangers at the bar wore mixed expressions of curiosity and relief. Perhaps the lunatic with the gun would be

46

subdued, or at least they would shut him up long enough for them to get out of there and go home.

Throwing his arms into the air, my father said, "Benny, you sonuvagun. What the hell are you doing here?"

Benny was shorter than my father, a cherubic guy with a round face, very little hair, a dark complexion and an easy-going manner belied only by his reptilian gaze. He stepped toward my father, taking him by the shoulders and staring into his bloodshot eyes. "What am I doing here? I was in the mother lovin' neighborhood and I decided to stop by." Benny, unlike my father, almost never cursed. Mother lovin' was a strong statement coming from him. "Whadda you *think* I'm doin' here?"

My father stared at him blankly, as if it might be a trick question.

"Gimme the gun," Benny said and, without waiting to debate the request, deftly pulled the revolver from my father's hand and shoved it into his own coat pocket. "Now siddown and tell me what this is all about."

Benny led my father to a stool and sat him down beside the sleeping Ray. Blackie asked Gus for a drink and Benny gave the bartender a nod. As Gus poured yet another scotch, Blackie said, "They don't believe me, Benny. They don't believe we got the biggest deal in the world right here." He held out an unsteady hand and pointed to his own palm. "Right here. Blood money is what we've got. Go ahead. Tell 'em. Tell 'em the truth."

"Do me a favor," Benny said. "Shut up, okay? I'm sure you've already done enough talking tonight."

The man at the bar who knew my uncle clearly agreed. Figuring it was safe now, he stood up and said to my uncle, "Vincent, okay for me to go?"

Uncle Vincent had remained near the door, his posture stiff, his expression a mask of restrained anger. He hadn't even noticed the guy until then. "Joe, yeah, sure," he said. "Sorry about all this."

Joe got to his feet with some difficulty. "Your brother's an interesting guy," he said.

"Yeah. He sure is."

Joe cautiously made his way past my father and headed out the door, but the other three strangers sat right where they were, willing to wait for whatever would happen next. Free drinks are hard to come by that hour of the night.

"Hey," Gus the bartender called out to them. "Show's over. We're all clearing out."

Benny agreed. "We got a tab here? Any damage done?"

Gus managed a short laugh. "Damage? Only thing that got shot was my nerves."

Benny said, "No trouble, then." Gus told him what was owed and Benny pulled out some large bills and paid three or four times the amount. Then he helped Blackie to his feet and led him toward the door, where my uncle was waiting.

When they came face to face, Vincent said, "Jesus Christ, John. I live around here, you understand that? Isn't it enough that you ruined my daughter's wedding and broke my goddamned kitchen window? I have to face these people. They're my neighbors, for Chrissake."

Blackie stared at his brother for a moment, his eyes struggling to focus. Then he turned back to the three strangers who were trying to make it to their feet. "Look guys, this is him. My brother Vincent. Best fucken brother in the whole damn world." None of the three men said a word, probably less afraid of Blackie pulling out another pistol than making another speech.

Blackie returned his uneven gaze to his brother. "You see, Vinny? You don't have to worry. They don't even know who the fuck you are." Then he turned to the bar. "You're a good egg Gus. A good egg. You put up with me tonight, right Gus? Hold on." Blackie staggered over and carefully placed several more bills on the wooden counter.

Gus said, "Hey, you don't have to do that Blackie."

"I do," my father said, his head moving slowly up and down. "Sure I do." Then he steadied himself. "You coulda called a cop. Coulda taken a run at me. But you clocked it right." When he turned to leave, Benny grabbed hold of his arm, helping him to stay aloft.

"Hey Benny, tell everyone. Tell 'em we got the world by the tail. Tell 'em Benny. Tell 'em about our deal."

"Shut up," Benny said, "let's just get outta here."

Blackie thought it over, then said, "Right, right, let's get outta here." As he made his way to the door again, he reached out and gave my uncle one last little slap on the cheek. "Best fucken brother in the world," he said, then he and Benny were gone.

CHAPTER FOUR

Sitting in Benson's, after Frank and I were done sharing memories of that night at Jonesy's, he asked the obvious question. "What about you? Blackie ever say anything more about it. After that night I mean."

I shook my head. "Not a thing."

"Must've been something to it, the way he kept talking about it and Benny kept shutting him up."

I looked down at the remains of my second drink, wondering where the rest of it had gone. "Good old Benny."

"This note is telling you to do more than just say hello to good old Benny, eh?" Frank was studying me carefully now.

"I told you what it says."

He shook his head back and forth, very slowly, as if I'd just told him something really sad. "It'd be a lot better if we were looking at the letter together, know what I mean?"

Oh, I knew exactly what he meant.

I swallowed what remained of my vodka, stood up, reached in my pocket paid the tab. "I'll give you a call. I've got some stuff to take care of in the office." As I stood there facing him, I realized he hadn't bothered to sit down yet. I also noticed I was taller than he was, as if it was the first time that ever occurred to me.

"Aren't we having lunch?"

"Lunch? Damn, I'd love to, really." I made a big show of looking at my watch. "I'm sorry, Frank. By the time you got here, and after all the family chit chat. I've got to get back. You know how it goes."

He gave me a benign smile, as if to say, "You poor bastard, you ended up a Working Stiff."

"How long you in town?"

"Another couple of days. You have my number at the hotel now. Call me. Get me a copy of the letter. We'll figure this out together. It'll be fun."

"Sure," I said. "Fun. So what about Benny?"

"I hear he moved out west. Las Vegas," Frank said.

Las Vegas. It might have been worth putting up with Frank for half an hour if this was true.

"I don't have a number yet," he told me, although this time I thought he was the one lying. "But I'll get it."

"I really should give him a call," I said, trying to make it sound like, what the hell, what else have I got to do with my time?

"Maybe we should go see him. Together."

"Who? Benny?"

"Yeah. Benny. Who're we talking about here?"

I knew Benny was not a big Frank fan, but I said, "It's an idea," then held out my hand.

Frank gave me one of his toothy smiles, which he followed by slapping my hand away and pulling me into another bear hug. I hugged him back, not because I felt like it, but with his arms around me I couldn't just stand there like a mope.

"Don't make me chase you down now," he said with a smile.

Even his smile didn't improve the way that sounded. "No," I told him, then walked out of Benson's as if I had someplace to be.

Which I did not.

They weren't expecting me at the office until later in the afternoon, and I was in no mood for work just then. I found a pay phone around the corner from Benson's and called my cousin

Nicky to say the thought of buying him lunch suddenly sounded like an excellent idea.

* * *

I GOT TO THE CAFÉ ON 57TH STREET just as Nicky arrived. He looked me up and down, checking out the navy blue suit, then reached out and touched the red tie. "What's with you? Job interview?"

"I had a meeting."

"Excuse me, big shot."

"Actually," I said, "I saw Frank for a drink."

"You had a drink with Frank and didn't call me?"

"I didn't think of it, tell you the truth. We had some business to handle."

"You had business with Frank? This I gotta hear."

We decided to sit at the bar—Nicky was short on time—and ordered sandwiches and beers. I told him about the box of papers, my discussion with Frank and why I wanted to find Benny. I also showed him the letter, which I had in my pocket when I met with Frank.

Nicky read it, then started laughing. He said, "What a pisser your father was," then slapped me on the shoulder as if this was some great big joke I wasn't getting.

A lot of people thought my father was more entertaining than I did, so I had a gulp of my beer and waited for Nicky to stop laughing. "That's it?" I asked him. "That's all you've got for me? That my father was a pisser?"

Nicky was nursing his beer. He had to go back to work, but I had decided I didn't, so I finished mine and called for another.

"You think this is for real?" he asked me.

"You knew Blackie. He was pie in the sky and all that, but he wouldn't go to the trouble of writing a letter like this if there wasn't something to it."

Nicky agreed. "But years have gone by. Anything could've happened. Something might've even happened before he died."

"Then he would've ripped up the letter. And it's dated just a month before he died, don't you think that's kind of significant?"

Nicky conceded the point. "What about the years since?" He shook his head. "Benny might have the money. Or someone else. And you've got two big problems, even if this is for real."

"Only two?" My new beer came and I took a long pull. After the vodkas at Benson's and these drafts, I was happy to have only two big problems.

"First, the letter doesn't have enough decent clues to get you off this barstool and start looking. Unless we're missing something obvious."

"We have Benny."

"What do you mean 'we,' paleface?"

"Go on."

"The second issue is right there in the letter. He's telling you the money is stolen. That means trouble, right? Maybe with the law, maybe with the guy it was taken from, which would be a whole lot worse, knowing who your father dealt with. Either way, trouble."

That last thought had occurred to me, but I hadn't worried about it, at least not yet. I stared at him, opening my eyes as wide as I could. "Fear? Is that what I'm hearing from you? Fear?"

"No bucko. Common sense. You've heard of it, I assume. As I say, given the type of people your father hung with, you should consider who the rightful owner might be."

I took another swallow of the lager. "Let's go see Benny."

"In Las Vegas?"

"Sure, why not?"

"Why not? I'm just a little busy at the moment, living my real life. Look, I know this is weird for you after all these years, and you've had some drinks, but the expression wild goose chase must still mean something to you."

Nicky is fond of trite sayings and overworked quotations. It's part of his dependable nature. I knew he wouldn't go to Vegas with me before I asked. Nicky's not the jump-on-a-plane kind of guy, which was all right just then. He knew me and he knew Blackie, and a dose of reality was what I needed. What I also needed was his take on whether he thought I was losing my mind. So I asked him.

"Of course you're losing your mind," he told me. "Who wouldn't be knocked for a loop, finding a letter like this." He shook his head as he thought it over. "It might have been different if you had this letter right after he passed away. But the trail is cold now. Remember, time and tide wait for no man, and I'm afraid this boat has sailed."

See what I mean about Nicky and trite expressions?

I said, "Don't make me seasick when I'm drinking."

∗ ∗ ∗

I WAS FEELING PRETTY MELLOW by the time Nicky headed back to work, so I went to the pay phone in the back of the restaurant and called my office, made an excuse about a stomach virus, then returned to my seat at the bar. I stared straight ahead, above the tops of the liquor bottles lined up against the wall, studying my reflection in the antique, cut-glass mirror. I didn't think I looked drunk yet, at least not from that distance. I decided another drink would be a good idea.

I don't drink alone in bars very often, but there I was, doing that very thing for the second time in three hours. I looked around for some company—even a casual conversation with a stranger would have been welcome—but at that hour of the day there was no one sitting still long enough for me to start a chat. People were hustling through the tail end of their lunches and clearing out, while the bartender was busy tending to the cash register. Left on my own, I felt I should be doing something other than just sitting there drinking, so I reached into my pocket and pulled out the copy of Blackie's letter. It only took me an instant to realize I didn't want to read it again, so I put it away and took out a scrap of paper and my fountain pen. I'm partial to fountain pens, even though they can tend to be a mess. There's something about the flow of ink onto the page that appeals to me. Maybe it's the old-fashioned style I like. Anyway, I unscrewed the cap, wiped the nib clean with a paper cocktail napkin, then pressed the piece of paper flat on the counter with the palm of my hand and started making a list.

I enjoy making lists. It helps me create a sense of order when I'm feeling confused. It also helps me remember things I'd otherwise forget. The need to buy new razor blades, for instance, after I've been scraping my face with the same one for about a month and a half. It's the sort of thing I won't think about after I walk out of the bathroom unless I write it down.

Leaning over the zinc-topped bar I began making a list of anything I could remember needing, trying to look busy in case anyone was wondering why I was sitting there at three in the afternoon, all alone, drinking a beer.

After a while, I got tired of the list, somewhere between toilet paper and silicone spray for a squeaky closet door, so I ordered another draft, got up and went back to the pay phone and called my friend in the phone company. Now that I knew Benny might be in Las Vegas, she might be able to help me track down his number.

She did. It was unlisted and under his wife's maiden name, which I just happened to remember. She gave it to me.

The phone was against the wall between the doors to the men's and ladies' restrooms. Staring at the chrome plate and silvery-square buttons of the telephone, I wondered what it was going to be like to speak with Benny after six years. I tried to script the first few lines, just to give me something to go with if it got awkward, but I was short on clever ideas at the moment. I thought, what the hell, and punched in the numbers.

This was before cell phones were everywhere, and I must have been a little tipsier than I thought, because I got the numbers on my phone card wrong the first time and the call didn't go through. I tried again, using an operator for assistance, then listened as a phone rang somewhere in Nevada, feeling more nervous than I thought I would. I noticed my hands getting sweaty and considered hanging up, but then someone picked up the phone on the other end and I heard a familiar voice say, "Yeah?"

"Benny," I said.

"Who wants to know?"

That was classic Benny.

He sounded a little older, although that might have been my imagination, and I found myself trying to picture what he looked like. Pretty much the same, I guessed. Benny always looked the same. I told him who it was and waited for him to say something.

"Jeez, kid, how the heck are you?"

Benny's not an effusive sort, but he sounded glad to hear from me. I told him I was fine and he asked how my mother and sisters were doing. I told him about everyone, keeping it simple, speaking slowly and trying not to have my words run together where he'd make me out for drunk.

When I got stalled somewhere in the middle of a boring story about my sister, he gave me a reprieve, interrupting long enough to ask why I had picked this afternoon to call after so many years.

I told him about the letter.

He paused for a long time. Then he said, "I'm not talkin' about no letter from Blackie," quickly adding, "and I'm definitely not talkin' about it on the phone."

"It sure would be good to see you," I told him.

"It'd be good to see you too, kid, as long as you're not gonna bug me about any letter from your father."

"Sure, all right. Maybe I could come by and see you," I said, trying to make it sound as casual as I could, like I was around the corner or something.

"Yeah, maybe."

"Okay," I said, and asked him where he lived.

Benny, ever the man of few words, recited his address, said, "Take it easy, kid," and hung up.

CHAPTER FIVE

So there I was, about to enter my father's world, dealing with Frank and Benny, stolen money and who knew what else, fulfilling all of my mother's worst fears.

Or was I?

I was an advertising account exec, which does not do much to prepare you for life's grand adventures, not to mention its more sinister dangers. I admit that I've never had my father's physical courage, perhaps because the life he led was so unlike mine, or maybe we were just wired differently. Either way, I felt I was about to head down the rapids with no sense of how to maintain a steady course, not even sure I would stay afloat—but what else was I to do?

Added to that was the reality of my financial situation, a euphemistic way of saying that back then I was existing week to week, working hard throughout the year in the hope my year-end bonus would clear up my credit card debt so I could start all over again in January.

A quick trip to Las Vegas was going to be a budget buster, but what choice did I have?

Destiny can really be a bitch.

I passed the next couple of days without speaking to Frank or Benny, or Nicky for that matter. When I wasn't at work, I spent my time reading through the rest of my father's papers and short stories, sorting through his photographs and war record, looking for something, anything that might lead me somewhere other than a flight to Las Vegas.

In the end I booked the trip and Saturday morning boarded the flight.

Riding high above the Midwestern plain states, wondering how my father's old friend was going to react to this whole thing. I knew if I was going to persuade him to play Abel Magwitch to my Pip, there were a few hurdles I had to leap—the fact that my father's note contained about as much solid information as a glass of water, the six years that had passed since he wrote it and his warning that Benny didn't want anything to do with it.

It occurred to me, looking out the window as America slipped by beneath me, how odd it was that Benny settled in Nevada. He's as true a New Yorker as there is, always was, always will be. You wonder about a guy like that, living near the desert, where there's no cold weather or traffic jams to complain about. There's not even a crowded street where you can double park your car without getting a ticket, just to prove that you have pull with the local cops. And where do you get decent Italian bread?

Nevada. Made no sense to me. Benny doesn't even play golf.

I rented a car at the airport, followed the lines on the map the agent drew for me and, after a couple of wrong turns, pulled into one of those nondescript planned communities with a thousand small houses that all look pretty much the same, except for the landscaping on their tiny patches of front lawn.

I found Benny's place and stopped at the curb, watching as he stood there, garden hose in hand, watering some red and yellow flowers. Whatever my doubts had been, it seemed he'd made the adjustment to Southwestern living. He looked healthy, maybe even a bit younger than the last time we met. Typical Benny, though, he was wearing a black, long-sleeved knit shirt, buttoned right up to the neck.

I got out of the car and, when I slammed the door shut, he turned toward me. He didn't say a word. He just stood there nodding slowly.

I said, "Hi Benny. It's great to see you."

"Yeah," he said, "you too."

I walked toward him and we shook hands. "Isn't that shirt a little warm for this climate?"

"What's the difference?" he answered. "Everything is air conditioned, right? Your car, your house, the restaurants, the casinos. Pretty soon they'll air condition the friggin' streets out here."

He still had that chunky build on a frame that only stood about five and a half feet tall. He had less hair than the last time I saw him, although what remained had taken on a strange, orange-brown color that must have come from a bottle. His dark olive skin managed the sun quite nicely, and his face was still unmistakably a Benny original, not a straight line or sharp angle to be found. His eyes were dark and warm, and it occurred to me that if he gave up his signature scowl he could model for some kind of cuddly bear on a children's cartoon program.

I laughed. "I'm sweaty just looking at you."

"Yeah, well, you live out here a while and your blood thins out. Come inside, I'll buy you a beer."

We sat in his living room, a wave of cool air blowing from a wall vent that provided relief from his dark, East Coast clothing. The room was furnished with a couch, two matching chairs and some tables that were all obviously sold in a set.

"Where's Selma?" I asked.

"Out at the store I think. She'll be glad to see you."

I didn't think so, but I nodded anyway and drank some of the cold beer he handed me. It's amazing how quickly the hot, dry air out there can make you thirsty.

"You didn't waste any time coming out here."

I shrugged.

"So how long you in town for?"

I looked around, as if the answer might be written on a wall someplace. "I don't know."

"Uh huh." He stared at me, waiting.

I said, "This is a great place Benny, but what made you choose Vegas?"

"I like the warm weather, you know. And Selma didn't want to move to Florida with all the old Jews."

I hesitated. "Wasn't Selma Jewish?"

"Still is," he told me. "Funny life, eh?"

"It sure is," I agreed.

Benny waited for me to say something else. When I didn't, he asked about my mother and sisters. I told him they were still fine, since I'd spoken to him three days ago.

"Mom sends her regards," I lied. If my mother knew I was coming out here she would have burned my plane ticket.

"She never knew quite how to take me, your mother. Good lady, though."

"Thanks. I think she knows you were the only real friend my father ever had."

Benny stared at me for what seemed a full minute. "All right," he finally said. "Let's have a look at the friggin' letter."

I considered making a big show of going out to the car and looking for it in my suitcase, or saying something like, "Oh, the letter, right," but I pulled it from my pocket and handed it to him.

He took so long, I tried to decide if he was memorizing it or if he was the slowest reader in the universe. I thought he might go on studying it until nightfall when he looked up and handed it back to me. His eyes were pretty moist, and I knew it wasn't me he was seeing.

"Some guy, your father. Best friend I ever had."

"That's nice to hear," I told him. I certainly loved my father, even if there were times I didn't love everything he put me through. But it was a totally different matter to see him through Benny's eyes. Was he a reliable friend? Loyal? Generous? I knew how much fun he could be, but could you count on him when the shooting started?

61

Benny said, "I told you on the phone I want no part of this. Your father warned you about that in the letter. What'd you think? You were gonna come out here and con me?"

"No," I said, "but I needed to come here and ask. To find out what it's all about."

His round face gave way to an uneasy little smile. "You got a lotta your father in you, you know that? This is something he'd pull, showing up here like this."

I have to admit, I felt happy to hear him say that, but I tried not to look too pleased.

"You wanna know the story, is that it?"

"I do," I said. "My father always talked about making a huge score, but this is something else." I held up the letter for him to look at again, just in case he'd forgotten about it. "I want to know what money he was talking about."

"Money?" he asked, suddenly looking a bit puzzled.

"Sure," I said. "The stolen money."

Benny pulled the letter out of my hand and looked it over again. "Oh sure. The stolen money." He handed the letter back to me and really smiled this time.

"I'm sorry," I said, remaining as serious as I could which was not too difficult, since I didn't get the joke. "What's so funny?"

"Blackie, that's all," he said. "So what happens if I tell you what I know? What do you do then, you chase this pot o' gold to the end of the rainbow?"

"I'm not sure," I admitted. "It depends."

"On what?"

"On the risks, I suppose. On where the money came from. Like if it was from drugs, for instance, I'd want no part of it."

"Nah, Blackie never touched narcotics, you know that. It wasn't his style."

"All right, what then?" I folded the letter and put it back in my pocket. "Did he rob a bank?"

That made him smile again. "Come on, kid. You can do better than that." He finished his beer as he watched me. "You ready for another?"

I drank off what was left in the can and said, "Sure."

When he stood to go the kitchen, I went with him. I wanted to make sure he was going to keep playing this guessing game, if that's what it would take.

"You wanna eat something?" he asked over his shoulder as he leaned into the refrigerator.

"No thanks. The beer is fine."

He handed me another cold can and we went back to our matching chairs in the small living room.

"Look kid, you oughtta let this go. I did. It's the smart move. You're a nice boy. You don't wanna get yourself in a jam."

"No," I agreed with him, "I don't. But I can't let it go, can I? He left me this letter for a reason. I can't just ignore it."

"I understand." He paused, thinking it over. "You know, people do some strange stuff. They make mistakes. A guy like Blackie, he made a lotta wrong turns. Now all these years after he's gone, it shouldn't matter." He shook his head, obviously unhappy with that approach to the subject.

I waited.

"What does your mother know about this?"

"Not much," I said, "or at least she's not willing to talk about it. The envelope was sealed, not sure she ever read the letter. She just says I shouldn't be chasing my father's fantasies."

"She's right. Leave it alone." He sat back in his chair, looking comfortable, and I was afraid he was getting comfortable with the idea of leaving it alone.

"I notice you haven't said it's not for real. Or that the money isn't still there, wherever *there* is."

He puffed up his round, chubby cheeks and blew out a stream of air, looking like one of those sculptures that symbolize the winds of summer and winter. "You're right," he admitted. "I'm not saying that."

"So give me something, anything." I was leaning forward, doing my best to convey earnest desperation. Benny didn't seem impressed.

"Go get married. You're not married, right? Have some kids. Don't get involved with your father's crazy schemes."

I gave up the curious son angle and did the best I could to give him a serious man to man look. "You know I can't do that Benny."

"I suppose not," he admitted sadly. "But what are you gonna do if all you have is the letter?"

"I don't know. I'm starting with you."

"You haven't shown the letter to anyone else?"

"No, although I told my cousin Frank about it." I didn't see any need to bring Nicky into the discussion.

He sat up again. "You told Frank?"

"I just told him there was a letter. I didn't show it to him or anything."

"Well don't. Frank's a bum, you don't want him involved."

"All right."

"Did you tell him you were coming to see me?"

"I said I might. He's the one who told me you were living out here. I didn't have anyone else to ask," I told him, sounding as apologetic as I could.

"Damn," he said, which coming from Benny was a strong statement of disapproval.

"Does Frank know anything about this?" I asked him.

Benny didn't answer me. Instead he asked, "Did your father ever tell you about our days in the south of France, at the end of the war?"

"Not much. When he talked about the war he mostly told me about your tour in India."

His smile returned as he mulled over those memories, but only for an instant. "Did he ever tell you about our friend from Marseilles?"

"No. I don't think so."

The "Uh huh," I got in response made it clear that I'd given the wrong answer.

"Did he have something to do with this?" I asked.

Once again, he didn't answer me. "Your cousin didn't mention anything about France or about a guy there, did he?"

"Frank? No, he claimed he didn't know anything. I only spoke with him so I could find out where you are."

"Uh huh. Well watch out for him, will ya? I never trusted that creep, I don't understand why Blackie did."

"I think he saw Frank as being like him in certain ways."

"I guess so. In style, maybe. Not in here." He pointed to his chest, in the vicinity of where his heart would be.

"So you think Frank knew something about this? Before I told him about the letter?"

"Knowing your father's big mouth? Yeah. That's my guess. But don't tell him another thing about it, kid. Nothing."

I took a moment to deal with the notion that my father would have entrusted this secret to my cousin and not me. Benny read my mind.

"You're not like him, believe me. Your cousin I mean. You never were."

I nodded.

"If I could make the whole thing go away, I would. I don't want to see you in trouble or getting hurt." He paused. "I don't know how he talked me into the idea, but we were friendly with this Frenchman, and he was a straight shooter and so we figured, what the hell, we take a shot. I didn't realize how big this thing would get. None of us did. When we realized that we backed off."

"You mean you never really did it?" Whatever *it* was.

"Oh, we did it all right. And then we knew we had to let it go. It's like robbing a bank and realizing all the bills are marked or numbered or whatever. You got 'em but you can't use em, *capisce?*"

I nodded. "So why would my father leave me the letter?"

He shook his head. "He probably figured if you wait long enough, even the hottest rock cools off. That's all. I think he was wrong and believe me, the guy in France feels the same way."

65

"So that's it, then?"

He gave me a look as grim as a heart attack, and said, "That's it. Rip up the letter. Stay away from Frank. Tell him you saw me and I had no idea what Blackie was talking about. Period. End of discussion."

I fell back against the sofa cushion and took a long drink of cold beer.

"Look, I know you're disappointed. I know you miss your father. So do I. But what am I supposed to do, get you all screwed up, because of something we did all those years back? I don't wanna give you the old song and dance about how I love you like you're my own son, but believe me, Blackie wanted a different life for you. You've got that life, you've done good. Stay with it. Run with it. Don't get into this, okay?"

I could see that he meant it, that the case was closed. "Can we talk again?"

"Sure. Any time. Just not about this. You get in a jam on this and I can't help you. How do those corporate stiffs say it? I'm outta the loop, know that, right? I got no more influence, no pull. I'm retired." He lifted his hand to show me his small bungalow, as if that would convince me he was truly retired. "You wanna stick around, say hello to Selma?"

I knew what Selma thought of my father, which wasn't much. Funny how the wives of Serious Guys never like other Serious Guys or anything having to do with them. I suppose they need to blame someone for what their husbands become, and I didn't see any purpose in waiting to say hello so she could ask me what the hell I was doing there. She was a tough old bird, that Selma. "Maybe later," I said. "I better check into a hotel."

"You got a reservation?"

I said I didn't, that I was told finding a place for a night or two wouldn't be a problem.

"Go to Caesar's. Ask for Johnny Wendt at the front desk and use my name."

"I will. Thanks."

"You staying in town long?"

I managed to laugh for the first time that day. "I came here for this, as you know. I guess I could leave now."

Benny nodded. "I'm sorry kid, I really am. I'm glad to see you, though. And maybe it was worth it, you coming here I mean, just so I could tell you what I told you."

"To drop it, you mean."

"That's right. And to steer clear of that cousin of yours."

He stood up and so did I, then I followed him to the front door. We said our goodbyes out in front, next to his yellow and red flowers, under the heat of the sun as it was setting somewhere in the desert.

We didn't hug or any of that stuff, but we shook hands for quite a long time.

"Listen to what I'm telling you," he said. "I wouldn't do you any harm."

"I know that, but you know I can't just forget it and do nothing," I said. Then, as I was walking away, I stopped and turned back. "Thanks for always being such a good friend to Blackie."

He nodded, but didn't say anything else, so I got in the car and drove into town.

CHAPTER SIX

After I left Benny I went to Caesar's Palace. As he suggested, I asked for his friend, a manager there who got me a room at a discount. After checking in, I went upstairs, dumped my bag on the bed and went back down to get something to eat.

Dinner for one is a bore, so I hunted for a spot where I could have a quick bite before heading to the casino. One of the hotel restaurants pronounced itself a "New York Style Deli," which sounded good enough for my purposes.

My father always got a kick out of people around the country who claimed to hate New York, then coveted everything to do with the city, flocking to delis that proclaimed themselves "New York Style," or restaurants that served New York Style Cheesecakes or New York shell steaks. What the hell has New York City got to do with shell steaks? When was the last time you spotted a herd of cattle in Central Park?

I sat a small table where I was served a sandwich stuffed with corned beef sliced so thick and fatty that if they served it on Broadway the place would have been out of business in a week.

I thought of what my father would have done, and called the waiter over.

"This sandwich is full of fat," I said.

The waiter was a skinny young guy with a dark Mexican face and heavy accent.

"Corned beef, man," he replied, as if that was an answer.

One time my father complained about a serving of veal marsala. When Blackie didn't like the waiter's response, he picked up the cutlet and slapped the guy across the face with it. Somehow, I didn't see myself taking a swing at this Chicano with half of a corned beef sandwich.

"Right," I said. "I know it's *supposed* to be corned beef." I picked up the top piece of rye bread to show him the grizzly mess that lay beneath. "Looks more like corned fat to me, don't you think?"

He stared at me with a look as blank as a handball wall.

I thought about calling over a manager or something, but it felt too ridiculous. I mean, it was just a corned beef sandwich after all.

"Forget it," I said, then watched him shrug his narrow shoulders and walk away.

I did my best to cut away the pale fat, then wolfed down what remained of the sandwich and washed it away with a couple of Heinekens. It was time to play blackjack and donate some of my money to the local economy.

I found a quiet table with a couple of players and sat down. My heart wasn't really into gambling, and I made one bad pull after another, alternating lousy hands with some poor decisions the other players did not appreciate. Blackjack players tend to be critical of mistakes that ruin their hand and kill the flow of the shoe.

I didn't care.

After losing enough to feel sufficiently beat up, I stood, collected the few chips that were still mine, and found my way to the sports lounge. I needed a lift, and the sports parlor is an assault on the senses if ever there was one.

The room was huge, with high ceilings and walls lined with banks of large monitors displaying what appeared to be every sporting event going on around the world at that moment. Football, basketball, soccer, dozens of different racetracks—you name it and you can watch it. And bet on it, of course. The din is incredible as players cheer, moan, holler and curse at the images on the wall. An ever-present cloud of thick gray cigarette and cigar smoke hung in the air like a Calder mobile.

In the middle of all this was a large square bar. I found an empty seat, ordered a Jack Daniels and watched the proceedings. I was getting tired, but there was enough energy in the room to keep me going. The bar stool was comfortable, with a padded seat and a nice high back. I'll bet there isn't an uncomfortable chair anywhere in Vegas.

Someone behind me said, "I thought I might find you here."

I turned at the sound of his voice.

"I checked the blackjack tables first," Benny told me. "You like blackjack, just like your father. Am I right?"

"You're right," I said.

Benny was wearing the same gray slacks and dark, long sleeved shirt he wore that afternoon. He looked around the room as if it were the first time he'd ever seen the place. "Some joint, eh?"

"It is."

"You got any action going?"

"Not yet. I thought I might wait for a really exciting bowling tournament to come on."

Benny smiled. "Johnny take care of you? Get you a room all right?"

"He was great, thanks. Can I buy you a drink?"

Benny shook his head, not turning me down, more like he couldn't believe the question. "Blackie's kid buying me a drink," he said. "Isn't life something?"

"Yes," I agreed. "It really is."

The bartender was looking in our direction. Benny said, "Hey Carl, how's it going?"

The bartender told him it was going fine. "Black Label, Benny?"

"Lots of ice."

"You got it."

"My father's drink," I said.

"Yeah. I used to drink Dewar's. Blackie told me to stop being such a cheapskate."

"Life is too short to drink cheap booze."

"That's what he always said," he recalled with a smile. When the bartender served him, Benny asked me, "You drink this stuff?"

I shook my head. "Uncle Vincent and I got together a few weeks after my father's funeral. He wanted to talk things over, so we went at a bottle, neat."

"Dangerous."

I laughed. "We started toasting every memory we could come up with. I passed out at the table for a while, but he didn't notice. I still have the bump on my head where I went down."

"C'mon."

"Just kidding. I drink vodka or Jack Daniel's. Safer for me."

"Same proof, no?"

"Sure. Different memories, that's all."

He nodded, said, "*Salud*," then we touched glasses and drank.

Benny and I spent some time looking around the room, commenting on the games. I asked him if he wanted to sit down.

"Nah. I sit too friggin' much as it is." He drank some of his scotch and I waited for him to tell me why he was there. "When you going back?"

I said I was leaving in the morning.

"You booked the flight already?"

"Yes," I replied.

He asked me which flight and I told him.

"American, eh? I got a friend at the airport, maybe get you an upgrade."

I thanked him, and explained I'd already done that. "I travel a lot for my ad agency, have a load of frequent flyer miles."

He looked impressed. "So, the early flight on American."

"No sense in sticking around," I told him, "and I've got to get back to work on Monday."

Benny took a deep breath and let it out slowly. "I know you came a long way to see me. You respected what I told you, that I wouldn't talk about it over the telephone."

I waited.

"You always showed respect," Benny said. "And you were always a smart boy."

"Thanks."

"Don't thank *me*. Your father was a smart guy, it figures he'd have a smart son. He could be a little nutty," he said with a deferential raising of his hand, "but Blackie was smart. Don't ever let anyone tell you different."

I felt like thanking him again, but took a pass.

Benny sipped some more of the scotch, then moved a little closer and lowered his voice. "I realize finding this letter, especially after all these years, it's like, uh, it's like Blackie talking to you from the grave. I don't want to get sentimental, but you know what I mean, right?"

I was glad he had no intention of becoming any more sentimental than discussing my father's grave. "I know exactly what you mean."

He placed his hand on my shoulder. "The thing is, kid, even if a guy talks to you from the grave, that doesn't mean he's making any more sense than he did before he was dead. You understand that, right?"

"I think so."

"Good." He squeezed my shoulder, then took his hand away and backed up a little bit. He took a moment to check out the room, as if someone might be watching us. "The last thing I want for you is that you should have any trouble. I don't want that on my head. Your father would haunt me the rest of my life."

As he struggled with that idea I started to feel rotten that I'd come to Las Vegas to bother him. I said, "I have the same problem, in a way."

"Right," he said, then reached into his pocket, took out a small piece of paper and pushed it into my hand. "The guy in France. That's his name." He gestured toward the paper with a tilt of his head. "I don't know where he lives anymore, but I'm pretty sure he's still in the south, someplace near Nice. I haven't seen him since Marseilles, but your father talked to him every now and then. He may be dead himself, for all I know. He was older than we were."

"You haven't seen him in more than thirty years?"

He smiled a sad smile. "Yeah, I guess that's right. Hadn't thought of that. More than thirty years." He paused. "Point is, he's the only one who could tell you anything about this. After a while I didn't want to know about it anymore. Your father and Gilles. It became their thing."

I unfolded the slip of paper. It said Gilles de la Houssay, and I did my best to pronounce the name. "That how you say it?"

"Close enough."

"What am I supposed to do with this?" The question came out sounding harsher than I intended, but let's face it, this wasn't exactly the sort of clue that would send Sam Spade scurrying for his shoulder holster and booking passage to the Riviera. "What I mean, is what should I do next? Isn't there anything else you can tell me?"

Benny looked around the room again, then shook his head back and forth very slowly. "This is it for me. I think you should let the whole thing go, which I told you enough times already. But now you have all I got to give. See if you can find Gilles, see if he'll talk to you." He made another quick nod toward the paper in my hand. "That's it."

And I knew him well enough to know, this time he really meant it.

CHAPTER SEVEN

Benny and I stayed at the bar for a while longer, then he left and I went to play some more blackjack. After a couple more drinks, and a winning streak that got me back to even, I headed upstairs to bed. I felt a little drunk, a little tired and emotionally spent, so I was disappointed to wake up at four in the morning. Although my body was in Las Vegas, I guess my brain thought it was still in New York and decided it was time for me to get up.

Alone in a hotel room in the pitch dark, I was wide awake, with nothing to do but think.

The human brain is a magnificent thing, but the one feature it lacks is an on-off switch. You can stop yourself from doing just about anything, except thinking. You can close your eyes and stop seeing. You can tune people out and not listen to what they're saying, even without putting your hands over your ears. You can stop moving, walking, talking. You can even hold your breath for a while. But your noggin just keeps going, asleep or awake, whether you like it or not.

I have friends who claim that meditating stops your mind from working, but it didn't work for me. All you do when you meditate, instead of allowing your mind to run off in its own directions, is to focus on a solitary thought like a one-word mantra, or the picture of waves crashing on a beachy shore, or some other repetitive image that's supposed to be peaceful and soothing.

God save us from the gurus.

Rather than some deep breathing exercise, I preferred to lay there and worry about things, so naturally I thought about my father. And, being in Las Vegas, I thought about the time he decided he was going to teach me how to play poker.

I was thirteen and I wanted to buy a junior golf permit, which cost twenty-five dollars. I had a couple of friends who started playing golf, I tried it a few times and it was fun. Van Cortland Park and Mosholu were the municipal courses near where we lived in the Bronx, but they cost ten dollars a round without a permit. With a junior permit it was only three.

Blackie didn't like the idea. He believed I was too young to play golf.

"Golf is for old men," he said. "Kids should play baseball and football. What kind of pussies are you hanging around with? Next thing I know, you'll be coming home with a tennis racquet."

I didn't think of my friends as pussies, and I liked golf. I was too skinny to play football, and couldn't hit a baseball very far—I was all glove, no hit, which doesn't get you chosen for the starting nine at that age. I was good at stickball, since I was fairly coordinated and you don't need a lot of strength to power a rubber ball with a broom handle. But how much stickball can you play?

I wanted the golf permit.

When Blackie came home one night after a few cocktails, I figured it was a good time to bug him again about the twenty-five dollars. With some drinks in him, I thought he might be feeling generous.

"What's the matter, don't you have any money of your own?" he asked me.

I felt like telling him, sure, I have that two million in the trust fund you set up for me, except I don't feel like going to the bank this week. Instead, I said, "I have about six dollars saved up."

"Okay, big shot, I tell you what. You bring your bankroll into the kitchen and we'll have a little poker game. You and me. One on one. I'll give you a chance to win the money and teach you a little lesson in life."

I already knew how to play poker, although I don't recall which of my friends taught me. Poker is just something you seem to know how to do, except maybe you get confused about whether a flush beats a straight, but only in the beginning. It's not like chess or bridge, where someone has to sit you down and explain all the moves and the rules and the nuances. Poker is just something you learn how to do, almost by osmosis, like checkers.

Since Blackie was a little snookered I figured I had a chance. I hurried inside, pulled out the money coins I had hidden in a tin box, and ran back to the kitchen. When I got to the table my father was waiting with a deck of cards, my mother standing over him, serving up a lecture on what a bad example he was setting and how gambling was evil and that there had to be something seriously wrong with a father who would even suggest that he play cards for money with his own son.

When my father saw me standing in the doorway he started shuffling the cards. Ignoring my mother, he asked, "You know how to play poker?"

"Sort of," I told him.

"What you don't know you're about to learn. Siddown."

I looked at my mother, giving her one of those imploring looks that said, come on Mom, give me a shot here.

She said something like, "I can't believe this," then stormed out of the room, leaving me to work it out with my father.

"Table stakes?" Blackie asked as I sat down.

"Huh?"

"How much are we playing for?"

"I don't know," I admitted. "I need twenty five dollars for the permit."

"I don't want to hear about the damned permit after tonight, you understand?"

I nodded.

"Put your money on the table."

I opened my hands and spilled my collection of coins and bills onto the speckled mica table top.

Blackie put down the cards and counted my money. I had six dollars and twenty-five cents. He reached into his pocket and pulled out a roll of bills. "Table stakes means you can bet anything on the table. You understand?"

"You have a lot more than I do."

"That's all right, I can't bet any more than what you have in front of you."

Seemed fair to me.

"And we ante fifty cents a hand."

I agreed, feeling proud that I knew what it meant to ante. I slid two quarters to the middle of the table.

"Cut the cards," he told me, and I did. "Five card draw, all right?"

I only knew two games at the time, five card draw and seven card stud. I was grateful he picked one of them. "Sure," I said.

He dealt out the cards, then asked me if I wanted to bet.

"Not yet."

"You don't say, *not yet*. You pass."

I nodded earnestly. "Okay. I pass."

"I bet two dollars," he said.

Two dollars! The fifty cents ante already made this the largest poker hand of my life. I looked at my cards. I had a pair of jacks, so I nervously slid two dollars to match his and asked for three cards.

"Dealer takes two," he announced. He took my discards and dealt me three new ones. Then he replaced his two. After he looked at his hand he explained that he had the right to make the next bet since he was the opener.

"The opener?"

"The player who made the first bet," he said impatiently, his whiskey breath filling the air between us. "You passed and I opened, so

I'm the opener. Unless there were other players and somebody raised, then the last raiser would be the bettor. I thought you knew how to play this game."

"I forgot that part, I guess."

"Three dollars and seventy-five cents," he said, throwing four singles on the table and pulling out a quarter.

"Three seventy-five?" That was exactly what I had left. I stared at the cards I'd drawn, which included a third jack. Then I looked at my father. "If I lose, that's it?"

"That's it."

I wasn't exactly the Cincinnati Kid, but I had an idea he was bluffing, trying to bull me out of the game on the first hand. I slowly pushed all my money to center of the table.

Blackie looked surprised. "What have you got?"

"I think you have to tell me first, right?"

"Don't be a smart ass."

I shook my head, then slowly laid out my cards. "Three jacks," I said nervously.

"Sonuvabitch," Blackie said as he threw his cards face down on the table.

"I won?"

He shoved the cards at me. "You deal," he said.

The next few hands Blackie stayed with his scorched earth policy, trying to scare me out with large bets. I dropped out a couple of times, but after eight or nine hands I'd won more than twenty-five dollars. I was feeling pretty excited. "Well, that's it for me, Dad. I quit."

"You what?" he asked in an angry voice. You would have thought I just told him I'd thrown his television out the window.

"I have the money for the permit. That was the idea, right?"

"Did I tell you not to mention the permit again?"

"You said after tonight. You said I shouldn't mention it again after tonight."

He started to get out of his chair. "Are you razzing me?"

I felt my insides get a little shaky. "No, I'm not, I'm really not. I just thought what you said—"

"I don't give a good goddamn what you thought. You can't quit while you're winning."

"I can't?"

"You gotta give me the chance to get even."

"I do?"

"That's right."

"Then how does the game ever end?"

I don't know if that concept had never previously occurred to him, but it seemed to take him by surprise. And made him even madder. "The loser says when it's over."

"But Dad, if I lose I have no more money. You could keep losing forever."

I knew the concept was right, but the way it came out...

"You think I'm gonna go on losing to you forever?" he hollered.

"That's not what I meant."

"I'll bet it's not."

By now my mother was back at the kitchen door, providing her version of a Greek chorus, reminding my father that she had warned him, that these were the wrong lessons for a father to teach his son, but all she did was stoke Blackie's anger.

I sat there as they got into it, occasionally glancing at the pile of money in front of me. As the volume of their shouting increased, so did my fear that I was not going to be allowed to keep the money I won.

I wasn't.

In the middle of his argument with my mother, Blackie announced that I was not entitled to my winnings since I had not given him a chance to get even.

I couldn't believe the utter stupidity of his reasoning. "Why would anyone bother to play poker," I asked, "if no one is ever allowed to win?"

He turned from my mother, glared in my direction, then got unsteadily to his feet and grabbed all the money off the table. All of it, not just my winnings, but my original six and a quarter as well.

I stood up too. "What about my money? What about the money I started with?"

"That's the price of learning a valuable lesson," he sneered at me, and made his way out of the room, into his bedroom, slamming the door behind him.

To this day I have no idea what valuable lesson he was referring to, but I can tell you that I never played another game for money with my father, not for the rest of his life, certainly not when he was drinking.

That said, when I woke up in the morning, I found twenty-five dollars next to my bed, which neither of us ever discussed again. As I may have mentioned, Blackie was a mass of contradictions.

* * *

WHEN DAWN FINALLY ARRIVED that morning in Nevada, I was already showered and dressed. I headed for the airport, boarded the flight for New York and settled back in a comfortable gray leather seat, grateful for the frequent flyer miles that got me to the fancy upstairs compartment they used to have on the 747. A Bloody Mary seemed a reasonable idea as I prepared for several hours of wondering what the hell to do next about Blackie's letter. All I had so far was Benny's refusal to help and the name of a Frenchman who may or may not still be around.

As I sank into a bog of confusion, a young woman's voice intruded with a polite "Excuse me."

She was seated just across the aisle to my left and, as I turned in her direction, she apologized for interrupting whatever I was doing, which was obviously nothing. Unless you consider staring into space doing something.

She had a pretty face, if you're partial to a firm line at the jaw, well drawn but delicate features, deep blue eyes and a healthy tan. I had given her the once over as I got on the plane, but when she barely glanced at me in return, I sort of forgot she was there.

"I'm sorry," I said to her now, "did you ask me something?"

She pointed to a magazine sticking out of the seat pocket in front of me. "I was wondering if I could have a look at that. If you're not reading it right now."

That was a silly thing for her to say, wasn't it? I mean, how could I have been reading it if it was in the seat pocket? I pulled out the magazine and handed it to her. "I'm too busy doing nothing to read."

She thanked me as she took the magazine.

"You come here often?" I asked.

She looked around her, then back at me, cold comment on an old line. "You mean this airplane or Las Vegas?"

"I meant Las Vegas."

"I work here." She opened the magazine and sat back.

"Ah," I said.

A few moments later, she said, "I'm sorry, did you lose a lot of money in the casinos or something?"

"Why do you ask?"

"You seem a little, uh, distracted."

"Oh. No, I really wasn't thinking about the casinos at all. I was only in town for one day."

"You came to Las Vegas for one day?"

"Business," I said, making that sound as important as I could.

"Was it a successful trip?"

I shook my head. "I guess that's what I'm trying to figure out."

She didn't seem in a big hurry to resume looking through the magazine, so I asked what sort of work she did in Nevada.

"Hotel management," she told me.

"Oh," I said again, falling back upon some of my cleverest repartee. I often rely on "Oh" or "Ah," or my favorite, "Huh?" to keep a conversation going.

She asked if I lived in New York.

"I do. Born and bred. What brings you east?"

"Other than this airplane?" She smiled, which was the first time she tried it on me. It was quite a smile.

I said, "Yes, other than this airplane."

"I grew up in Queens," she told me. "Visiting, then going on from there."

I nodded. "You want a drink?" I asked.

"Why not," she agreed, closing the magazine on her lap. She told me her name was Donna, so I introduced myself.

The stewardess came over and I suggested a Bloody Mary. "It's a morning kind of cocktail. Chock full of Vitamin C."

Donna ordered a screwdriver instead, just to stay with the citrus thing I guess, and I asked for another Bloody Mary.

She told me she had a graduate degree from the hotel and management school at Cornell, spent a few years in New York, then a couple of years ago landed a job in the front office of one of the big complexes on the Strip. She was learning the casino trade from top to bottom.

"You visiting family back home?" I asked.

"No, just friends. My family moved to Florida a few years ago."

"Ah. Florida."

"I'm looking forward to just walking around the city for a couple of days. I miss it. Las Vegas is awfully provincial, for all its glitz. When you work in the industry, which almost everyone does, it becomes a very small town."

"Never thought of it, behind all that glitz."

She showed me her smile again. "What do you do?"

"I write."

"Newspaper? Magazine?"

"Advertising."

She nodded.

"You said you were going on from New York. To see your family in Florida?"

"No. Taking some vacation time in Europe."

"Ah."

"What sort of business brought you to the land of Sodom and Gomorrah? Your agency doing work for one of the hotels?"

"No, it was personal."

"Sorry. I didn't mean to pry."

I told her it was fine, since I'd been prying into her life for the last several minutes. "I needed to look up an old family friend."

"Things work out?"

"I'm not sure," I admitted. "But it was good to see him."

She studied me for what seemed a long time. "Well that's something, right?"

"Yes," I said, "I suppose it is."

CHAPTER EIGHT

As Donna and I continued our transcontinental chat, I found myself thinking about a place where my father spent a lot of time, back in the day. A place that might help me make sense of his letter.

Arthur Avenue is a street in the Bronx, but the name is used to describe the surrounding area, a neighborhood in the truest, old-fashioned, New York sense of the word. The apartment buildings are tenements, three and four stories high, no doormen or any of that swanky Manhattan stuff. At ground level you'll find some of the best Italian restaurants in the city, which means they're among the best anywhere in the world, except Italy.

Arthur Avenue was my father's main stomping ground, where he hung out, where many of his friends worked and where several of them met for their Saturday lunches, which they called the Club.

I had a feeling I might find some answers there, in his old neighborhood, among that old crowd. Just before our plane set down in New York, I invited Donna to dinner.

"Look," I said, "I've got my car at the airport, you need a ride into town and I can promise you a great Italian dinner. Not a bad deal, right?"

"You sure you're not a lawyer?"

"Huh?"

"You sound like you're pleading a case."

"Really?"

"You make a dinner invitation sound like an argument to a jury." She gave me a flash of her killer smile.

"All right, what's the verdict?"

"Well, the jury is still out on you," she said, "but I'll be happy to go to dinner."

Getting off the plane I had nothing but a carry-on, so I waited with Donna at the claims area for her suitcase.

"This is it?" I asked as I lifted her bag off the luggage carousel.

"That's the only one."

"You travel light," I said.

"You mean, for a woman?"

"Ouch."

"Carry my bag and you're forgiven."

We headed to the long-term parking lot, climbed into my eight-year-old Karmann Ghia convertible and headed up the Van Wyck Expressway toward the Whitestone Bridge.

The Roosevelt was opened in the early fifties by Antoinette and Anthony, a couple who emigrated to the States from Sicily, opened their *trattoria* and named it in honor of the late, revered President of their adopted country. Anthony presided over the bar and dining room while his wife, Antoinette, ran the kitchen like a small fiefdom. As far as my father was concerned, she was the best cook in the city.

Blackie became a regular during his days as a liquor salesman, after which he would stop by almost every Saturday afternoon to have lunch with other guys from the Avenue. That was how the Club got started.

The Club was not any sort of formal organization. There certainly was no golf course or clubhouse because, as you figured out already, Blackie and his cronies were not country club material. Serious Guys never are, and never want to join any organization—with one notable exception I need not name. Those lunches at the Roosevelt became a ritual, a collection of men who had known each other for years, who gathered on Saturday afternoons with only a few rules, all of which were strictly enforced.

No women. No discussion of your own business. And every member would have to contribute money every week to the Fund.

The Fund was based on the charity-begins-at-home concept, available if one of the members was in financial straits. Or one of the good kids in the neighborhood needed a few bucks for college. Or a friendly politician in the area needed help. Basically, the Fund was a way of giving the group a reason for being, other than the chance to share stories and the enjoyment of Antoinette's cooking.

At times, when I accompanied my father on his Saturday morning rounds, he would take me to those lunches at the Roosevelt. Most of the men at the table liked to say they knew me since before I was born, and they never seemed to mind my being there, even though I was the only kid that ever sat at their table.

I knew how to act with respect and to keep my mouth shut, which was pretty much all they wanted from me.

There was a lot of talk at those lunches about big real estate deals and other investment opportunities where they would all have a chance to make a fortune. Those discussions weren't considered a violation of their rule against promoting your own business, because they were outside their normal occupations and presented a chance for the others to participate in something really huge.

As far as I knew, very few of those longshots ever came through, but during the flight from Las Vegas, I found myself trying to recall my father mentioning anything of a plan that involved the south of France, or whatever the hell he was talking about in the letter.

I was also wondering if there might be someone around Arthur Avenue who remembered.

* * *

DURING THE RIDE I TOLD DONNA about the Roosevelt and the Club and how going back to Arthur Avenue was like a trip down

Memory Lane for me. She seemed interested, or was too polite to say she wasn't.

"When was the last time you were there?"

"I go to Arthur Avenue for dinner every now and then, but not to the Roosevelt. Too many ghosts, I think. I haven't been there in years."

"The way you talk about it, I thought you were there last week."

"I guess seeing my father's old friend in Vegas made me feel a little nostalgic."

"Nostalgia is good," she said. "It's honoring your own history."

"I like that," I told her.

"I mean it. People who think it's corny must be ashamed of something, don't you think?"

"I don't know," I said. "I'd have to think about that."

Donna laughed. "Don't jump to any dangerous conclusions."

When we walked into the Roosevelt I could see the place hadn't changed much. Except for the people. I'm not sure what I expected, but I felt disappointed not to recognize any of the men at the bar. It was an early Sunday evening, so there were a few guys staring up at the television as the late afternoon football game wound down, but not a familiar face among them. I stood with Donna beside me, just inside the door, thinking maybe this wasn't such a great idea after all.

Then I spotted Ralph.

Ralph was Anthony and Antoinette's oldest son. He must have been about fifty years old by then, a huge man who stood well over six feet tall, with broad shoulders, a thick neck and a head that made him look like he wouldn't need a helmet to play on the offensive line for the Packers. His hair was wiry and cut very short, just like his father had worn his. He was talking to the bartender at the far end of the room, and they were having a laugh about something. I remembered him years ago, when he was trim and muscular, running errands for his parents, working in the kitchen, lifting boxes filled with vegetables and mopping the floors. Now he was dressed in a dark suit, white shirt and dark tie, and it was obvious he was in charge. When he spotted us he grabbed two menus and made his way to the front. His legs were so long he seemed to take the entire length of the room in about three easy strides.

"An early dinner, folks?"

I smiled at him. "Hi Ralph," I said. "Long time no see."

It took a few seconds, but when he recognized me he took my outstretched hand and started pumping it hard enough jack up a Peterbilt.

"Blackie's kid," he said. "Blackie's kid. Jeez. How the hell long has it been?"

"Before my father died. Six, seven years, at least."

"Jeez. I remember you as a skinny little geek, always talkin' books and stuff. You become a professor or what?"

"Not exactly. Advertising," I told him.

Ralph nodded slowly. "Almost the same thing in a way, right? Words. You were always good with words."

"I'm not so sure anymore," I told him. "Say hello to my friend Donna."

"Hi Donna, good to meet ya." He shook her hand, somewhat more gently than he had mine, then turned back to me. "What happened to you all these years? You been in jail, you been outta the country, what? You don't come by to say hello?"

"I don't know, Ralph. Too many memories, maybe."

He gave me a gentle slap on the shoulder. "I know what you mean. It's not the same without the old crowd. And I'm here every day."

"It's your place now, huh?"

"Hey, if not me, then who?"

I told Donna that Ralph's father, Anthony, was probably the sweetest guy who ever lived.

"Too sweet maybe," Ralph told her, but he seemed genuinely pleased to hear me say it. "Not nearly as tough as my mother, right?"

"Who ever was? And who ever made a rigatoni Bolognese that good?"

"I come pretty close."

"You cook here too?"

"Nah, I'm what you call the supervising chef. Fancy, eh? I got all the recipes up here," he told us proudly, pointing to his sizable head. "Come, sit down."

He led us past the strangers at the bar to a table toward the rear of the dining room, not far from where they used to set up the large, round table for the Club. It was late for Sunday lunch and early for dinner, so the room was fairly empty. In the quiet, I imagined hearing the murmur of familiar voices.

"What happened to the table for the Club?"

"Still got the big round top stored in the back. We pull it out once in a while for parties, groups, you know. But it's not the same. This place used to be filled with nothing but neighborhood people. You remember."

"Sure."

"Now the Avenue's a big deal. Actors and actresses show up. Politicians from downtown. Suits from Wall Street and Madison Avenue." He thought about how that sounded and added, "Hey, no offense. You're family."

"No offense taken."

"How about a nice Chianti Classico?"

"Great."

"I'll get you a good bottle." Turning to Donna, he said, "Jeez, last time I saw him I think he was drinking soda."

"Beer," I told him.

He laughed. "I'll be right back."

"What a nice man," Donna said as we watched Ralph head off.

"He's like his father," I said. "Just taller."

When Ralph returned with the wine, I asked him to join us for a glass.

"This is your idea of a romantic dinner with your lady friend, having me at the table?" He slapped me on the shoulder again. "What happened? I always thought you was a smart kid."

"Come on, Ralph, it's early, you're not busy yet."

He dropped his large frame into a chair, opened the bottle and poured us each a full glass, with none of that sniffing the cork or any phony tasting ceremony. We all toasted and drank.

"This is great wine," I told him.

He smiled. "Of course," he said.

Then I asked him about the guys from the Club.

I knew that both of Ralph's parents had died years back, but was saddened to learn how many of the other men from the Club had died. When I first sat at that table I was so young that most of them seemed old to me, even then. Yet somehow, when you're growing up, you never expect old people to get any older.

"We still buy our pastries from Gerry, though," Ralph told me.

"Gerry Egidio? No kidding."

"The one and only. Sonuvagun has more money than Midas, but he shows up for work every day. Must be eighty now."

"God bless him," I said, although I don't know why. As I may have already mentioned, I'm not the least bit religious. Must have been the setting.

"Yeah, Gerry takes good care of himself. Not the like the rest of us." He spread his hands across his generous gut. "Gerry's smart enough not to eat his own *cannolis*."

I laughed.

"I know he'd love to see you. You should stop by and say hello."

I knew I would do just that.

Gerry Egidio was the most articulate member of the group. Like most of the others in the Club, he was raised by immigrant parents and had limited schooling, but he educated himself while working hard, and became the premier baker in the area. He had a brood of children, I don't remember how many, and since he was older than my father, all of his sons and daughters were adults by the time I was allowed to attend those lunches. Gerry was always glad to see me, curious to discuss what I was studying in school and the books I was reading.

He had wavy, silver hair, an olive complexion and dark intelligent eyes that were framed by steel rimmed glasses. He wasn't a man who smiled a lot, not like a some of the other guys at the table who were quick to show how sociable they were, but his eyes would light up when we started discussing something that interested him, like whether the nineteenth century novelists had it all over contemporary writers. Contemporary to him meant Fitzgerald, Faulkner, Joyce and, of course, Hemingway. He argued for the older classics and was a big fan of the Russians, particularly Dostoevsky. In those days I leaned more to Salinger, Golding and Knowles, which he said was appropriate to my age, assuring me that taste in all things eventually changes.

He turned out to be right, except when it comes to Salinger.

Gerry liked my father, but was one of those people in my life who were adamant about my pursuing college and beyond. And not having anything to do with *the life*.

"You know," I said to Ralph, "I was actually hoping to talk with some of the old crowd."

"Yeah? You writing a book or what?" Turning to Donna, he said, "We always figured he would write a book some day. Maybe about the club?"

"Maybe I will. Some day."

"What then?"

"Something came up. Some old business. You remember my father's friend Benny?"

"Do I remember Benny? Of course. Great guy."

"Yes, he is."

Ralph gave me another playful clap on the shoulder. "Well if you got business around here, you better not wait another ten years to stop by." He drank off his wine, stood up with his empty glass in hand, and said, "So, I'm gonna make the two of you dinner, right? A little antipasto, rigatoni Bolognese, some veal with a side of escarole. Good?"

"Better than good," I said. "Donna?"

"Perfect for me."

"Okay." Ralph refilled our glasses. "Now forget all these old timers and talk to the girl about something interesting, you chooch." He shook his head and gave me a big smile before ambling off to the kitchen. "You bright guys, you don't know anything."

As it turned out, Ralph wasn't entirely wrong.

CHAPTER NINE

Donna and I were quiet on the ride back to the city, tired after the flight and the dinner and the wine. I pulled up to her hotel and we sat in my car, not speaking for a few moments. I was trying to figure the right thing to say but came up empty.

"I'm only in town for a couple of days," she reminded me.

"And you have friends to see."

"You seem to be the busy one, all these meetings with people from your past."

I nodded.

She stared straight ahead, looking out the windshield. Then she smiled. "Las Vegas and New York, that would be quite a commute."

"I guess so."

She started to get out of the car, then turned back. "It really has been nice meeting you."

"That's it, then?"

She squinched up her eyes, trying hard to look confused. Then she smiled. "What'd you expect? An invitation to spend the night?"

I gave her a perplexed look of my own, like I was thinking it over, which I actually was. "Will I see you again?"

"It depends."

"On what?"

She didn't respond, so I leaned toward her, took her gently by the shoulders and drew her to me. As we kissed, she placed her hand gently on my cheek, which I think is a terrifically intimate thing to do when you're kissing.

When she sat back, I asked, "How about dinner tomorrow night?"

"I've got a lot to do before I leave for Europe," she said.

"You've got to eat dinner."

She studied my face, as if it had words printed all over it. "All right," she said.

After we got out of the car and I carried her suitcase into the lobby, I thought about kissing her again, but there were a lot of people around and Donna looked like she was ready to say good night, so I let it go.

Walking out into the balmy autumn night, I was feeling a lot better than I had all those hours ago, when I boarded the plane for home.

* * *

I TEND TO WAKE UP QUICKLY, not like people who ease their way out of sleep slowly, as if they're pulling off a turtleneck sweater, careful not to stretch the fabric as they emerge into the light. That's not how I operate. My eyes pop open and I'm up, simple as that.

The morning after I got back from Vegas, I jumped out of bed and made for my father's box of papers.

It was so obvious. Benny had given me the name. Gilles. But he was also telling me there must be something about him in the box.

There was.

It took a while, pouring through the photographs with faces I didn't recognize and letters from people I never knew, but then I found it. It was a letter from one Gilles de la Houssay, the name Benny had written out for me. The letter was still in its envelope, postmarked the year before my father died.

It was written in English, the penmanship excellent, a chatty note from an old friend. How are you? When are you coming back to visit us in France? That sort of stuff. At the end he wrote, "I know you are impatient. It has been a very long time, but you must act with caution. Let me hear from you soon." Then he signed off.

The return address was a place called Roquebrune. I checked my atlas and found it, a small town in the south of France.

I know what you're thinking. If Gilles had something to do with this, why hadn't my father mentioned him by name in his letter, why only mention Benny?

I wondered the same thing.

There was also the possibility that Gilles might have died, as Benny said.

Or maybe Blackie wasn't sure how Gilles would react if I showed up, a total stranger asking him a lot of questions.

I decided on the most likely answer—Blackie wanted to be certain I got to Benny before I spoke with anyone else. I had done that, and now I knew I had to find Monsieur de la Houssay.

* * *

I spent Monday morning in the office, working on a small account we had recently signed. It was a Cadillac dealership on Long Island, which is not the sort of client that tends to inspire madcap flights of creative fancy. It's tough enough trying to come up with original material for a new car, with everything that's already been done about new cars in the past fifty years, but the age of long, big-finned sedans was over, and even the Cadillac had become a stubby version of its prior self. Try inventing a meaningful ad campaign about that, especially when there's something much more important you want to be doing.

Taking a break from studying photographs of the client's showroom, I called a friend who worked for an international company with an office in Paris. She got me a listing for a Gilles de la Houssay living in a town called Roquebrune, somewhere just north of Monte Carlo. She gave me the address and phone number.

For all I knew, this M. de la Houssay could be a different fellow altogether, not the Gilles my father knew. He lived in the town named on the postmarked envelope, but what did that mean? This M. de la Houssay could be Gilles, Jr. Or Gilles the nephew. Or Gilles the cousin.

I took a deep breath, picked up the handset and dialed the number.

Listening to that funny overseas ring, my nervousness turned to concern. What if no one answered?

And then, after what seemed a long time, someone did.

When he said "*Bonjour*," I just knew he was the guy. It was the age of his voice, or something in it.

"Is this Gilles de la Houssay?" I asked.

"Yes it is," he said, in heavily accented English. After a brief pause, he added, "And you, I presume, are young Monsieur Rinaldi."

I didn't fall off my chair or anything, but I was more than a little surprised. "Yes," I admitted, sounding as if that made me guilty of something.

"Our mutual friend has been in touch with me," he said before I could ask the question.

Of course, I told myself. Benny. "He told you I might be calling?"

"He did." For some reason, I could imagine M. de la Houssay smiling at the phone. "He also told me why."

I waited, but he didn't seem to have anything more to say, so I decided to get right to it. "You know about my father's letter."

"*Mais oui*. And *you* know, as our friend has told you, this is not a subject to be discussed on the telephone."

I nodded, even though there was no one there to see it. "I understand that, but I really want to speak with you."

"I know," he said in a kind way that almost sounded like an invitation.

"I think we should meet. Would that be all right?"

He sighed. "I am not sure that it will benefit you in any way, but for me to meet the son of my dear old friend would be the delight of a lifetime. That much is certain."

And just like that, without the burden of reason or the control with which fear too often ruled my insular life, I was confirming his address, bidding him *au revoir*, and preparing to buy a plane ticket to France.

Then I realized I needed to pay a visit to my boss.

Harry was a short, heavy guy with a quick mind and a quicker temper. He wore a perpetual scowl that led some to say that the only way you'd ever see him smile was to turn him on his head. I always thought turning him on his head would be quite the trick, since he weighed more than a washing machine. Not what you'd call a health nut, the most exercise I ever knew him to get was a brisk walk back and forth to the men's room.

Harry had yellow stains on the fingers of his right hand from the ever-present cigarette he seemed to hold more than he smoked, burning them right down to the end. Even in those days, smoking was not allowed in our office, but that didn't stop Harry—he had a portable smoke-eater, kept his door shut, and figured he made enough concessions to modern values. He wasn't giving up the cancer sticks and no one complained, at least no one who wanted to keep their job.

His testy disposition, combined with the constant flow of nicotine, led to an ulcer, which caused him to switch his regular drink from scotch and soda to scotch and milk—convincing himself that the dairy ingredient provided a sufficient buffer for the ravaged lining of his oversized stomach.

I should mention again that this was 1979, just after that golden era in Madison Avenue advertising celebrated decades later in a popular television series, where the men wore trim-fitting suits with narrow lapels and narrow ties; drank heavily at lunch, in the office and after work; and chased women with abandon, since a woeful inequality of the sexes was the order of the day.

Which is not to say that people didn't drink or flirt when I started in the business, but this was a darker time, just after New York City almost went bankrupt and the disastrous Carter administration had spent almost four years destroying the country. Interest rates were inflated beyond all reason; our foreign policy was a debacle; the business world was struggling; and income was tight.

As to Harry, even in the face of those bleak economic conditions, I knew that behind his bluster he was basically a compassionate guy who recognized that I was one of his hardest working account execs, and felt sure he'd be understanding when I strolled into his office that morning to tell him I needed some time off to attend to family business.

"Are you batty?" he hollered. "I need an entire print and TV campaign for this dealership in two weeks. What the hell am I supposed to do without you?"

I told him it felt good to be needed.

"Spare me your pale attempts at humor." He lit a cigarette. "Can't this family business wait a couple of weeks?"

"It can't. But it shouldn't take long. I can bring the material with me. I'll work on the road."

"The road? What are you now, a traveling salesman? I hear you just spent the weekend in Vegas." He nodded in response to my surprised look. "That's right, I keep tabs on my people. So where's your next stop?"

"Monaco, I think."

"Monaco? You think? What is that, like maybe you're wrong, maybe you meant Sweden?" Harry wasn't given to expending a lot of unnecessary physical energy, so I knew he was fairly worked up when he lifted his corpulent frame out of the chair and started pacing around the room. "Monaco, you think. Maybe you mean Russia. Or

South Africa. Why don't you just throw a dart at a map? While you're at it, why not throw a dart at my head and put me out of my misery."

"I need to do this," I explained as calmly as I could. "Worst case, I'll only be gone a few days."

"Worst case for who? The client? Me? The firm?"

"I'll work on it while I'm gone, I promise."

Harry was running out of steam. He could only rant for so long before he got winded, so he sat down and puffed on his cigarette.

I said, "You know me, Harry. If I tell you I have to do this, then I do."

Harry thought that over. "What if I say no?"

I never really argued with Harry. Even when he would holler about something, I would let him finish, then work things out the best way I could. This time, I met his gaze through the small haze of gray smoke and said again, "I have to do this."

I think my tone took him by surprise, because Harry is rarely at a loss for words. He just sat there without speaking.

"It's only a few days."

He finally waved a pudgy, dismissive hand in my direction. "Do whatever it is you have to do. But take the goddamned paperwork with you."

"Right," I said. I got up, started out of the office, then turned back. "I really appreciate this, Harry."

"I know, I know," he said as he inhaled a lungful of poison. "I'm a fucking prince."

Back in my office, as I was pulling together automobile brochures and graphic layouts, the phone rang. It was Frank.

"I thought you were getting back to me."

"It's just been crazy," I said.

"Hey, I knocked myself out getting a number for Benny."

I couldn't imagine that "knocking himself out" consisted of more than one phone call. "I found him myself," I said, "but thanks."

"You could've told me you got to him, saved me a headache, eh?" He paused. "You speak to him? How is he?"

"He's good, he's really good. He asked for you," I lied.

"And the letter, when do I get to see this mystery note?"

"Right, the letter. Uh, we'll have to get together."

"Lunch. They let you out of your cage for lunch, don't they?"

"Sure, uh—"

"Great. One o'clock." Before I could respond, he gave me the name and address of a restaurant and hung up.

CHAPTER TEN

When Frank insisted we meet for lunch, I knew it was pointless to argue. He would catch up with me sooner or later.

He chose an Italian restaurant on East 27th Street, a place he said was owned by a friend. The dining room was light and airy, with white stucco walls, high ceilings and large overhead fans that turned very slowly. I strolled to the back, where Frank was already seated with a colleague.

Colleague is a generous description.

I wasn't surprised to find that Frank brought someone with him. It was an old Blackie move, having a flunkie in tow, just in case you needed help of one kind or another.

"This is Lou," Frank announced as I approached.

I responded with a look that said I needed a better explanation than the lug's first name.

"Big Lou is the best," was all Frank offered.

I am still not clear what Big Lou was best at, but I can tell you he certainly was big. He was dressed in a black suit with a white shirt he wore open at the neck, three buttons worth, to display a hairy chest and an assortment of gold chains that would have given a smaller man a backache hauling them around. His complexion was pock-marked, his eyes as dark as his suit, and his black toupee the kind of piece that gives wigs a bad name.

Frank said, "Whatever we want to talk about, we can talk about in front of Lou."

I was about to tell my cousin that there wasn't a single thing I wanted to discuss with either of them, but Frank clearly read my impulse to turn and walk out.

"Lou," he told his compatriot, "say hello to my number one cousin."

Big Lou unfolded himself and got slowly to his feet, introducing himself as Lou Grigoli or Grisanti or something like that. It was hard to concentrate since he blocked out most of the light in the room.

Lou offered his hand, which was the size of a small ham, and I was glad to have all of my fingers returned without injury when he was done squeezing it.

"Sit down, sit down," Frank urged us.

Lou and I sat down.

"Well," Frank said, "glad you managed to break away from the office." He turned to Lou, gave him a conspiratorial wink and the two of them chuckled.

"Yeah," I said, "they unlocked the shackles."

Lou must not get out much, because he had himself a long laugh over that one.

"Very good. Shackles. I like that."

"I'm glad you're pleased," I told him, which brought his laughter to an abrupt end.

"All right," Frank jumped in. "How about some snacks, eh?" He called out to our waiter by name and began ordering for the three of us.

That's Frank. He grew up in Rockland County and lives in Florida, while I'm a lifelong New Yorker, but he comes to town, chooses the restaurant, knows the waiter by name and starts ordering for everyone.

After he called for just about every appetizer on the menu, he looked up and said, "While we wait for the food, how about you bring us a bottle of Pinot Grigio."

"I prefer red," I said, and asked the waiter, whose name I didn't know, if I could order red wine by the glass.

"Forget that," Frank said, sending the waiter off to bring the Pinot Grigio. "Try the white first, you stubborn bastard." He turned to Lou. "My cousin is like a brother to me, you understand what I'm saying?"

Lou replied with a look as nuanced as a panel of sheetrock.

"I don't drink white wine," I said.

Frank looked at me and said, "You'll never change," then reached over and gave me an affectionate slap on the shoulder.

What the hell am I doing here? I wondered.

The waiter brought the Pinot Grigio, then the prosciutto, melon, salami, provolone and grilled vegetables Frank ordered. I resigned myself to eating, drinking and dealing with the numbing sensation of the clock ticking away, one second at a time.

"So what gives with your treasure hunt?" Frank asked.

I didn't recall any mention of a treasure hunt, so I said I'd rather not discuss it.

We ordered our main courses, which Frank was generous enough to let me do for myself. Then he took some time to choose a red wine before asking, "How was your trip to Vegas?"

Since I also had not told him that I had been to Vegas, I tried my best not to appear surprised. "Short," I said.

"You make any dough at the tables?"

"I didn't bankrupt myself, so I figure it was a win."

That broke Lou up again. "Your cousin's a funny guy," he told Frank.

Frank asked me how it was to see Benny, after all these years.

"A little strange."

"How so?"

I shrugged.

"That's it? No details? What's the problem? Is it Lou? I'm telling you, you don't have to worry about Lou. Right, Lou?"

Lou had already demonstrated his penetrating sensibility by observing that the parmigiana cheese was "very cheesy tasting, if you know what I'm saying," later adding that he was happy about the Pinot Grigio because—and I want to get this down verbatim—"It's good and cold like it should be." Now, in response to Frank's inquiry as to whether he could be trusted, he held out both hands, looked me in the eyes and said, "That's right, guy. You don't have to worry about Big Lou."

Boy, was my mind at ease.

"Look Frank, I don't mean any disrespect to your friend." I smiled at Lou, any respect I might be feeling was inspired only by the size of his shoulders, which were large enough to fill a steamer trunk, lengthwise. "There's nothing to tell. I saw Benny, he has no idea what I'm talking about, and that's really all there is. The rest of our discussion was about family, which I prefer to keep to myself." I turned back to Lou. "No offense."

Lou nodded with his hands, which is no mean feat if you stop to think about it. "Family business," he said. "I know about family business."

The waiter returned with the red wine and let Frank have a taste. "You'll love this Barolo," he told us.

It's incredible, how self-confidence isn't tied to ability or skill or knowledge. It's more like a virus that some people catch and others never will. I happen to know for a fact that Frank couldn't tell a good Barolo from a lousy St. Julien, not without a waiter and a scorecard. Yet here he was, giving me his toothy smile, raising his glass to mine and saying, "*Salud.*"

I was waiting for Lou to observe that the red wine was definitely warmer than the white when Frank took another run at me.

"Look cuz, I can see you don't want to talk about it, but did you at least bring the letter? I could read it in silence, if that's what you want."

"I don't have it," I told him. "But it doesn't matter. It's a dead end."

"Uh huh." He showed me his smile again, as if to say that we both knew I wasn't nearly as good a liar as he was. Refilling my glass, he looked at me with a coldness I had not seen from him in a long time. "You sure that's the way it is, or is that just the way you want it?"

I stared back at him without blinking. "Is there a difference?

"I think so."

"Either way, it's done."

As the meal thankfully wound down, Lou turned to Frank and reminded him that they had a pressing engagement downtown, the prompt sounding very well-rehearsed, delivered by the big man in monosyllabic style.

"You're right, Lou," Frank said as he had a theatric look at his watch, "I didn't realize where the time had gone. Sorry, cuz, we've gotta blow out of here." The two of them rose, as if on cue, said their hasty goodbyes, and hurried out, sticking me with the check.

I had no way of knowing the cost of that lunch would be the least of the problems they would create for me.

CHAPTER ELEVEN

I left the restaurant, stared up into the cloudless blue sky and decided to walk home. It was a beautiful day, and I thought it might be good to clear the old noggin.

As I strolled along, I thought about Frank. And Donna. And Blackie.

I became so lost in thought that, by the time I reached the United Nations, I stumbled into the middle of a political protest.

A crowd was gathered, some of them carrying placards, all of them yelling and chanting, mostly at each other. It had something to do with the endless violence in the Middle East.

Pro-Israeli zealots and pro-Palestinian extremists were screaming and jumping up and down and accomplishing nothing useful that I could see.

I moved off to the side, watching the ebb and flow of picketers and dissidents, fascinated by the crush of demonstrators as they spilled into the street, blocking traffic and ignoring the admonitions of policemen carrying bullhorns, cautioning them to disperse before they got themselves arrested.

Big problems deserve big solutions. Was this the best they could do?

I decided to turn west even though it was out of my way, not just to get away from them, but to stroll up Madison Avenue. Putting the political strife behind me, I returned to my own problems while passing some of New York's finest shop windows—Paul Stuart's beautifully tailored clothing, Tourneau's endless array of watches, a bookstore that sells first editions and the impossibly chic fashion shops further up the line.

Funny though, how my thoughts kept returning to the protest outside the U.N.

By the time I got to the sixties, I turned east for home. I only had a few hours before I picked Donna up for our dinner, but I knew I was not going back to work, that there was something I needed to do first. Reaching my apartment building, I got my car out of the garage and drove up to Arthur Avenue.

Sometimes you don't stop by Memory Lane for ages, then you're suddenly camping out there like it's where you live.

I parked around the corner from the Roosevelt and took a walk down the street to Egidio's Pastry Shop. It was a warm fall afternoon, and the sun felt good as I stood out front, staring at the window. Beautiful cakes were on display, placed on paper-lined shelves alongside trays of luscious *cannolis* and the largest Napoleons I've ever seen. There were racks of breads, piles of cookies and all sorts of other goodies. If you stood there long enough you could probably gain three pounds just looking at the stuff.

Gerry Egidio loved all his shops, but this was the original. I waited outside for a minute or so, thinking about how long it had been since I'd seen him, how awkward it was going to be to ask him to play twenty questions about my father. I took a deep breath and walked in.

There he was, behind the counter, giving instructions to two ladies about how to organize pastries on a large metal tray. When he turned in my direction he hesitated, then his businesslike demeanor softened.

"Unbelievable," he said.

I couldn't help but laugh. "You recognize me?"

"Recognize you? If I didn't know any better, I'd think it was your father thirty years ago." He came around the counter and shook my hand, holding it in both of his. "This is wonderful, wonderful to see you."

"You too," I said.

"Ralph stopped by this morning, said you were at the Roosevelt last night for dinner." He let go of my hand. "I'm happy to see you. Come," he said, and led me to one of the small wrought iron and glass cafe tables that were set off to the side of the shop. We sat, and he called to the ladies behind the counter, asking them for espresso and *biscotti*.

He wanted to know everything about me, and I told him. He knew I'd finished college and heard I'd done graduate work. He said it made him very proud. He recalled how much he enjoyed our discussions at those Saturday lunches at the Roosevelt, and how disappointed he was that I never came by to see him anymore.

I told him I felt odd about visiting the old neighborhood since Blackie died.

He nodded.

We drank espresso and talked about his children. When he told me he was seventy-eight, I said I couldn't believe it.

"You look exactly the same as the last time I saw you, you really do."

He smiled. "I try to stay in shape, I don't eat too much of my own *pasticcino,* and I keep working. That's the trick. Retirement is a death sentence."

He really did look the same. Same wire-rimmed glasses, same healthy olive complexion, same measured smile and those same dark, intelligent eyes.

"I'm a grandfather seven times over," he announced, then went to his wallet for photos.

"You're kidding," I said. I knew there was nothing unusual for a guy his age to have grandchildren, or even great-grandchildren for that matter, but I thought astonishment was the appropriate response.

"Three girls, four boys."

As I looked at the snapshots, I figured he must be a fine grandfather.

"Best thing in the world," he told me.

"That's great," I said.

"Ralphie says you're not married yet."

"I'm not," I admitted.

"It's time for you to find a nice girl, no?"

I ignored the question and continued to study the photos. Then I said, "My father wouldn't even be sixty yet, you believe that?"

"Yes," he said solemnly. "He cheated himself out of a lot of things, your father. But this," he said, tapping the snapshots with his forefinger, "this is the greatest experience in life."

I handed him back the pictures, then watched him take a sip of the dark coffee.

He placed the demitasse cup down and gave me an even, serious look. "You're not here because you missed my pastries or because you wanted to hear about my family. All these years, you never stopped by, then last night you see Ralphie and this afternoon you come to see me. What is it, son?"

When he used the expression "son," it kind of took me by surprise. I know it's just a figure of speech, but I drew a deep breath before I responded. "I want to show you something," I told him, "then I need to ask your advice."

"All right," he said softly.

I reached into my jacket and pulled out a photocopy of the letter. "I found this in my father's papers. My mother gave them to me a few days ago. It looks like he wrote this about a month or so before he died."

Gerry took off his glasses, trading them for a pair of reading spectacles he kept in his shirt pocket. He took his time going over the letter, reading it through twice. I watched him, thinking, if I can't trust Gerry Egidio, what is there to believe in?

109

When he finished he looked up, shaking his head back and forth, very slowly.

"Does it mean anything to you?" I asked.

He grinned and his eyes narrowed, making him appear years younger. "Blackie," he said. "He was a rogue, your father. He always broke my stones about working so hard, never having enough fun. He teased a lot of us in the group, but especially me."

"I remember."

He looked away now, staring at the trays of pastries and breads and cakes that lined the far wall of his shop. "I really miss him, maybe more than I miss anyone in the club. And that's funny, because we couldn't have been any less alike. Except for one thing. We both knew you were a smart boy. We both wanted you to be educated. My own kids, I did the best I could. They had some schooling, but none of them were really students. My sons are all in the business now, did I tell you that? They don't work as hard as I did when I was their age." He uttered a short laugh. "They don't even work as hard as I do now, but I guess that's how it goes, from generation to generation."

He gave me a look, as if that was something we should both think about. "You were different. You were intelligent, and your father saw that. As crazy as he was—and you should forgive me if I have to say that he was a little crazy. As crazy as he was, he saw it. It made him proud too. Don't think it didn't."

I couldn't bring myself to reply.

"So now you found this letter." He waved the paper gently in the air. "One of Blackie's schemes, one of those big deals he was always trying to cook up. And all these years later you want to make the mistake we all hoped you would never make."

"I'm not sure what to do," I admitted. "That's why I'm here."

He pressed his lips together and had another look at the paper. "I suppose you've already spoken to Benny."

"I did, yes. He knows what it's about, but the only thing he would tell me was that it has something to do with a man in France, an old friend of my father's named Gilles."

When I mentioned France, I saw something light up in Gerry's eyes, then fade just as quickly.

"This must have something to do with the time my father was in the Army. In France," I said again, hoping to get another rise out of him. "I think it was toward the end of the war. I thought maybe he said something to you at one of those lunches."

He switched eyeglasses and leaned against the back of his chair, folding his arms, staring at me. "I understand he left your family with very little."

"Nothing, is closer to the truth," I admitted.

"Then whatever he meant by this letter, if it amounted to anything at all, he would have told your mother, wouldn't he?"

"Not necessarily. I realize you don't know my mother, but she's a lot different than he was."

He nodded. "I understand. And I understand that this letter, coming to you all these years after he's gone, it makes you feel you need to do something about it."

"Exactly."

I waited as Gerry let his gaze meander around the room again.

"All right," he said at last. "There were times your father talked about something he and Benny did at the end of the war. Said they had a friend in France, and that some day they'd all be rich. It wasn't the only time he said he'd be rich, but this was something else. The war was over for so many years by then, and far as I know he never went back to France. If he had something going on there, what was he waiting for?"

"I have the same question."

"Most of the men in our crowd were in the service. Even I did my part, although I was too old for combat. Those days, in France or Italy or the Pacific, they were special to us." He shook his head again.

111

"Which certainly doesn't mean I'm encouraging you to go any further than this conversation. If he did something, stashed money or whatever nonsense he got into, it's ancient history now. You can see that, can't you?"

"I guess so."

"And his death, the way he died just after he wrote you this letter, that's part of it too, isn't it?"

I felt every drop of blood within me go ice cold. "What do you mean?"

"I didn't mean anything. I'm sorry."

"What are you saying? What has this got to do with his car accident?"

He removed his glasses again, shifted in his seat, sipped at his coffee, all without ever taking his eyes off me. "I don't know what to say." He hesitated. "I'm just trying to help you, that's all."

"I know, but help me do what?"

Gerry managed to smile again, although this time it came to him with difficulty. "To forget it? To stop asking questions you shouldn't be asking?"

I thought it over. "Sometimes I feel I've spent too much of my life not asking questions I should have asked, or worrying and thinking but then not doing anything. I went to college and graduate school, I work at my job, and where has it gotten me? I feel like half of my life I'm reaching for something, and the other half I'm playing it so safe I never get there."

The way he looked at me, I felt like an idiot.

"I'm sorry," I said. "It's just that I don't have anywhere else to turn for answers. I don't know anyone else I can trust, anyone who knows me and knew my father."

"I understand," Gerry said in a quiet voice that sounded as sad as I suddenly felt.

"What should I do?"

"I think you knew that answer, even before you came to see me." He waited for me to say something. "You're going to try and speak with this man Gilles?"

"I am," I said. "But I want to know what would you do?"

He hesitated before saying, "I think I'd do the same thing. I'd want to at least talk to him." Then he said, "Damnit, just remember, you're not your father. Whatever you do, remember that." He rubbed his eyes with the palms of his hands.

"Sometimes I think maybe I've run too far from who he was. I know that sounds nuts, but I do."

He said he understood. Then he made me promise to be careful. "Next time I see you," he warned me, "I expect to hear about the books you've been reading, not about old letters." He handed me the copy of Blackie's note, which he'd been holding all this time. "Come back and see me soon."

"I promise," I said. And I meant it, not just because it felt so good to see him, but because there was another part of our conversation we had not finished.

* * *

ON THE DRIVE BACK TO MANHATTAN I thought about my father's death.

Blackie had pulled one of his disappearing acts, which he would do every now and then when he was on a bender, or off "doing work," as he called it. My mother would become nervous when he disappeared for a day or two, and when he returned they would argue about why he couldn't phone from wherever he was, just to say he wasn't going to be home that night, that day, whatever. Blackie would tell her he couldn't, that was just the way it was. He couldn't.

This time, though, it ran into a few days before she heard from one of his friends.

I was living in Manhattan, so I didn't even know he was gone. It was my sister Kelly who called to tell me that Blackie had been away for three days and that my mother had just received a phone call. That's when I learned Blackie had been in a car accident.

In the hospital, my mother didn't want us to visit him, not until he'd healed up a bit. She didn't want any of us to be upset.

I told her that was nonsense, I was his son and I was going to see him.

Blackie was in the intensive care unit, an awful, insensate mess. His face was mostly bandaged, the uncovered areas badly bruised and cut and having turned various shades of purple and black and red. He lay there with his eyes closed, his breathing shallow and irregular, tubes and wires running from his arm and his nose and his chest to all sorts of monitoring devices, with hanging bottles crowding the small area. I sat there quietly for a couple of hours, just watching him, waiting to see if something would happen. I held his hand and spoke to him. He tried to mutter a few things, but mostly he slept.

I saw the doctor, who explained that the facial injuries were the least of it. He said that Blackie had suffered massive internal injuries, and the specialists were worried about how his heart was going to take it. He'd had a second coronary earlier that year, and his condition was very weak.

As I've said, he died two days after the accident without ever regaining consciousness. We were told he had been driving alone, that his car swung out of control on the Saw Mill River Parkway, and he crashed into a tree.

I recalled the car Blackie was driving in those days, a brown Eldorado with a white convertible top. I remembered that the car showed up in the driveway a few days after we buried my father, looking as good as new, supposedly having already been repaired. I remember saying how odd it was, that the car was fixed up that quickly, but my mother never responded. She sold the car as soon as she could, explaining to us that there was as much owed on it as it was worth.

My mother never discussed the circumstances of his death again.

* * *

AT THE ENTRANCE TO MY BUILDING I used the house key to let myself into the lobby, took the elevator upstairs and trudged wearily down the hallway.

Somehow, before I reached my door, I began feeling more alert. It was as if I had awakened from an uneasy sleep, knowing that something was wrong. I'm not sure how I knew, I just did.

I had already inserted my key in the lock when I noticed the scratch marks on the brass. It was one of those things you see but it doesn't register right away. Then it did. I hesitated, just before I turned the key, when it occurred to me that someone might still be inside.

I opened the door and quietly stepped inside, carefully measuring each movement. I stopped in the foyer, listening, hoping not to hear anything. There was silence, except for the sounds outside from the noisy streets of New York. I walked slowly toward the living room.

The contents of my father's box were scattered all over the coffee table and floor. I stood there for a moment, not ready to move again just yet.

I considered turning and walking out, then felt a rush of anger that told me, no, this is my goddamned apartment, I'm not running anywhere.

Maybe it wasn't the wisest instinct at that moment, but that was how I felt.

I turned for the bedroom, where I opened the closets, then looked in the bathroom where I pulled back the shower curtain, then moved to the kitchen. I don't know why it all began to strike me as funny, perhaps it was the absolute absurdity of the situation, or the fact that the apartment was too small to effectively hide anyone, but I even opened the refrigerator and dishwasher, just to amuse myself. Then I returned to the mess in the living room.

I drew a deep breath and let out a long sigh—it felt like the first breath I'd taken since I opened the front door—then dropped onto the couch, in front of the box, and stared at the mess that had been left behind. As I began sorting out the papers and photos, the first name that leaped to mind was, of course, Frank. Who else had I talked to about the letter? Nicky. Gerry. Benny. None of those names made for a likely suspect. Frank was the name that kept flashing across my mind.

I re-organized my father's papers, knowing the one thing they had not found was his letter, since I'd already hidden the original in a file at my office, the only copy still in my pocket. I assumed the note and envelope from Gilles de la Houssay went unnoticed and, when I found it, I experienced a momentary sense of relief. There was no reason for anyone to attach importance to an innocuous letter from an old friend. I put it down on the table, then went back to organizing the other papers, feeling sad and angry and lonely as hell.

CHAPTER TWELVE

That evening, shaking off the upset of the day and doing my best to dismiss the ghosts for now, I took Donna to dinner at *La Cote Basque*. There are some small benefits to working for a large advertising agency, one of which is the ability to get a table at a great restaurant on short notice. It was the best place I could think of and, if it was showing off, I thought *what the hell*. She wasn't going to be in town for long and, the way things looked, neither was I.

This was not the time to worry about my personal budget.

Unfortunately, it is no longer with us, but back then *La Cote Basque* was the most romantic spot in the city, with flowers everywhere and generously sized tables set far enough apart to provide the illusion of elegant intimacy. The food was even better than the decor.

"This is beautiful," Donna said as we were seated by the *maitre'd*.

The man nodded in appreciation and asked if we would like an aperitif. I ordered a bottle of champagne.

"I haven't asked you. How was your first day back in New York?"

"I started by sleeping late," she said. "Still on Rocky Mountain time, I guess."

"You see any of your friends?"

"I got around a bit," she said. "It was good to be in the city again."

"Visit your old stomping grounds in Queens?"

"Not yet. How was work?"

"I didn't spend much time in the office."

"Still taking care of your family business?"

I nodded, although after lunch with Frank, my discussion with Gerry Egidio, and having my apartment vandalized, I didn't feel I had taken care of anything.

"You manage to solve the mystery?" she asked.

"The mystery?"

"You know what I mean." She seemed a little embarrassed to be intruding.

"Oh," I replied, "*that* mystery."

She uttered a sweet laugh. "How many mysteries you have in your life?"

"More than I would like at the moment."

She responded with a look of concern I hoped she was faking. "Maybe I should know a little bit more about you before things go too far."

"I think I'm fairly safe to have dinner with."

Her deep blue eyes studied me for a moment. "I was thinking beyond dinner."

"In that case, ask me anything." The Laurent Perrier was served, and I watched as she took a sip, then delicately licked the champagne from her lips.

"So," she said with a sweet smile, "figure out what the letter was about?"

Falling in love is easy. It's the part that comes afterward that's tough.

Look at the romances portrayed in movies—I use motion pictures as a reference point for a lot of things because I believe they form the common bond of our time. I'm partial to the old black-and-whites Blackie introduced me to, and I grew up learning from the moral examples set by Clark Gable in *Test Pilot* or Cary Grant in *Mr. Lucky*, which were the catechism of a churchless family.

The ancient Greeks shared the experiences of the *Odyssey* and the *Iliad* as if they lived those adventures themselves, grand epics that were retold from one generation to the next. Other civilizations relied on their own myths to create a unifying ethic. The Bible came later, then an assortment of other tomes dealing with principles and beliefs. I am not referring to the sort of books we read now, the kind you run through in three days on the beach and immediately forget. I mean real books, by writers like Tolstoy and Dostoevsky, Dickens and Hugo, Melville and Conrad.

Now we share a heritage fashioned in large part by motion pictures. We all know where Rick's *Café Americain* was located, where Dorothy was going when she flew over the rainbow, and what Charles Foster Kane meant when he whispered "Rosebud."

In romantic films—which means just about every film ever made, since even the goriest action flick has a love story in there someplace—the guy and girl seem to fall in love in the twinkle of an eye. According to Hollywood, it doesn't take much more than a twinkle. They have the couple bumping into each other in a crowded elevator or an airplane, turn up the soundtrack, cut out the dialogue, send them walking along a beach or sharing a glass of wine as they gaze out at a sunset, and wham!, the music comes down, the actors start talking again and we know they're madly in love.

Hello?

If that's all it takes to fall in love—some accidental physical contact, a few shared moments and something to laugh at—then every morning at rush hour, the New York City subway system would turn into a gigantic orgy.

But we watch these films and buy into it, even though we know what's coming. The man and woman will have issues. Then some action or tension that will pull them back together. And, in the end, we'll see them fall in love.

But then what?

That's where they hang us out to dry. They don't tell us what happens next or what to do about it. Sure, there are movies where one of the lovers dies just before the credits roll or, once in a great while, where the affair ends badly. But in most films, the ones that finish with a juicy kiss or clever remark as the fadeout comes, they don't explain how to sustain the excitement, the wonder, the enchantment of that heady experience of falling deeply and passionately in love. I suppose that's why it's called escapism, right? But I don't want to escape. I want to stay right there, with the music playing and the sun setting.

I want the whole Hollywood thing.

Maybe those movie makers are right, maybe falling in love can be as easy as picking fruit from a tree, staying in love is like a grab for liquid mercury. The harder you try to get ahold of it, the more likely it is to slip away, especially for me. I'm cautious to begin with, and particularly when it comes to women. Like a lot of guys, I think I come by it honestly, through years of disappointment and doubt and even insecurity.

For instance, when Donna asked me if I figured out what the letter was about, I couldn't recall ever mentioning anything about the letter to her.

"Where are you?" Donna asked.

"I'm sorry?"

"I lost you there for a minute." She was studying me with those clear blue eyes, wearing her excellent smile.

I looked around the dining room. "Just thinking about what a great place this is," I lied.

"You can do better than that."

"I don't know, just got wrapped up in an old memory, that's all. It's been a crazy couple of days."

"Is it about the letter?"

"Yes," I said, "the famous letter."

"Anything new?"

"Not much, I'm afraid. Except that I'm going to France."

"France?"

"It's either that or start seeing a psychiatrist. I thought the trip would be cheaper in the long run."

"Probably more fun, too."

I agreed.

"That's very exciting. Why France?"

Why indeed? "My dad had a friend there. He might be able to help sort this out for me."

"You know him?"

"Never heard of him until Saturday."

"Well then, it really is going to be exciting, isn't it?"

"I would say so."

The waiter came by to hand us menus and describe the specials, then left us on our own to consider the assortment of tempting offerings. After lunch with Frank and her mention of the letter, I wasn't feeling all that hungry, but the fellow spoke with a beautiful French accent that made everything sound delicious, and after more champagne I had no trouble finding my appetite. Donna suggested I choose for both of us, so when the waiter arrived to take our order, I told him we were going with his suggestion of the tuna appetizer followed by an herb encrusted rack of lamb for two.

He gave a slight bow, then left me with the *carte de vin*. Without looking up from the list, I asked Donna if she'd ever been to France.

"Never."

"It'd be a great place to start your trip to Europe."

"Is it as beautiful as they say?"

"Paris is more beautiful than they say."

"Have you been there many times?"

"Only once," I said. "I've also been to the south."

"The Riviera?"

"Uh huh. And Provence. And the wine country, Burgundy and Bordeaux."

"That's strange."

"Strange?"

"It sounds like you've been all over France, but your father never mentioned he had a good friend over there."

"Good friend?"

"I was just assuming that. They must have known each other pretty well if you're flying off to see him."

"You're right," I said, "but I took that trip after my father died."

"Oh," she said, as if she might have gone too far.

I looked up from the list. "Let's talk about something else."

"Okay," Donna said. "Tell me about Paris."

I took my time describing what I knew of the City of Lights which, I assure you, is a whole lot less than what you'd find in a cheap guidebook. Then we talked about anything else I could think of.

It was after polishing off the champagne and a bottle of Gruaud Larose, somewhere between dessert and cognac, that I returned to the subject of my trip.

"You're going to Europe, right? I don't know what your plans are but why not start by coming with me?"

She looked at me like I was slightly daft.

"I don't know where you're heading," I said, "but as I mentioned, France isn't a bad place to start."

Donna replied with a slight tilt of her head. "Is this your extravagant way of propositioning me?"

"It's not what I meant."

"No? Maybe I should feel insulted then." She was smiling again, so I figured she wasn't feeling insulted. I also thought she wasn't taking my invitation seriously.

"I mean it," I told her.

I know, maybe I overreacted. The dinner, the wine, her blue eyes and great smile. Her light brown hair that seemed all soft and wavy and carefree. The slinky white dress that showed off her pure, tanned skin, with the colorful silk scarf draped casually over her shoulders, not hiding the delicate curves of her neck as it plunged to her breasts.

Then, of course, there was my desperate curiosity. How did she know about the letter?

"You're serious," she said.

"I am," I admitted. "Does it sound crazy?"

"Crazy? As in, I just met you? As in, I just arrived in New York yesterday? That kind of crazy, you mean?"

I paused a moment. "I'm trying to think if you left anything out."

"Is this restaurant part of the plot? Get me in a French kind of mood?"

"Strictly coincidence, I promise you. Look, maybe it's overkill after a couple of dinners together, but it seems like a great idea to me."

Donna laughed. "Don't sell our relationship short. It's not just two dinners. Remember the plane ride here."

"Ah, right."

She leaned back in the comfortable chair, her eyes narrowing slightly. "I suppose you think I'll sleep with you."

"I hadn't really thought about that," I lied, "but we don't have to rush anything."

To my disappointment, she agreed. "No," she said, "we don't."

"Although separate hotel rooms might be a hassle."

"And expensive." We were quiet for a while. Then she said, "Sorry to state the obvious, but I barely know you. I mean, this has been fun, and it does sound like a great idea, but—"

"Got it. And I know you have your own plans. Forget the whole thing, maybe we can see each other when I get back."

"When are you leaving?"

"I'm thinking about tomorrow night."

"That's fast work," she said, then laughed a charming laugh. "How long will you be gone?"

"A few days. I don't know. Three or four."

She gave me a pout any Parisian woman would have been proud of. "And who am I going to have dinner with in New York, while you're running around France?"

"You have friends in town."

"I do. But none of them have asked me to dinner in Paris."

"Monte Carlo," I corrected her. "Paris on my way home. From there you can go anywhere else you were planning to go in Europe."

She lifted her wine glass and took a sip.

"You thinking about this?"

"Don't you want me to?"

"Of course. It's just that, I, uh, I'm not the impulsive type, and—I mean this in a good way—I've never known anyone impulsive enough to do something like this."

"You've never known anyone like me. Period."

"That may be true."

She paused for a few moments. "Well, I have to admit, it's the most incredible invitation I've ever received."

"I guess that means no."

"Actually, it means yes."

CHAPTER THIRTEEN

Early the next morning I was alone in my apartment, sorting out any number of issues. Such as the improbability of Donna accepting an invitation to join me on a trip to the south of France. My decision to fly off and visit a man I'd never even heard of until a couple of days ago. The question of whether to call the police to report someone breaking into my apartment. The comments Gerry Egidio made about my father's death. And the need to cover my responsibilities at work.

Consumed by all of this, I was startled by the unfriendly sound of someone pressing my door buzzer in three quick bursts. I was not in the mood for guests, but that was far from my main concern.

I took the box from the table, shoved it on a shelf in my bedroom closet behind a pile of sweaters, then went to the door where the buzzer was making another series of angry noises.

"Who is it?" I asked.

"A couple o' guys knew your father," came the reply. "We gotta talk to ya."

I looked through the peephole, which makes every apartment its own sort of speakeasy. Two rather wide men were standing there, looking uncomfortable or unhappy or both. Maybe they didn't like being up this early.

One of them looked vaguely familiar.

"I'm not dressed," was all I could think of to say, realizing how lame that sounded.

"Who gives a shit?" a second voice asked. "We didn't come here to dance with ya."

"We were friends o' Blackie's," the first voice said. "We gotta talk with ya."

I figured, hell, if they gotta talk with me, they were gonna talk with me some time or another. I opened the door.

"What's this about?" I asked.

They pushed past me like I was the swinging door in a Dodge City saloon and made themselves comfortable on my living room couch. I followed them inside.

"It looks like you don't remember me," the smaller, familiar looking man said as he had a look around. He was in his sixties, mostly bald, with a wide nose you earn from finishing second in too many fist fights. He didn't offer his name to help me along.

"I'm sorry," I said, shaking my head as if I should feel bad about offending two thugs who had just bulled their way into my apartment at seven thirty in the morning. "I don't."

He smiled, a not altogether unpleasant smile. "Blackie and me, we went back a long way. I saw you when you was a kid. Probably wouldn't a' recognized you either, if I saw you on the street or something."

I couldn't think of anything worthwhile to say about that, so for a change I kept my mouth shut.

"Let's get to it," the younger, larger man said.

Blackie's friend said, "You remember your father's, uh, his, uh, friend, Big Mike?"

"You mean his boss?"

"Yeah. I didn't wanna say it like that, but yeah. You knew Big Mike, right?"

"I knew who he was."

"Yeah, well, you know when your dad died—I feel bad to have to bring this up—but when your dad passed, he and Mike had some unfinished business."

"And you're coming here to discuss this now? Six years after Blackie died? Not to mention, I heard Mike died too."

"Yeah, yeah." Blackie's old pal was shaking his head, like he couldn't believe it either. "Time passes, eh? But the business goes on, if you know what I mean. Mike is gone, but someone takes over."

I was still standing there, wearing nothing but a white terrycloth bathrobe and shearling slippers, staring down at two hoodlums who had come by to roust me about something that happened more than six years ago. My entire life, it seemed, was suddenly being lived in the past.

"Look," I said, "I don't want to seem rude, but if you knew my father and you remember me, then you must know I never had anything to do with his business. Never," I repeated, thinking how proud my mother would be to hear me say that.

"I know, I know, but—," the older man said, leaving whatever thought he might have had hanging on that last word.

The younger man interrupted with an impatient shake of his head. "What is this," he wanted to know, "old fucking home week? Look kid, your father was into the boss for some scratch back when, never straightened it out. Now we hear you got something might belong to your father, which means it belongs to the boss. Or a piece of it. Or whatever. You gotta make good for your father, plain and simple. You with me on this?"

"Am I with you?" I asked. "I have no idea what you're talking about."

"No, eh?"

"No. Really, no. I don't know who you are, I never had anything to do with Big Mike, and I can't imagine why you'd come to see me, all these years later."

The way his eyes widened, I realized my answer had not made him happy.

"I don't think you're in any kind of a position to be a wise guy here."

I looked at him like he was speaking a foreign language. "A wise guy?"

The older man intervened, saying, "Let's take it easy, all right?" No one said anything for a few seconds, so I guess we were all taking it easy. "We got a job to do. We need to know if you got something from Blackie, which in turn would be something belongs to our friend, you understand?"

I can't explain why I wasn't afraid, but I wasn't. At least not yet. Maybe it was all those years of hanging around with my father, meeting guys like this, feeling more comfortable than say, a normal Working Stiff would have felt in the same situation. Or maybe I figured if they were going to hurt me, they would have started off that way, just to set the tone. Or—and I know this may not sound logical—but if they were the ones who broke into my apartment and found nothing, then they had to be more confused than I was if they needed to come back the very next day.

Mainly, I found myself wondering how they heard anything new about my father in the first place. There was only one reasonable answer.

"What exactly did my cousin Frank tell you?"

They looked at each other, two guys without an ounce of subtlety between them, trying to make it seem this had nothing at all to do with Frank.

"Never mind," I said. Then I turned to Blackie's old chum. "Look, I really do not understand. So, is there anything else, or are we done here so I can take a shower and get to work?"

The younger man stood up. He appeared to be in his mid-forties and built like a linebacker. "You college boys always gotta have the last word."

If I had not felt scared up to then, I was at least aware that he had not gotten up to shake my hand. I reflexively took a step back, but he reached out fast enough to grab a bunch of terrycloth robe and slam me against the wall.

"Hey, take it easy," I said, hoping to sound more angry than afraid. I don't think I succeeded.

"Yeah, take it easy, Silvio," the other man agreed as he scrambled to his feet "We ain't gonna get nowhere like this."

Silvio stared into my eyes with a look that told me he would have no problem punching the hell out of me, whether or not it would get him anywhere. He let go of my robe and took a step back.

"Good guy, bad guy," I said. Sometimes I just can't keep quiet.

The older man stepped forward now, all efforts to evoke any friendly history with my father gone from his face. "Don't misunderstand this situation, kid. You're nothin' to me, except I got a job to do. If I want Silvio should break your neck, believe me, you're as good as dead. Now we don't have to get nasty about this, do we?"

I didn't see the need for things to get any nastier than a broken neck, so I shook my head.

"Good. Then just tell us, where's the thing?"

I took a moment to rearrange my robe. Then I said, "I really have no idea what you're talking about. If you tell me what you're looking for, that might help." Silvio made a slight move and I flinched. God, it pissed me off that I flinched, and now I really did get angry. "You can pull all the rough stuff you want, but it's not going to get you anywhere. I told you, I have nothing to do with my father's business."

Silvio studied me carefully, none of us speaking as he looked me over from head to toe.

He said, "You tell us you got nothin', we hear something else. What am I gonna do with that?"

"You mind if I ask you who told you, and what it is I'm supposed to have?"

Silvio was quick, I'll give him that, because I never saw it coming. The back of his hand lashed out across the side of my face with enough force to knock me off balance.

"What the fuck," I said.

"Fuck this," Silvio replied, holding a large fist up to my face.

"Knock it off," the other man said calmly, then turned back to me. "You see, here's the problem. You say you don't know nothin', you think we're off base, and you'd be happy for us to just get the hell out of your place, right? But then you ask a question about who told us what, and you ask about this guy Frank, and all that makes us think, like, 'Hey, maybe he does know something, or why would he ask.' You see my problem?"

Keeping an eye on Silvio, I said, "Natural curiosity, okay?" They didn't answer, they just kept staring at me. "I let you in here because you said you were friends of my father. Does that sound like I've got something to hide? No. So how about we forget the whole thing and you just go away."

The older man smiled at me. "We'll go away, but we're gonna be talking again. You can count on that."

He tapped Silvio on one of his broad shoulders and they made a move to leave. But Silvio turned back and took a swing at me, his bowling ball-sized fist stopping just short of my gut as I doubled over and put my hands up in a pathetic effort at self-defense.

Silvio laughed. "Some tough guy you are. Tough with your mouth is all, you fucken wimp." And that's how they made their exit, with Silvio laughing at me all the way out my front door.

It would have hurt less if he had punched me.

When I heard the door slam shut I fell into a chair and stared up at the ceiling. They had never mentioned the letter, not once. Which left me to wonder again, what the hell *did* they know and was it Frank who told them?

Then I started thinking about the look in Gerry Egidio's eyes when he mentioned my father's death, and the time Blackie got himself into trouble, the year he died. I knew a little of the story from Blackie, a bit more that Benny told me after the wake. I wondered about the connection that all of that might have to Gerry's comments the previous morning and the visit I just had from those two goons.

Blackie was running a bookmaking operation for his boss, Big Mike, spending his afternoons with the rest of a small crew in an apartment off Tremont Avenue in the Bronx. Well before personal computers and cell phones, they would work the landlines, confirming betting lines and booking action for local sports gamblers and horse players. After closing down for the day, they would set out on collections and payoffs, visiting neighborhood bars, restaurants, retail shops and the other haunts where their customers could be found. A couple of times a week, Blackie delivered a recap of the bets together with the profits—there were always profits—to the main office downtown. That's where his boss raked off most of the take as payment for bankrolling the business, providing protection and for generally allowing them to do what they were doing. Which didn't leave all that much for Blackie and his cohorts. Not a fair split, my father came to believe, which is when he decided to do a little past-posting.

Past-posting is more creative than mere theft. The idea is to bet on horse races that have just finished, which is a fairly reliable way of ensuring a result. The bookmaker starts by inventing an imaginary customer, giving him a name, then booking some bets and reporting them to the downtown office. In the beginning, you make mostly losing bets and you cover the losses, just to show this imaginary gambler is a good payer. Then a few of the picks run in the money, which is easy enough to arrange, since the horse race is done by the time you record the wager. Timing is important, of course. You have to set up the paperwork in advance, picking a few different horses, then using the slip for the horse that won, looking over your shoulder at the other guys you work with, to be sure no one sees what you're up to. As I say, this was long before online betting and off-shore accounts, where everything is recorded and time stamped. If you were very careful and not too greedy, you might skim a few dollars from the home office and no one is any the wiser. Or so you hoped.

Unfortunately, someone always gets wiser.

When my father got called downtown for a private meeting, he suspected it was not an invitation to lunch, and he prepared himself for the interrogation.

"Impossible," he said to his boss. "We're being past-posted?"

They were seated at a small round table in the private club off Grand Street where Mike held court. The club was a dark, wood paneled room with dim lights and an espresso machine. I was there once or twice, although never allowed in the back where the Really Serious Men sat.

Blackie's boss, who I met a few times, was a squat, beefy man with blunt, pugnacious features and a piece of stone for a head. His manner was gruff, his speech unfriendly, and his eyes had all the life contained in a pair of dull pebbles.

"That's right," Mike told him. "One of your men thinks you got a customer sending in horse bets too close to race time."

"No shit," my father replied with a shake of his head, undoubtedly wondering who the rat in his small group might be. "How could that happen?"

His boss shrugged his broad shoulders, indicating he could not possibly care less how it happened. He said simply, "You gotta cover."

As the man responsible for the operation, Blackie had to pay for any losses caused by cheating or stealing or past-posting, regardless of the how or the who or the why. When it comes to problems, the mob isn't interested in the story, it's all about the money.

Later on they go after the guys who were in on the scam.

Since there was no actual customer for my father to get the money from, and since he'd already spent the thousands he'd been raking in over the past several months, there was no way for him to clean up the mess without some help. That's when he went to his brother.

He was too embarrassed to admit to Vincent what he'd done. He thought it should be enough to tell his brother he was in trouble and needed the money.

It wasn't.

Uncle Vincent said he had his own obligations. Mortgage payments on the house in Rockland. New carpeting he was having installed. A diamond ring he bought my aunt for their anniversary that he was still paying off. He couldn't come up with any real dough on the spot, not like that.

My father didn't explain why he needed the cash. He also didn't mention any of the money he'd loaned Vincent over the years when my uncle was down and out—money Vincent had never thought about repaying while he was laying in carpet and buying his wife a ring. It wasn't Blackie's style to bring it up. He just turned away from the best goddamned brother in the whole world and went off to look for another way to solve the problem the best way he could.

Looking back at things that morning, I began to guess at how it all worked out in the end.

* * *

I finally got myself out of the chair, showered and dressed, then sat down again to make a couple of calls, the first to my younger sister, Kelly.

"I was wondering when I'd hear from you," she said.

"Meaning what?"

"Meaning that Mom told me about the goodies she gave you. When do I get a peek?"

"Any time."

"Okay. Now tell me about the letter."

"Mom told you there was a letter?"

"Of course. She claims she never opened it. Amazing, huh?"

"I believe her."

"I do too. Now tell me what it said."

I did. I also recounted my visits with Frank and Gerry Egidio, and described my trip to Las Vegas to see Benny.

"You went to Las Vegas and didn't tell me?"

"It was no big deal, just an overnight thing. It was good to see Benny."

"And?"

I gave her a brief rendition of what Benny had to say, which was easy enough because what he said was so disappointingly brief. Even so, Kelly made me go over it twice, not allowing me to leave out a single detail.

When I was done, she asked, "What else?"

"What do you mean?

"Come on, what else?"

I took a deep breath, then described the break-in the day before and the visit I just had from Blackie's old pal and his sidekick, Silvio.

"My God. This isn't funny."

"You hear somebody laughing?"

"Have you called the police?"

"No, and I'm not going to."

"You have to."

"Think about it. This letter is about something a little less than legal, right? Do I want the police involved?"

"You're being threatened."

"Not yet I'm not, not really. And what would the police do anyway?"

"All right," she sighed, "but you know who dad was. Whatever this is, it can't be good. Don't be foolish."

I figured I was already being foolish, but said, "I'll be fine."

She paused. "What else?"

"That's it."

"Are you sure?"

"On the plus side of the ledger," I said, "I met a girl."

"Tell me."

I did.

When I got done with that, there was absolute silence on the line.

"What? What's wrong?"

"Let me get this straight," Kelly began. "In the middle of all this, you just happened to meet a girl on the flight back from Vegas who just happened to go to dinner with you and now, you should pardon the simplicity of this summary, just happens to be willing to get on a plane and fly off with you to France. Who, by the way, seems to know about Dad's letter even though you don't think you ever mentioned it to her. Have I got all this right?"

I almost laughed. "Not exactly."

"Tell me, please, tell me what I've missed."

"Well for starters, she didn't just happen to go to dinner with me."

"No?"

"I asked her."

"You asked her. Well good, that's very good."

"And it was actually two dinners."

"Great. She had two dinners with you, and you've talked her into going off to the Riviera tomorrow."

"Uh, tonight."

"Tonight. Excellent. These dinners must have been something. You must be a magician with a fork and knife."

"Did you say fucken knife?"

"Have you taken time to count your marbles lately. I think a couple may be missing."

"That's why I called. I need a reality check."

"Okay. A, I think you should stay away from our cousin. We all know what kind of person Frank is, but I'm afraid you don't see that as clearly as everyone else. B, I think Benny has your best interests at heart. If he says you should let it go, you probably should let it go. C, I know you well enough to know that you're not going to listen to him. So D, how are you going to track down this Gilles person?"

Did I mention that Kelly is a psychologist with a very well ordered mind? She often gives lists like that.

"I already spoke with Gilles. Sounds like a nice old man."

She hesitated before saying, "Dad wouldn't even be sixty yet."

I nodded to myself. "I mentioned that to Gerry Egidio yesterday. Benny says Gilles is older than that."

She waited.

"You think this all too strange."

"I think you're strange." She sighed loudly into the phone. "You're really going to France to meet him?"

"It's not a conversation we can have on the phone. He made that clear, and so did Benny. I have to ask him about something they were involved in more than thirty years ago. He's not going to discuss it on a trans-Atlantic call someone might be listening to. For that matter, he can't even be sure who I am. Not without meeting me."

"I guess that's right," she admitted.

"You have a better idea? Other than just letting it go, I mean."

Kelly was quiet again.

"Hello, you still there?"

"I'm thinking. Give me a second, for god's sake."

Kelly's profession is better known for questions than answers, a perverse calling based on the proposition that we will feel less psychic pain if we can identify the source of that suffering. Assuming you buy into that premise, you subject yourself to years of counselling sessions, only to determine the reason you're a mass of neuroses is because your mother didn't breast feed you long enough, or your father didn't show up at your Little League games or your grandmother forced you to kiss your grandfather's corpse when you attended his wake at the age of four. Tell me, if a teething infant understood the source of its pain, would it cry any less? I don't think so. When you hit your thumb with a hammer, does the knowledge of how that blow was struck reduce the ache? Nah. Sometimes, I think knowledge intensifies the hurt. Isn't ignorance supposed to be bliss? Take a look at some of the morons you have to deal with in life. They seem incredibly untroubled, don't they? Knowledge can be overrated.

"Are you listening?" Kelly demanded into the telephone.

"What's that?"

"Did you hear what I just said? I love being asked my opinion and then having it ignored."

"Sorry, sis. Lost in thought."

"What else is new? What I just said was, I think you need to go. To get closure about this."

"Closure," I repeated. A psychologist's word.

"You should meet him and hear what he has to say. What harm can there be in that?"

"I wonder."

"You going to call Benny before you leave?"

"Right after we hang up."

"If you won't call the police, at least Benny might be able to tell you something about those two thugs."

"I'll keep you posted."

"You better," she warned.

"I actually think I might be doing myself a favor, getting out of town for a few days."

"Oh, great. My big brother, taking it on the lam."

I ignored that and asked her how her kids were doing. She has two little children, one of each.

"They're good. You ought to visit them some time, like before they head off for college in fifteen years."

"I will," I promised. "I really will. Say, uh, you think you could mail me some recent pictures of them?"

"What?"

"Photos. If you've got some extras laying around. Something to hang on my refrigerator door or something."

"You're kidding, right?"

"Forget it."

"No, no. I will, I'll send you a couple."

"Thanks."

"You be careful, okay?"

I told her I would, made her promise she wouldn't tell our mother where I was going, and said goodbye.

Then I pulled out Benny's number. It was still early in Las Vegas, but I wanted to tell him what was going on.

His wife, Selma, answered the phone.

I said hello, then told her who I was.

"You," was all she said, making the word sound horrible.

I decided to forego any niceties and asked, "Is Benny there?"

"No," she said, her angry voice faltering, "Benny's in the hospital. Now don't call here again. Not ever." Then the line went dead.

CHAPTER FOURTEEN

The next several hours were something of a blur. I packed, picked up the airline tickets, straightened things out at the office and found myself on a plane with Donna, heading for the Riviera.

My mind was in overdrive, feeling worried for Benny, suspicious of Donna, anxious about what my cousin Frank was up to, nervous about the two thugs that had visited my apartment and generally concerned about myself.

Even so, it never occurred to me that anyone outside that small universe might be interested in what I was doing.

Looking back, I guess I was a bit myopic about that, not to mention some other things that should have been obvious. But when you live in the real world, the workaday business world, you're not really prepared for being followed or having your apartment looted or being rousted by a couple of *guidos* from Little Italy. Those things don't happen to Working Stiffs and, if they do, it's tough know what the hell you should do to protect yourself.

Anyway, when we arrived at the airport in Nice early the next morning and made our way through immigration and customs, there was a guy was staring at me, and I asked Donna about him.

"Where?"

"On the far side, to the left. Don't turn around yet, I don't want him to see you looking at him."

Naturally she spun right around. Why do people always do that when you tell them not to?

139

"Which one?" she asked as she gazed across the terminal.

"The gray one," I told her, more quietly now.

"The gray one?"

"Yeah. Gray suit, gray tie, gray hair, gray face."

She started to laugh. "Oh, I see him, the gray one. And you think he's staring at you."

"Don't you?"

"Don't I what?"

"Think he's staring at me," I demanded impatiently.

"This is France. He might be staring at me."

"Ah." For some reason that hadn't occurred to me.

"He does look French," she said. "Maybe he's just a local guy meeting someone."

"All right," I said, not feeling entirely convinced. "Let's go."

We grabbed a taxi and, by the time Donna and I arrived in Antibes, the thing I needed most was sleep. I hadn't closed my eyes once on the plane, fretting my way through a seven hour flight and the five hour time change. Donna had napped soundly, but I mostly sat there, staring at magazines, or movies, or off into space. By the time we reached our hotel, I was ready to pass out.

The desk clerk was in no apparent rush, probably still working on his first *latte*. We went through an infuriatingly slow check-in process, then shown to our *chambre* on the third floor.

The room was small but full of charm, with heavy brocade curtains, old trompe l'oeil wallpaper and Provencal furniture made of dark wood with antique brass trim. It also featured a four poster bed, which had most of my attention at the moment.

"This is beautiful," Donna said.

"So are you," I informed her with appropriate chivalry, then announced I was about to fall face down on the bed and become dead to the world.

"Not so fast," she said, calling me over to the window. "Look at this."

The room had a magnificent view of Cap d'Antibes, a little peninsula surrounded by the blue Mediterranean. Majestic looking sailboats, huge yachts, fishing boats and other, smaller craft rocked gently on the early tide. The morning was sunny and warm, and Donna suggested we go for a swim.

"Really?"

"Come on," she said, "don't be a stiff."

"Even I wouldn't touch that line."

"Come on," she said again, then dragged me to the small luggage stand, where they'd placed our two bags, and began digging for her bathing suit.

"I didn't remember to bring one."

She said, "You're lying," and pulled a pair of trunks from my suitcase.

"Perfect," I said.

We discreetly took turns changing in the bathroom, slipped on the thick Turkish robes provided by the hotel, then headed down to the beach. On the short elevator ride, I nearly nodded off. Then, as if by magic, we were outside, facing the sun and the sea.

The beaches of the Riviera are not like American beaches. There are no big waves crashing on top of each other, nor is the shore lined with fluffy sand. The *Cote d'Azur* features a carpet of smooth stones that have been polished by eons of the sea's gentle ebb and flow. Wooden walkways crisscross all over the place, each path leading to the sea.

It was early by Riviera standards, and we were pretty much on our own. Most people were still sleeping off champagne hangovers and late nights at the casinos. We dropped our robes on two wooden-slatted chairs and walked toward the shore. I was moving a bit slower than Donna, so she took me by the hand and pulled me along.

"We'll have a nice swim. Once you jump in, it'll invigorate you."

"You promise?"

"Promise," she said.

"I won't have a heart attack and die?"

"Not today, no."

We reached the end of one of the boardwalks and, as we stood facing the onshore breeze, the morning didn't seem as warm as it had when we looked out from the window of our cozy room, the one with the big four poster bed I couldn't stop thinking about.

"How do you know the water isn't freezing?" I asked, but Donna was done with my whining. Still holding my hand, she took off, and in an instant we were diving headlong into the azure water.

"You see?" she said triumphantly as we came up for air. "You lived."

"Now if I only could feel my legs."

"Come on, let's swim out to the float."

It was immediately apparent that she was the better swimmer. Her slender arms came out of the water, reached high over her head and then sliced back through the sea like some sort of a machine. I did my best to muscle my way alongside her but, if we were racing, it was clear she'd be kicking me in the face.

"Nice of you to hold back," I said as we lifted ourselves onto the large, square wooden float that felt about five miles from shore. We sat there on the edge, dangling our feet in the cool water.

"I was a swimmer in school," she told me, then flipped her hair back with a quick snap of her neck.

Her smile seemed even brighter in the morning sun, droplets of salt-water running down her tanned face, the color of the shimmering sea no match for the blue of her eyes.

"I can't believe we're sitting in the Mediterranean," I admitted. "It's surreal, don't you think?"

She didn't tell me what she thought. Instead, she put her arms around my neck and kissed me on the mouth, taking her time to make it count, then jumped back into the water.

I swam a little faster on the way back. Maybe I had the tide with me, or maybe I just wanted to keep pace with her. Or maybe it was the kiss. Whatever the motivation, when we got to shore I was completely winded. We ambled up the wooden boardwalk to our chairs, and I helped her into the plush, white bathrobe. I gave her more than a little help, actually, taking the opportunity to gently rub her with the ter-rycloth. She was wet, and I didn't want her to catch cold or anything.

I pulled on my robe, then took her in my arms and we kissed again. There were a few people around now, arranging their chaises and organizing towels and so forth, but this was France, so I didn't care.

When I slowly drew back from her, I looked up and saw him walking along the quay, just above the beach.

"That's him," I said.

Donna turned, trying to find what I was staring at. The guy was walking slowly, not looking in our direction.

"Who?" she asked.

"The man who was watching us in the airport. You know, the gray guy."

"Of course. The gray guy."

"Come on, that's him, you see him walking?"

"Walking? Wow, that is suspicious. Is he still in gray, or has he changed his disguise?"

I was going to laugh, then decided to skip it. "He is, in fact. Still in gray, I mean. Gray pants, white shirt, gray head. Take a look."

She was still sort of smirking at me, but then he looked right at us.

"Shit," I said.

He never broke stride. He just stared at us for a couple of seconds, then turned straight ahead and continued on.

"I do recognize him," Donna admitted.

"So?"

"So what? He's having a look at the beach, is that so odd?"

"Maybe not."

With a delicate touch of her hand, she turned my face toward her. "I can only guess how much this all means to you. Your father and all that. But the rest of the world isn't interested. This is your own personal treasure hunt, no one else's."

I was about to say something, then uttered a long sigh instead. "I suppose you're right. Maybe I'm getting a little nuts. I mean, I don't usually jump on a plane to Europe on a whim."

"Neither do I."

I was going to remind her about the flight from Vegas, when she told me she was already planning to go to Europe, and how this trip was not quite the whim for her as it was for me. But I shook my head, deciding to let it go for now. "All right," I said, "but I'm telling you, if he shows up at our table for dinner tonight, you're going to have to rethink this."

Donna laughed her musical laugh. "Agreed. Now you need to relax, and I think I've got just the thing." She took my hand again and told me to come along.

Who was I to argue?

* * *

By the time Donna and I made our way up to the hotel room I was feeling a more pleasant kind of exhaustion, the kind where your muscles feel loose and calm and your brain is on holiday. I pulled the curtains closed, and the room enveloped us in a muted darkness. We slipped off our robes and grabbed a couple of towels from the bathroom. As I rubbed my hair dry, Donna pulled off her swimsuit, patted herself down and, tossing her towel on a chair, climbed into bed.

"This is heaven," she said.

I stood there looking at her. "I promised not to take advantage of you."

"You're not. Now take off that bathing suit and get in here with me."

I did.

The mattress was thick and set so high my feet would not reach the floor if I sat on the edge. The white cotton sheets were soft and cool, and the fluffy goose down duvet, covered in pale, beige paisley linen, seemed to float above us.

We were on our sides, facing each other, and I took her in my arms, our legs entwined. I felt the smoothness of her skin and the soft pressure of her breasts against my chest.

"This certainly is heaven," I agreed.

She held my face in her hands and we kissed, a long, moist kiss. I held her closer and our bodies seemed to melt together.

She drew her head back slightly and smiled at me.

I said, "Looks like our plan about not rushing things didn't take."

She kissed me gently on the lips, then whispered in my ear, "Someone once said that life is what happens when you're busy making other plans."

We kissed again, then I said, "I think it was Lennon."

"The communist?" she asked with mock surprise.

"The Beatle," I said.

We laughed, then for a moment neither of us spoke. We just stared into each other's eyes in that intimate way where you feel everything about you is laid bare. I'm sure I had a goofy smile on my face, but she looked positively beautiful. I was aware of her sweet fragrance and the warmth of her breath as it mingled with mine.

"I'm happy we're here," she told me.

So was I.

We made love, tenderly and passionately, feeling so right that I all but forgot my doubts and questions, losing myself in the intimacy of the surprising connection between us.

Just before we drifted off to sleep, Donna whispered, "I have to know something."

"Uh huh."

"Do you take a lot of women to Europe to get them to make love with you?"

"Not a lot." I kissed her lips. "Actually, never," I said, "but it works out nicely, don't you think?"

She smiled. "I have a confession then."

"Uh huh."

"I wanted to make love with you before you invited me to France."

"Damn," I said softly, "all that money wasted."

We kissed again before we nodded off, my arms still around her.

I awoke sometime in the afternoon, not knowing where I was or what day it was, all that usual jet lag disorientation. Donna had her back to me, sleeping the quiet sleep of the innocent. I was on my stomach, my face pushed into the pillow.

I managed to sit up without disturbing her. Although the room was dark, I could see there was still daylight at the edges of the curtains. I looked down at her, beginning to wonder again what the hell she was doing here.

I mean, I knew why *I* was there, which consisted of some rather questionable reasoning at best. Donna was another story, but I was annoyed at myself for going there.

"You're awake?" she muttered.

"No," I told her, "I'm sleep-sitting. I'm too lazy to sleepwalk."

She rolled over on her back, drawing the sheet up to her neck. "Hi." She smiled up at me. "What are you thinking about?"

"You, actually."

"That's nice," she whispered, as if she might fall back to sleep.

I brushed the hair off her forehead. "We should get up, or we'll never get our internal clocks straightened out."

"Who cares?"

I thought that over. "Come on. We need to make dinner reservations and I need to call my friend."

"I think you should call your friend first," she suggested.

146

It was after four in the afternoon as I sat at the small writing table and dialed the number.

After we exchanged greetings, M. de la Houssay chuckled gently into the phone. "It is hard to believe you are here."

"For me too," I agreed.

"You're in Nice?"

"Cap d' Antibes, actually."

"Ah, *bon*. Quite beautiful."

"It is."

"We should have dinner tonight, yes?"

"That would be wonderful."

He told me about a restaurant called *La Colombe d'Or*, in the nearby town of Saint-Paul-de-Vence. He suggested we meet at eight. "At my age," he explained jovially, "a great meal cannot be taken too late in the evening. *Comprendre?*"

I said I understood. Then I told him I had a young lady with me.

He surely seemed to enjoy laughing, because he started up again. "I should have known," he said. "What is the expression? Like father, like son?"

I didn't know how to respond to that so I didn't try.

"I could not possibly forfeit the opportunity to dine with a beautiful young woman. And I could not think of letting her spend the evening alone."

Being a Frenchman, I guess he just assumed she was beautiful. I said, "I would like her to come along, if that would be all right."

"But we do have certain matters to discuss, *oui?*"

"We do. I'm sure my friend will allow us some private time."

"Good. Until eight then."

"*Parfait*," I said, giving the French thing a go.

He chuckled again. "Forgive me, my young friend, but I must ask one question. Has anyone else accompanied the two of you on this trip?"

I told him it was just Donna and me.

"Ah, *bon*. And how many others have you told of your intention to speak with me."

I thought about that. "A couple, maybe. My sister…." I said, beginning to name them, but he cut me off.

"Later, when we meet."

CHAPTER FIFTEEN

That evening, preparing for our dinner with Gilles, I chose a navy blazer, dark gray slacks and a shirt of French blue, which I figured was appropriate to the circumstance. I also selected one of my two Hermes ties, just to stay with the Gallic theme.

While Donna was fixing her hair in the bathroom, making a lot of noise with some over-powered hair dryer, I tried to reach Benny again, without success. Selma had her answering machine on, so I hung up without leaving a message. I was worried, but there was nothing I could do about it now, and since Monsieur de la Houssay would also be unable to help, I decided not to mention anything about it.

I went to the window, to see if the man in gray was outside but, unless he was standing on the beach, I wasn't going to spot him from there.

Donna came out, looking sensational in a dark purple dress that made her tan seem positively luminous, the silk clinging to enough of her that I wanted to stay in the room a while longer. But we would have been late for our *rendezvous*.

I walked up behind her and kissed her on the back of the neck. "You look fabulous," I said.

She gazed at my reflection in the mirror. "I'm happy to be here," she said, and I decided, for now, that would have to be answer enough to all the questions I had.

When we got to the lobby I saw no one familiar or suspicious, and I realized I was becoming comfortable with my paranoia, which is not necessarily a good thing. I spoke to the concierge about transportation.

I may not have mentioned that I possess a somewhat underdeveloped sense of direction, but it is true. I can get lost driving around places as familiar as Brooklyn, so any thought of renting a car and attempting to find my own way around the Riviera was consigned to the category of bad ideas. Not wanting to leave our fate to the vagaries of local cabbies for a journey as important as this, I arranged a car and driver for the evening.

We stepped into the balmy Mediterranean night and climbed into the back of a small, four-door Mercedes sedan, only to learn that our chauffeur *du soir* did not speak a word of English, stubbornly refusing to acknowledge even my "Hello," as if he had never heard the word before. I looked out the window for help, and the doorman was kind enough to step forward and pitch in. I asked him to explain to our driver that we would be dining at *Colombe d'Or*, where he should wait for us to finish and then bring us back, making any stops along the way we might desire, assuming we would find a way to communicate those desires to him.

The doorman began that explanation, but the name of the restaurant was apparently all the information the driver wanted and, well before the instructions were finished, he pulled away from the curb with a sudden lurch, heading north out of Antibes to avoid the local traffic. I preferred the route along the Grand Corniche before we turned inland, so Donna could enjoy the view.

"*Monsieur,*" I said, making a game effort, "*la Grande Corniche, s'il vous plaît.*"

I might as well have been talking to the brake pedal.

I made a second attempt, this time in English, leaning forward so I was speaking directly into his right ear. Funny, how we tend to raise our voices a notch when trying to make ourselves understood in a foreign language. It doesn't work. Another favorite of mine is when we add a bit of accent to English, as if that might make the other person more likely to discern the message. A couple of years before, I was playing golf in Cancun and told my Mexican caddie, "Hey Pedro, I theenk you need to get behind me when I sweeng el clubbo." Pedro looked at me like I was bonkers, since I had almost killed him with a vicious three iron shank on the prior shot, and that was all he needed to get the point, language and accent notwithstanding.

The Frenchman at the wheel remained content to ignore me, regardless of my volume or intonation. When I made a last, desperate attempt, all it bought me was a reply in rapid fire French, where he either explained the reason for the route he was taking or told me to go screw myself, I couldn't be sure which. It all sort of ran together in that nasal way that French does, as if an entire sentence is made up of one incredibly long word with a lot of syllables.

I leaned back in defeat, opting to enjoy whatever view there was, telling Donna not to worry. "We'll come back through Monte Carlo," I said. "We'll stop at the casino."

Our destination for dinner was the town of Saint-Paul, site of an ancient monastery surrounded by huge stone walls that once served as both boundaries and fortifications. Located beside the town of Vence, north of the coast, it looks like something out of the middle ages, which I suppose is what it is, large, dark and imposing.

We arrived in plenty of time for our appointment with Monsieur de la Houssay, the driver winding the car around a tight curve and bringing it to an abrupt stop in front of the massive entrance to this old citadel.

When I began to speak, he said something that I made out to mean either he would come back for us later or, "Find your own way back, you ignorant American slob."

I hoped for the best, smiled at him and said we'd look forward to seeing him in a couple of hours. He grumbled something in response as Donna and I got out the back, then drove off as quickly as I could shut the door. I assumed he took his driver courtesy course in Paris, or perhaps Manhattan.

Donna and I walked through the tall stone gates and entered a bustling little village of shops and storefronts that was straight out of a Victor Hugo novel. Streetlamps of weathered iron and copper lighted the cobbled walkways. There was no room for automobiles on the narrow streets, so pushcarts were in active use. People busied themselves, walking here and there, as we looked for the restaurant.

I decided to forego asking directions, but not just because of the language thing, but because real men do not ask directions. Long before GPS was available on every smartphone, real men would drive around in circles for an hour and a half rather than pull into a gas station to confess their ignorance. If you were absolutely lost, you sent your wife or girlfriend inside for the information, because people tend to be nicer to them.

Since we knew from the hotel concierge that *Colombe d'Or* was situated within this fortress, I figured we would not go missing, and was pleased to locate the understated façade without making one of my usual wrong turns along the way. A friendly looking little man in a tuxedo greeted us as we walked in, but when he started jabbering away in French, I held up my hand. I'd had enough of that for one night.

I asked him if he spoke English.

"Of course, *monsieur*," he told me.

"I'm meeting someone, Monsieur de la Houssay. We may be early."

When I said the name, the man's smile widened. "Ah, *mais oui*, Monsieur de la Houssay. *Formidable*." Extending his arm, he said, "*S'il vous plaît*," gesturing for us to follow him.

The main dining room was large, with tapestries hanging on stone walls, candles lighting the tables, and soft music wafting through the air, just loud enough to be heard without intruding on the murmur of private conversations. Waiters in black ties moved about, not too quickly, but with assurance. As soon as you entered the place you felt more like a guest than a customer.

The *maitre d'* led us toward the back where he showed us through a double door at the rear of the dining area that opened into a beautiful open courtyard bordered in flower-covered latticework. There we discovered another group of tables set on a large, open-air stone patio under the star-filled Mediterranean sky.

We continued walking behind him to the far corner, where a distinguished older gentleman sat, a slight smile on his lips as he watched us approach.

When we reached the table, which was set for three, the *maitre d'* stopped. "Monsieur de la Houssay," he said as he extended his arm again, this time with a flourish, "your guests."

Monsieur de la Houssay pushed back his chair and rose slowly to his feet. He stood about five seven, with a trim physique that seemed well kept for his age. For any age, in fact. His face was tanned, the lines around his mouth and eyes not so much like wrinkles as evidence of his experience. His hair was thin, but neatly parted to the side and combed flat. He was dressed in a dark blue suit, white shirt and burgundy tie with a pattern I couldn't quite make out in the dim light of the evening. What I could make out were the clear, caramel colored eyes that made him appear younger than his years.

He came around the table, bowed slightly at the waist as he took Donna's hand and kissed it, then said, "*Enchanté.*"

Ah, those French.

He turned to me and said, "After all these many years."

We shook hands and then he held me by the shoulders. For a second I thought he was going to hug me and kiss me on both cheeks and do that whole continental routine, but all he did was stare at me with a thoughtful, intelligent gaze.

"It is as if I am looking into your father's eyes," he told me in his thickly accented English.

I smiled, since I couldn't think of anything else to do, while the *maitre d'* helped Donna into her seat. "An aperitif, *madame?*" the little man in the tuxedo asked her.

"Some champagne, perhaps," Monsieur de la Houssay suggested.

"That would be wonderful," Donna said.

"Excellent," I agreed.

"*Bon*," the man said, and went off to bring us champagne. I noticed that he did not need to ask which type of champagne our host preferred.

I waited for Monsieur de la Houssay to sit, then I did too.

"It is a great pleasure to meet you at last," Gilles said. Despite the heavy accent, his English was impeccable. "But I must confess, this is a bit strange for me, eh? As if there is someone else at the table with us." His smile turned a little wistful.

I nodded.

He said to Donna, "I hope you will enjoy this restaurant, my dear. You are comfortable?"

The table was made of heavy, old wrought iron with a round, glass top. The chairs were also wrought iron, with curved metal arms and seat cushions that made the otherwise stiff design rather cozy.

Donna nodded politely. "Very comfortable. It's a beautiful setting."

"It is," he agreed. "I hope you will not be bored as your young man and I share stories from the past."

"Not at all," she allowed with her luminous smile.

"His father and I met many years ago."

I waited for more, then said, "You and my father were close back then."

"Ah *oui*. It was a time when friends and enemies were more clearly defined than today. The world was more black and white than it is now." He turned to Donna. "You understand my terrible English?"

"You speak beautifully," she assured him, which inspired Gilles to reach across the table and give her a paternal pat on the hand.

"You are too kind," he said.

"No, she's not," I said. "You should hear my French."

He laughed. "I hope to have the pleasure to help you with it." He sighed. "Yes, it is a different world now. French, English and Americans drive cars made in Japan and Germany. Our countries buy oil from Arabians, then go to war against them. The Russians were our allies, then our enemies, and will certainly become our allies again. I wonder how long one must live to see the wheel spin completely around, eh?"

"That was one of my father's favorite expressions."

"Of course," he said with another smile. "He would say, 'The wheel turns.' He could never speak French, but he was very clever with English."

I was about to tell him that "the wheel turns" was not all that clever, but let it go. Instead I said, "I never heard him try to speak French."

"It was for the best," Monsieur de la Houssay told us with another chuckle.

A waiter arrived with a bottle of *Pol Roger* in a bucket filled with ice, and three champagne flutes. He placed our glasses on the table and then displayed the label to Monsieur de la Houssay. When Gilles nodded, we all watched as the waiter expertly uncorked the wine and gave Monsieur de la Houssay a taste. Another nod was followed by a polite, "*Merci*," and the waiter poured us each a glass.

"My dear," Monsieur de la Houssay said to Donna, "if you will indulge me, I must first make a private toast." He looked at me, held up his glass, and said, "To the memory of your father."

We touched glasses, making a sweet, clinking sound, and then drank.

He was staring intently at me again as he said, "It is as if I have been waiting for you to come to see me for a very long time. You understand?"

"Not exactly, no. I'm embarrassed to admit it, but I only learned about you very recently."

"I know."

"Benny?"

He nodded. "There is much for me to explain."

I was glad to hear it. "Why didn't you ever try to contact me? I mean, you knew about Blackie dying, right?" As soon as I said it, I regretted how critical it sounded. "I'm sorry, I didn't mean to—"

"Please," he interrupted my apology. Then he took another sip of champagne. "You are just like your father. You Americans are always, how you say, right to the point."

"But I didn't mean to sound rude."

"Rude? No, no, no. How can you be rude? After all this time, you must have so many questions. I understand."

I wanted those answers, but for now he turned to Donna and said, "One more toast, for the three of us. To love, eh?"

Who could argue with that? We all touched glasses and I had another taste of the dry, sparkling wine.

Returning his attention to me, he said, "Your father did not tell you of our days together."

"He told me nothing."

"Ah, Blackie. That was his way. Close to the vest, as he would say. And in this case he had reason to be careful. So careful. We all did." He nodded slowly, gazing absently into the clear night sky. "What great fun we had though."

"My father could be fun," I admitted. Turning to Donna I said, "He had his moments."

Gilles shook his head. "May I say, it is far different, far more difficult to be a son than a friend, especially when we speak of, how you say, a *bon vivant. Comprendre?*"

"Yes, I do," I said. "And I believe you're right."

"When you have feelings for a person, this also carries a certain burden, a responsibility which is different for each of us. Between friends, these emotions can be, eh, more casual, yes? With parents or brothers or sisters, it is much different." He stuck out his lower lip, looking very French as he did so. "Love is not only a gift, it is an obligation. It carries with it the duty of allowing the other person to have faults, to be less than perfect, to be, uh, to be human, if you see what I am trying to say."

I let out a long sigh. "Yes, I see. You know, I'm not sure I'll ever really understand my relationship with my father," I admitted. "But I think you just helped to remind me of how my own immaturity figures into that equation. And I must say, you've done it with exceptional grace."

"*Merci*," he said, his eyes shining with pleasure. "I understand much about fathers and sons, although God did not bless me with children." He shrugged his shoulders. "I loved my father very much, but he was a difficult man. He drank. He caused problems for my mother. He was very demanding of me. There was pain and disappointment and yet, he was my father, and what existed between us was unique. I believe these are the things that make my feelings for him so special. Am I making sense to you?"

"You are."

"I've had a good life, a fortunate life. No complaints, as they say. My wife was a wonderful woman."

I hesitated before asking, "Was?"

"Yes." The sadness in his eyes was plain enough. "She is gone, three years now."

Donna said, "I'm sorry."

"It is so much different without her."

Donna and I waited as he took a moment to remember.

Our waiter returned, this time to pass out menus. When he said something in French to Monsieur de la Houssay, his tone was very respectful.

I watched and listened as the two of them went back and forth discussing the food, not fully understanding their enthusiastic banter, but getting the general idea. Gilles then suggested he order dinner for all of us. That suited me fine, since it saved us all the ordeal of having the items on the menu translated, a practice I'd employed since the time I thought I was ordering a filet of something and wound up with the sautéed stomach lining of some large, deceased critter.

I told Monsieur de la Houssay I'd be pleased to have him order. "As long as it isn't brains or kidneys or anything like that, if you don't mind."

The old man laughed, but Donna looked at me as if I'd just called Gilles a dirty name. "It would be awfully nice if you would order for all of us," she told him. "Anything you like will be wonderful."

"I trust you both eat fish, yes."

We said that we did.

"Your father never would. Did he ever change?"

"He never did."

"*Quel dommage.* Although, one must admit, there is something to be said for consistency, *oui?*" He turned back to the waiter and began another animated discussion in French about this dish and that.

"Their special appetizing course is *extraordinaire*," Gilles told us after the waiter departed. "I ordered only one, for the both of you to share. Believe me, it will be more than enough."

"What about you?"

"Ah. It is the sad fate of a Frenchman, if you are fortunate enough to live a long life, you become unfortunate enough to have to deprive yourself of some of life's great pleasures."

I nodded.

"I will have a salad and I will enjoy watching as you indulge yourselves."

Donna told him he was too young to think of himself as old.

"Ah," he said as he lifted his glass to toast her, "you are almost as generous as you are beautiful."

No wonder women love Frenchmen.

When he turned back to me, his demeanor was more serious. "You have come a long way to meet me. I appreciate that."

"It was a little impulsive," I admitted.

"Impulsive?"

"Nutty. Foolish."

"Ah, yes."

"But I trust Benny, and he gave me your name."

He grimaced for an instant, and I wondered if he knew Benny was in some sort of trouble. Before I could ask, he reverted to that charming little grin of his.

"Benny," he said, "is a man worthy of trust."

For now, all I said was, "He certainly is."

"And thanks to him, we are here together, yes."

"Yes," I said. "We are."

"Then we have much to discuss." And, having said that, he began to describe his days with Blackie, at the end of the Second World War.

They met when my father arrived in Marseilles, shortly after Benny got there, following the fall of Berlin. They were attached to a detail charged with investigating subversive activities, which was the polite name given to a covert scavenger hunt for artifacts appropriated by the Nazis during their unwelcome stay in France. Gilles claimed he had no idea how my father came to receive that assignment, but I had a suspicion that some of the brass in the armed forces can be smarter than we think. The boys at the Pentagon may buy forty-two-dollar bolts and six-hundred-dollar toilet seats, but they also win the wars they get involved in—Vietnam being excluded for too many reasons we don't need to get into—and winning is what wars are all about. My guess was that Blackie and Benny, and, perhaps Gilles, were recognized by their superiors as having a unique set of skills in their hearts and heritage, so who better to track down stolen goods?

I said, "My mother just gave me some of his papers, and I saw part of that in his service record."

He nodded. "*Bon*," he said, then went on.

Gilles explained that their detail was a joint effort between French and American forces. In the days of Vichy and the German occupation of France, there were innumerable items that were separated from their rightful owners, and the French wanted them back. These included valuable wine, historical artifacts and artwork. Their unit was assembled to retrieve as much as they could, in clandestine manner, with as little fuss as possible.

"It was of the utmost importance that our missions were carried out in secret," Gilles told us.

I asked why.

"The thieves were not all German officers," Gilles explained with a touch of sadness. "There were many French collaborators who took advantage of the opportunities presented by the war. That became a public relations nightmare for the restored French government, particularly as they were singing the praises of the fabulous French Underground and their invaluable role in overthrowing the Third Reich."

I explained to Gilles that I understood the importance of public relations.

"The less that was revealed about these traitors, the better," he said. He interrupted himself as the waiter arrived with our first course.

It was immediately apparent why he ordered only one appetizer for Donna and me to share. The dish was served on a large rectangular tray separated into sections, each containing a different delicacy. There were several types of fish, such as sardines, shrimp, herring, succulent little pieces of salmon and others I couldn't identify. There was also a selection of marinated vegetables including green lentils, zucchini, eggplant and so on. Each taste turned out to be more delicious than the one before.

"I hope this is the entire dinner," Donna said.

The size and assortment was overwhelming.

"*Bon appetit*," said the waiter, and we thanked him. Monsieur de la Houssay ignored his mixed salad and watched expectantly as we made our way through the various offerings.

"Please," I encouraged him, "you must have some of this."

"Ah well," he sighed wistfully, "life is short, as they say." He got right in there with us, sampling the fish and other treats with as much gusto as if he were trying it for the first time. "This dish never fails to delight."

As we ate, the sommelier brought a bottle of chilled Montrachet and I realized we had finished the champagne without noticing our glasses being refilled. Gilles gave the white wine a taste, then nodded his approval. Our glasses were filled, the bottle was placed in the silver ice bucket on a stand beside the table, and the man bowed and walked away.

As I have mentioned, I am not much for white wine, but tonight I said nothing, and it was delicious.

"Your father hated the French you know," Gilles said with an indulgent chortle that graduated into a slight cough. "It is amazing," he continued when he caught his breath, "really amazing that we became such good friends. Frogs, he called us. Blackie would say, 'Lousy Frogs. How do they come to think they won the war?' He was quite a provocative one, your father." Gilles smiled. "I must admit, to a certain extent we shared the same cynical view of what happened in France."

Gilles said they spent many an evening over wine and cognac and cigarettes, arguing about the differences between the Italians and the French. "He was embarrassed by the fascists in Italy, of course, so he would, how you say, make fun of the French. He would say, 'The French are the weakest of all men. When Hitler knocked on their door, what happened? Did they fight? Did they defend their great country? No. They laid down and spread their legs like so many whores in *Pigalle*.' Forgive me, my dear," he said to Donna.

"It's all right."

"Blackie would say, 'Look at the French. They cried like women, asking Der Fuhrer not to hurt them, while their great DeGaulle went into hiding and the Americans and English were left to save them.' It made your father angry when the war was barely over, and the French were already claiming the victory was owed in large part to the Resistance." Gilles took a moment to remember. "He would say, 'If the Germans were looking for a master race, they could find it in the United States.' Blackie called the French a lot of inbred Poodles. He claimed America was a melting pot that took the best of so many cultures to breed strength and character."

This did not sound anything like my bigoted father, but I figured he was young then, and probably feeling all sorts of patriotism after they whipped the Nazis. I guess he refined his prejudices about the great melting pot when he got home.

Gilles spent more time giving us a description of what went on during the war, then said, "The truth is, the Resistance was very helpful to the Allied effort. There were brave men and women who fought and died, spies who were tortured, even children working as our couriers who were murdered. The Nazis were merciless but the Resistance went on." He shook his head. "Even your father admitted that you should not judge so many heroes because of the acts of a few greedy traitors."

"Traitors?"

"The collaborators who later claimed to be connected to the underground. I will come to that."

We fell into silence as two waiters arrived with a delicious looking veal roast. It was expertly sliced tableside, then served with an assortment of sautéed vegetables. Donna and I uttered the appropriate sounds of appreciation, especially as a bottle of Beychevelle was uncorked.

"Enjoy," Monsieur de la Houssay said.

As we ate and drank some more, he spoke of those days in the south of France when he and Benny and my father were together, engaged in research, reconnaissance and repossession. "There was much information as to where these valuables had been hidden, some of it good, much of it false, some of it outdated by the time we received it. We followed each lead, searching for these people and, of course, what they had taken."

He told us how their efforts led them to various places, including Paris, where most of what they were able to recover was safely delivered, and where they made time to celebrate their successes. Out of deference to Donna, Gilles was discreet in sharing the tales of Paris, only hinting at the more pleasurable aspects of those exploits. He was also careful not to go too far beyond general descriptions of their work, never venturing too near the subject that had brought me here.

When we finished our main course, he said, "I have asked them to give us some time before dessert. Or perhaps you would care for cheese. I think you need to digest first, yes?"

Donna and I nodded.

"Would you mind if I smoke?" We told him it would be fine, so he took out a pack of Gauloises and, after we declined to join him, he lit up and took a long, grateful puff.

Donna looked from me to him, then said, "Perhaps this is a good time for me to go and powder my nose or something. Maybe I'll take a walk around the village."

Gilles smiled at her, then reached for her hand. "You are a most understanding young woman."

When Donna stood, so did Gilles, which brought me quickly to my feet. "Don't be too long," I said.

"Don't worry. I'm easily amused." She kissed me on the cheek, which for some reason took me by surprise. Then she picked up her purse and strolled away.

"She is most discreet," he observed.

"Yes. I told her that you and I would have some private matters to discuss."

"*Oui*," Monsieur de la Houssay said as we sat down again, "and of course you have your questions."

I reached into my sport coat and took out the letter. It was the original, not a copy. I thought I owed it to him to show what my father had actually written. When I handed it to him, he held it, still watching me. Then he unfolded it carefully, took out reading glasses and put them on.

"I trust you will be patient with me," he said. "As bad as my spoken English is, my reading is worse."

"Please. Take your time. Let me know if I can help."

I watched him as he read, feeling sad that Blackie and Benny were not with us. As he went through the letter, I thought about how much fun it would be to sit and listen to the three of them talk over old times, recalling when they were young, when everything was still possible.

He finished, took off his glasses, folded the page and looked at me in a way that told me he was feeling just as melancholy as I. "Your father loved you very much."

"Thank you," I said.

"You now know, of course, that he and I occasionally spoke over the years. We also wrote letters, but not many. I knew of you, of how devoted he was to you."

Blackie's attitude toward me did not always feel like love *or* devotion, but I didn't want to ruin Gilles' view of my father, or of me, so I just nodded.

"Now you want to know about this letter."

"Yes. About the stolen money."

A large smile worked its way across his lips. Then he put his glasses back on, unfolded the letter and had another look. "Money," he muttered, pronouncing it *"moe-nay."* Then he began to laugh. "I am so sorry," he said as he removed the spectacles. "When you mentioned stolen money, I was reminded of how clever your father was."

I felt a sick feeling roll across my stomach. "Are you saying, there is no money?"

He handed me the letter. "Have a look. You see how the word appears only once in the letter?"

I had practically memorized the thing, but I scanned it again. "Right. Only once."

"With a capital 'M,' correct?"

"Yes, yes," I agreed, a little impatiently. "I don't get it."

"And you see the few water stains on the page? One of the droplets having fallen on the end of that one word, yes?"

"Yes, I see it."

"You did not think he wrote this in the rain, correct? Or that these marks were his tears? No, he was a clever man."

"Please, Monsieur de la Houssay. What are you saying?"

"I am saying that you are correct, there was no stolen money." He paused, taking time to have a long look at me. Then he said, "What we stole was a beautiful painting, my boy. What we stole was a Monet."

CHAPTER SIXTEEN

"Things are seldom what they seem."

That's what my father said toward the end of his letter, a take on the Gilbert and Sullivan song I heard as a child, and a lesson Blackie taught me years ago on a Christmas morning.

I was nine and Emily was eight, Kelly a couple of years younger. We were all done opening our gifts when my father left the room and came back with two packages. One was small, the other large.

"Here are the last two presents that Santa left for you and Emily," he said to me, "but Santa forgot to mark who each of them is for. We'll have to figure this out for ourselves."

"Ooh, ooh, ooh," we chanted, which is just another version of "Gimme, gimme, gimme."

"Let's open them first," I suggested.

"Sorry," Blackie replied with a shake of his head. "That's not how it works."

"I want to go first, I want to go first," Emily was saying as she eyed the larger package.

"I don't know about that," my father replied. "Your brother is older, so I think he should go first."

I liked that thinking, and immediately reached out my little hand to begin a physical inspection of the packages. Blackie brought me up short.

166

"No poking, touching, shaking, none of that. No peeling off any of the wrapping paper. You make a choice, and you keep what you choose."

I was no fool, so naturally I grabbed the much larger package, quickly tore away the paper and stood the large box on its end. Then I sat there, staring at the picture on the front. I had chosen something called Patti Playpal, a *doll,* for god's sake and, what was worse, it was huge, almost as big as Emily.

"Patti Playpal," Emily shrieked.

I wanted to die.

Emily wasted no time ripping away the colorful red and gold paper of the small box, and I turned away from the horror of Patti Playpal to see what she had uncovered.

It was a Fanner 50.

The Fanner 50 was the greatest toy cowboy gun of the era. Among its other wonderful features, it had a faux pearl handle that opened up, revealing a compartment that held a large roll of paper caps, and a smooth hammer that you could fan with the side of your hand, enabling you to snap off fifty loud shots in a row, sending a small cloud of smoke rising from the barrel. Hence the name.

"A Fanner 50," I groaned.

My father was smiling. "Things are seldom what they seem," he told me. "You made your choice, and I think there's a lesson in there somewhere."

A lesson? I wanted to strangle him. How could he do this to me? His own son. This was betrayal of the highest order.It was the worst moment of my young life.

He then repeated the admonition, that we had to keep what we chose, so I had to think fast. After running through a few ideas, some of which involved serious violence, I changed course. I took out the doll, told my sister and parents how happy I was, then informed them all that Patti Playpal would make a terrific target out on the street, where my friends and I could practice our aim, hitting it bows and arrows or rocks.

My mother tried to intercede, but I said fair is fair. If I wanted to fill the doll full of holes, or rip her limb from limb, it was mine to do with as I pleased. Right?

Emily started screaming, then literally dove through the air, shoving the small box at me and clutching Patti Playpal for dear life. If I had to guess, I would say it was the 'limb from limb' comment that put it over the top.

I owned that Fanner 50 for many years. Long past the age when I had any use for it, I kept it in the original box on a shelf in the closet. When I was away at college, my mother threw it out in one of her fits of Spring cleaning, but I wish I still had it. It was the best toy gun ever made, and another link to the past I shared with my father.

I was staring at Gilles as I looked at my father's letter again. It said, "*When Benny and I stole the Money in France we knew the risks.*" One of the water stains fell directly over the "y," which now turned out not to be a "y" at all, but a "t."

I took a deep breath, feeling as if the air had gone out of my lungs all at once. "A Monet? As in, Claude Monet?"

Gilles smiled at me.

"You mean these water drops were intentional?"

"*Mais oui.*"

I lowered my voice to a whisper now. "He was talking about a Monet painting?"

"Yes," he replied, probably thinking me an imbecile at this point, or at least slow on the uptake.

From that evening when I first read my father's letter, I had my doubts about the entire thing, concerns I carried all the way to France. Was there really any money? Whose money was it? What trouble would I be in if I found it? Would his old friend Gilles even acknowledge that he knew what I was talking about?

Through all of that, though, I assumed my father was talking about dollars, a heist, who knows what?

But he was talking about a Monet, and Monet paintings are worth millions of dollars. Millions.

I had more questions than I could organize, but the first one was easy. "Where is the painting now?"

"Of course, you will want to know that," the old man allowed, "but first there are other things you must understand."

I picked up my glass of Bordeaux and unceremoniously drained it. "I'm listening."

Monsieur de la Houssay leaned toward me. "Most of the artwork we recovered belonged to museums, some to large institutions, others to private collectors. It was a challenge, sorting out the proper ownership. Some of the owners had died in the war—some in battle, some in concentration camps—and others who survived had been wrongly deprived of what was rightfully theirs. Am I saying this correctly?"

"Yes sir."

"These were problems that have carried over to the present time. For example, Swiss banks refuse to, uh, divulge, is that the word, to divulge ownership of money that has, shall we say, a questionable source. *Comprendre?*"

"Money and property taken during the war. Especially from the Jews."

"*Exactement.* There were Jews throughout Europe who were fortunate enough to survive Hitler, yet still faced problems reclaiming their property."

Our waiter, seeing my empty wine glass, stopped by to fill it up, which finished the bottle. Gilles asked him to bring another of the St. Julien.

"You like the wines of Bordeaux?" he asked me.

"Yes, very much."

"There are also white wines from that region."

"I prefer red."

"As do I. Beychevelle is a very reliable Chateau."

"You were talking about the Jews."

"Ah." He took a moment to find his place. "It was horrible. Many Jews lost their lives, their families—I have said this already, yes? But it cannot be said enough. Many of those who survived had their property taken, as I have also said, and we were to investigate and recover everything we could with the least amount of, what is the word, uh… *publicité?*"

"Publicity?"

"*Précisément.* As I also said, our work was, how you say, clandestine. Hush hush, they called it." He laughed at the memory. "The Americans loved to say that, to say it was a hush hush operation. Americans, in so many ways, are young. Like children." He smiled at me. "I mean no disrespect. I find it a most charming, uh, attribute. Your father was very much that way."

I smiled. "He could certainly be charming."

Gilles returned to their days in the service, explaining the process used to identify the missing artifacts, then track them down. Most of the items were taken by Nazi occupiers, but some were pillaged by those French collaborators who later falsely claimed an affiliation with the Resistance. That was why the government wanted to avoid publicity. The government did not want that sort of immorality to taint the reputation of their best and bravest. The authorities also wanted to keep these issues away from the inevitable bureaucracy of tribunals and hearings and red tape that comes with winding up a war.

"Your father, Benny and I, we were diligent in our work, and very honest. Believe me, this was an assignment of great honor, and we were proud of what we were doing. Of course, we took certain liberties with some of the wine we recovered, sharing it with local maidens who were pleased to celebrate their freedom with us. We were popular, as part of the liberating force. I am sure you understand."

I laughed. "And I'm sure the local maidens were extremely grateful."

"Ah, indeed, indeed. What I am trying to explain, is that we never intended to do any wrong. We were patriots, and we retrieved millions and millions of francs in valuable treasures. I am sorry your father never shared any of this with you, it was a source of great pride."

"He felt the need to keep it a secret because of the Monet."

He nodded, then sat back in his chair and lit another Gauloises. "We were doing God's work, believe me. And then we met Jean Paul Quoniam," he said with obvious contempt.

The waiter brought the second bottle of Beychevelle, and Gilles waited until it was served before he continued.

"Quoniam was working for the Resistance at the start of the war. Then he came to believe that victory by the Third Reich was inevitable and turned coat. He sold out his countrymen, furnishing information to the Nazis from his participation in the underground movement, leading to the deaths of the many freedom fighters he identified. None of that could ever be proven, but I believe it to be true. When Vichy fell, Quoniam took the spoils he had accumulated and hid out in Alsace, where your father, Benny, and I tracked him down."

"You also found what he'd stolen?"

"*Oui.* He had paintings and sculptures that belonged to museums and individuals, including various Jewish families living in France, people he had identified to the Germans so they would be arrested and taken away. When he was cornered, Quoniam tried to buy his way out, like the coward he was. But we could not be bought," Gilles said, his voice strong. "You must understand, we did not make deals, your father and I. And Benny, of course. We were trusted with a sacred mission, and we believed in what we were doing."

Gilles told me of how they arrested Quoniam at gunpoint, then sorted through his treasure trove and cataloged the pieces. All the pieces but one.

"It was so beautiful. You cannot imagine what it is to hold it in your hands and look at it. You lean it against a wall and step back, your breath is taken away, yes? It was unmistakable, a Monet, there was no need to look at the signature to see that. A hazy sunrise with small boats beneath an orange morning sun. Beautiful. And without an owner."

"How's that?"

"It was incredible, but there was no record of this painting being stolen. Or missing. You understand? We checked every list, every claim. It was as if this painting came directly from Monet himself. We could not find any record of an owner."

I sat back in my chair. "*Provenance*, right? Isn't that the word?"

"Very good, yes. There was no *provenance*, we could find no history of ownership from the moment Monsieur Monet completed the last brush stroke on the canvas."

"Don't major artists catalogue their work?"

"You are well informed. *Touché*. But such records are not perfect, especially when one is dealing with a prolific artist. Even today, there are many, many cases in the French courts involving the authenticity of paintings. It is not an easy task, to recreate this history."

"And so," I said, "if there was no record of it, then finders keepers, was that it?"

Gilles burst into laughter that caused others dining on the terrace to turn in our direction. He leaned toward me again. "Ah, my friend, I can hear your father saying these same words to me, so many years ago." He drew on his cigarette and exhaled, his movements as elegant as could be. "Yes, it was there, in our hands. No owner. No history. No one making a claim."

"And so you decided to keep it? Simple as that?"

"Ah, if only it had been so simple. You see, after his arrest, the weasel Quoniam tried to make deals with everyone he met *en route* to prison. He knew every piece he had stolen and, when he was confronted with an *inventaire* of his plunder, he raised the issue."

"*Inventaire*? Like inventory?"

Gilles smiled. "Yes. Quoniam insisted there was a Monet not on the list. He could see that it was not there and accused us of taking it.

By then, of course, we had no choice to give it back, even if we wanted to. We had to say he was lying. Our impulse, as you gave me the word before, was not to include it in our list since we had not found an owner. Once we did not record the paining, we had no choice but to deny the accusation."

"This guy Quoniam was a liar, a traitor, and a thief. Why would anyone believe him?"

"It was not a matter of belief. It was a matter of caution. It was, as I have said, a difficult time for France. There was paranoia and, in this case, I have to admit, it was justified." The admission saddened him, even now. "If we could have found the owner we would have given it up. Perhaps, if there was a way to explain its exclusion from our list, we would have given it back then and there and the matter would have been complete. But we could not, not without admitting our improper intent, so we never did. And in all these years, no one has ever stepped forward to say, 'There is a missing painting that is mine,' 'my father's,' 'my grandfather's.' You see?"

"What if it belonged to a Jewish family that was wiped out in the Holocaust? I'm sure you considered that possibility."

"*Mais oui*. And we tried to find whatever we could, especially after we were investigated ourselves. We came to believe the painting had never been outside France. As your father would say, how could one steal something that no one seems to own?"

"He had a point."

Monsieur de la Houssay managed another sad smile. "Perhaps. Unfortunately the authorities would never see it that way. The intelligence agencies have never completely given up the suspicion Quoniam created. Still, as you properly said, no *provenance* exists. Not even a description of this painting in Monet's records. It could not be identified even if it were hanging on the wall of this restaurant."

"Could it be a forgery?"

He uttered a brief laugh. "My young friend, this is no forgery. This is Monet."

"And all these years later, the police still suspect—"

"Oh yes, I see the surprise on your face. Why do you think this became so difficult? This episode, in many ways, deprived me of my friendship with your father and Benny. Our contact became very limited. It was a great price to pay, I assure you."

I nodded.

"And the ownership, even the existence of this painting, remains an unsolved mystery."

I held my breath and asked, "But you still have it?"

Gilles let out a sigh. "No, I believe that you have it."

I drew back. "I didn't even know about a painting until twenty minutes ago."

"I believe you," he replied patiently.

As I was about to ask what he meant by that little paradox, Donna returned.

"I'm sorry," she said, a bit out of breath as she took her seat. "I know you two have things to discuss, but there's something I think I should tell you."

Gilles and I waited.

"I took a walk around the village," she said. "It's awfully nice, by the way. Then I came back, thinking I'd sit inside, near the bar, until you came for me."

"And?"

She turned to me. "Guess who was sitting at the bar when I got back?"

At that point, I don't think I could have been shocked by anything.

"The man in gray," she said.

CHAPTER SEVENTEEN

"The man in gray?" Gilles asked.

I explained that I thought there was a man watching us, and how Donna thought I was nuts.

"Aha," he exclaimed in a whisper. "Interpol."

The two of us stared at him. "Interpol?" Donna repeated.

"Yes. Not to worry. Does this man have gray hair, ordinary features, medium height and weight?"

Donna said he did, which only describes about a half billion people in the world.

Gilles got to his feet. "*Pardon*, allow me a few moments."

Donna and I stood up too, then watched him slowly amble toward the doors that led him inside.

"What's going on?" she asked as I fell back into my chair with a dull thud. She took her seat beside me.

"I'm not sure."

"Did he tell you what you needed to know?"

"Some of it. I'm still having a hard time putting it all together."

"You mean putting together what he told you and what Benny told you?"

I felt a slight shiver run up from the base of my spine.

"Benny?"

"Wasn't that your father's friend in Las Vegas?"

What she said seemed fine, it was the way she said it that sounded too familiar, too knowing.

"Yes." I looked at her, and her sparkling blue eyes danced away from my gaze.

"God, this is just awful," she said.

I found myself staring across the courtyard at an elderly couple enjoying their candlelight dinner. They appeared to be French, and I guessed they were talking about their children, or maybe their grandchildren. Perhaps they were just discussing what they were going to do tomorrow. They looked like they fit together. When I turned to Donna again, she was watching me, her eyes rimmed with a touch of red.

"Is there something you want to tell me?" I asked her.

She hesitated, then said, "Everything has gotten so complicated."

"I couldn't agree more," I said, then spotted Gilles coming through the courtyard door. "We should talk about this later"

"We will. I promise," she whispered.

As Monsieur de la Houssay made his way back across the stone terrace, I noticed how gingerly he walked. He seemed older than when he was sitting at the table animated by the obvious pleasure he took in sharing his stories with us. Donna and I watched in silence as he eased himself into his chair.

"Well my young friend, I can assure you that you are not crazy. The man who has been watching you is an old friend of mine, although some may find that hard to comprehend. His name is Frederique Durand, and he would very much enjoy meeting with us. I invited him to join us for dessert, if you have no objection."

I leaned against the back of the wrought iron chair. "Who is he?"

"Inspector Durand is an officer of the law, and has more than a passing interest in our, shall we say, our situation." Then, turning to Donna, he said, "Some more Beychevelle, my dear? This second bottle has breathed enough, please have another glass with us."

I found myself wondering about the oil painting of a Provençale landscape Blackie brought back from France. I knew enough to know it was no Monet, but it was a painting, the only painting he had ever given me.

As for a *Monet*, if Gilles was correct and I had the thing, I never noticed.

Gilles had described the Monet oil in great detail, the small boats, blue sea, orange sun and the shimmering reflections on the water. I'd seen Monets like that, but only in museums. Gilles also said that the painting was pretty fair in size, about a meter across and two thirds of that in height.

Not something I would miss if I had ever seen it.

While I was running through the possible whereabouts of the Monet, I had some random thoughts about Donna. There's a screen in my brain that displays headlines twenty-four hours a day, like the building in Times Square, and believe me, while the rest of my tortured mind was trying to work everything out, my cousin Frank's name was brightly flashing there.

And what about Gilles? He wanted to introduce me to Interpol. What was I missing?

What if I was the target of an elaborate plot to recover the painting, or worse, to steal the painting back from those who had stolen it in the first place? What if there was no painting, that this was all about something else entirely?

My stomach began to ache.

Gilles read the look on my face. "I know," he said warmly, "this is all a great deal to absorb."

"I'd say so."

"Please, before we meet with Durand, ask me anything you wish."

I shifted in my chair, then did it again, as if it had become impossible for me to find a comfortable position. Which it had. "Forgive me, Monsieur de la Houssay, but we've never met before tonight. I never even knew you existed until a few days ago. I came to France to ask you some questions and, frankly, I'm more confused now than when I boarded the plane."

He waited.

"I showed you my father's letter. You've shared some wonderful memories about the end of the war. But—and please try and understand, I don't mean to be insulting—but I don't have any way of knowing if you're really who you say you are."

I expected him to start giving me a list of things that might prove who he was, evidence of his background, all of that. Instead, he remained silent so I could continue.

"Now you want me to meet someone from Interpol. What if you're from Interpol? What if this is all some elaborate setup?" I realized how ridiculous I sounded and turned to Donna, who appeared even more bewildered than I was. Worse than that, I still wondered who *she* was.

For an instant I thought about the grumpy driver who brought us from Antibes to the restaurant. If I could have located him right then, I might have happily jumped in the back of his sedan, returned to the hotel, grabbed my passport and gone home. I remembered the ad campaign I needed to write for that car dealership in Long Island, and how Harry was going to be all over me when I came back without ever having opened the file. It occurred to me I might use a Monet sunset with a car superimposed in the foreground. The copy would read, "For that continental feeling with the assurance of American quality," or something like that.

Gilles interrupted my silent but growing sense of anxiety. "May I say something?" he asked politely.

"Please. Please do."

"I think you would agree that I have asked you for nothing. Not one thing. You, of course, have asked questions of me, and I have done my best to respond."

I nodded dumbly.

"Then let me explain something more." He glanced at Donna. At this point she was not about to go anywhere, and I was not about to ask her to. "This situation has made me something of a local celebrity over the years. The legend we discussed is old, but still very much alive. At first, I was thought a scoundrel, but the reputation of a scoundrel ages well, and in the end has a certain charm. Other than this one episode I have lived an exemplary life. I have been a moderate success in business. I held public office, as an elected official in Roquebrune. Your father found that very amusing." He lit another cigarette and exhaled a small cloud of smoke. "I have enjoyed this little cat and mouse game over these many years, always knowing I would never have the pleasure of owning the item myself." He was obviously taking care not to mention the painting in front of Donna. "Your father was the dreamer who believed it would bring us riches. I understood the truth. Once we were suspected, I could never be involved again. It was the same advice I gave to your father over the years." He paused, his bright, hazel colored eyes looking directly into mine. "That is why Benny advised you to forget this entire affair. Which you have not mentioned to me."

That got my attention, since I had never told him what Benny said. As I already said, I also never told him about my discussion with Selma a couple of days ago.

"Ah yes, you failed to mention what Benny advised you, but I know because he shared that when he called me with the news that you would be coming."

I looked at Donna, whose was fixed on Gilles. Turning back to him, I said, "I'm sorry, I feel like a jackass. Benny gave me your name and I—"

He responded with another tolerant smile. "Your upset and confusion are understandable." He took a moment before going on. "I have mentioned that in some ways I have outlived my years. Unfortunately, the doctors now agree. So I am happy, if my time is short, to have this chance to meet you." He carefully tapped the ashes of his cigarette into the crystal ashtray. "And understand, I take no offense at your questions. If anything, I am fascinated to have this opportunity to see your father again, in you."

I began to say something, but Gilles held up his hand.

"My condition affords a certain freedom," he said, "since there is nothing left for me to fear. My only concern is that my friend's son does not suffer for the mistake of our youth."

"I'm so sorry to hear that. About your health, I mean."

He offered a melancholy tilt of his head in response. "Sorrow should be reserved for the death of the young, eh?" His heavily accented English made his sadness in speaking these words all the more poignant. "I lost many friends in the war. They never had the chance to live beyond their youth, to enjoy the full life I have had. Please, do not waste your pity on me."

I managed a wan smile. "I'll try to remember that philosophy."

He took another long and grateful pull at his cigarette. "Now you must decide if you really want to find it, yes?"

"And do what with it? Turn it over to the authorities?"

"Ah, no." He smiled. "I could never suggest such a thing. It would not be a fitting end to all these years of intrigue. No, if you find it, it is yours to do with as you please."

Donna was looking at me. She didn't speak, she just nodded slightly.

"Sorry if I'm confused about this, but why do you feel we should meet this Interpol inspector?"

"To assure him that you are here for one reason only, which is to visit an old friend of your father. We can say, if it is necessary, that you learned of my illness and decided to come and have dinner with me during your brief vacation in France."

"And my father's letter?"

The smile returned to his thin lips. "What letter?"

CHAPTER EIGHTEEN

Frederique Durand was indeed the man in gray I spotted at the airport and the beach.

We joined him in the lounge, where we he was seated at a small cocktail table. When we approached he stood, gave Donna a brief nod, then shook my hand as Gilles made the introductions. With a slight smile, Gilles asked the Inspector to show us his identification. Durand seemed puzzled by the request, but politely obliged with another slight tilt from the waist. He assured us, as he displayed his credentials, that he had not come in any official capacity. To the contrary, he explained, his old friend Monsieur de la Houssay had told him of our visit, and he was therefore a bit worried about Gilles and, by association, Donna and me. I was anxious to hear what, precisely, he was worried about.

Durand was younger than Monsieur de la Houssay, somewhere around sixty. Up close he didn't appear so gray, although he was wearing the same suit I'd seen him in that morning, the one that matched the color of his hair. His eyes were dark brown and his complexion, contrary to how it appeared from a distance, was robust. He looked quite fit, and had a calm, formal manner.

He invited us to be seated and asked if we might like dessert. Following our enormous dinner, for which Monsieur de la Houssay insisted on paying despite my repeated protests, we all agreed that even one additional morsel of food was simply out of the question.

Since my stomach had become more a barometer of nerves than a depository for nourishment, I was happy to be done with the eating portion of the program. Inspector Durand said that he had already taken his dinner at home, so we all sat in the lounge, ordered coffee and shared a bottle of Sauterne.

By now, I decided there was no reason to exclude Donna from the proceedings. I figured I would learn more from her presence than her absence.

"Frederique," Gilles announced with a glance in his friend's direction, "is, how you say, an anomaly. Although he is a great detective, he is not by nature a suspicious man. He is, you would say, *réaliste*. Am I correct, *mon ami?*"

The Inspector responded with a bemused look. "Our host refers, of course, to the legend of the Monet."

Earlier, I might have fallen off my chair at the casual reference by a police officer to the puzzle I was trying to unravel, but by now I was beyond surprise, and more than happy to get to the matter at hand. Donna was either confused by the reference to a Monet or a terrifically subtle actress.

"Ah, yes, the legend," Gilles replied cheerfully. "You see, my young friends, how quickly the Inspector reveals his true beliefs."

I turned to Durand. "May I ask what those beliefs are, Inspector?"

He nodded slowly. "Gilles is a shrewd man. For years, the fable of this mysterious painting has permitted him the opportunity to play a part based on an incident which I understand he has just shared with you. Or, as we say in my profession, the alleged incident." Durand's English was flawless, his accent far lighter than Monsieur de la Houssay's. "You recall the Hitchcock film that was set here, on the Riviera?"

"*To Catch a Thief*. Cary Grant."

"Just so. That provides the perfect pose, so to speak. Some around here even felt that character was based in part on Gilles."

"Nonsense," Monsieur de la Houssay said with a brief laugh.

"Whether or not that is true," the Inspector went on, "the legend exists."

I studied Durand carefully now. "You keep referring to this as a legend—"

"Indeed," Gilles interrupted. "The Inspector never believed, does not believe and will not believe that there really is a missing Monet. Am I stating this correctly?"

The Inspector gave another of his stiff nods. I figured he would have been great in the Court of Versailles, with all the bowing they did in those days. "Gilles is correct. No one has ever admitted to seeing this painting. There is no record of its ownership. The principal players, which I am led to understand include your late father, denied any involvement from the outset. The only proof of its existence, if it can be called proof, is the claim of the late Jean Paul Quoniam, a most despicable man. My friend Giles has allowed the legend to go on, and he may do as he wishes, with this I have no quarrel. He romanticizes this *escapade*"—he pronounced it in the original French—"and if he is amused by the rumors of his participation, I have no quarrel with that either. My only concern has always been that the wrong people might believe the painting exists. As time has gone by, such a painting would have become increasingly valuable, making it more of a lure for others to claim this prize for themselves. Is my English clear?"

It was Donna who said, "Oh yes, Inspector. Very. You speak beautifully."

Durand smiled, then took her hand and gave it a little kiss. "You are too kind, *mademoiselle*."

Those Frenchmen, I'm telling you.

"No doubt there are many possessions that were stolen by the Nazis and their co-conspirators," Durand went on, "items that remain unclaimed, even to this day. The *Jeu de Paume* in Paris was filled with plunder taken from Jewish families, as well as others considered enemies of the Third Reich. Notorious collaborators, like Hans

Wendland, created false documents in an effort to authenticate the *provenance* of many of these stolen artifacts. You understand?"

I told the Inspector I was learning. "What about Monet's record of his own work?" I asked. Monsieur de la Houssay had answered the question, but I wanted to hear it from Durand.

"Ah yes," the Inspector admitted. "There are certainly works from Monet's *ouvre* whose whereabouts cannot be accounted for. This is the only reason my friend retains his *crédibilité*."

I nodded. "So, you've been keeping an eye on us, not because you're looking for this painting, and not because you thought we were any sort of threat to Monsieur de la Houssay—"

"But because you might have attracted the attention of others who could be," Durand finished my thought.

"Which I don't think we have" I said, shooting a quick glance at Donna.

"Ah, but you may be incorrect I that belief," the Inspector disagreed.

"We have?"

"Did you not notice the man sitting on the beach this morning? The same man who took a taxi outside your hotel and followed you here tonight?"

"You're joking."

"I am not joking," the Inspector replied in a serious tone.

"I can vouch for that," Gilles said. "Frederique is a charming dinner companion, but he has absolutely no sense of humor when it comes to his profession."

Durand nodded his agreement.

I asked what the man looked like, and the Inspector described someone in his thirties, not tall but well built, with an olive complexion and, despite Italian features, unmistakably an American.

"Don't tell me. He had on plaid shorts and a camera around his neck."

Durand smiled. "I began watching you upon your arrival at the airport. I believe you noticed me there, this is true?"

"Yes."

"That was well done. Unfortunately, your powers of observation did not extend to this other man. You see, I was doing nothing to disguise my interest in you. He was. I am convinced there are people who know you are here."

I leaned back in my chair, trying to wrap my mind around all this. "He followed me from the States?"

"With all respect to my old friend, I do not think there is anyone left in our community who believes Gilles has this painting."

"I am forced to admit," Gilles conceded with a wry smile, "this is true."

"However," the Inspector continued, "there may be others who believe you have come here to get it. And, whether you do or not is beside the point. If they believe it, then there is reason for concern."

Monsieur de la Houssay shrugged his shoulders. "I told you, Frederique does not believe the legend, but he is a good friend."

"Thank you," the Inspector said.

I stood up. "I know this may be an imposition, but would you gentlemen mind if Donna and I took a short walk? I need to clear my head, and there are a couple of things she and I need to discuss privately."

"Please," Monsieur de la Houssay protested. "Frederique and I need the exercise more than either of you. And *mademoiselle* has strolled through the village quite enough for one evening, I am sure." He got to his feet slowly, the Inspector offering a hand. "We will stretch our legs for a few minutes and then return."

"Thank you," I said, then watched the two old friends saunter off together. When they were out of earshot I turned to Donna and asked, "Is there something you want to tell me?"

She shook her head slightly, but offered no response.

"You're sure?"

She stared at me, her eyes welling up as she said, "What do you want me to say?"

I took a deep breath. "You must realize I have questions."

She hesitated before saying, "So do I."

"Such as?"

"Such as, I don't know what the Inspector is talking about, and I don't know about anyone following us. Except him."

"What about us?"

"Us?"

"You must realize by now, we met at a very unusual moment in my life."

"I know."

"Which is making me suspicious of everything and everyone."

"Including me?"

"You have to admit, it's a bit strange that you just happened to meet me on that flight from Vegas, just happened to be on your way to Europe, and just happened to jump on a plane to France on my half-assed expedition."

After another pause, she said, "You're wrong."

"Which part do I have wrong?"

"Most of it. All of it." She looked away.

"Come on, Donna," I said, reaching for her arm and gently turning her toward me.

"Trust me," she said. "That's all I can say right now."

"That I should trust you?"

"Yes, that's what I'm asking," she told me, then got up from her seat. "If you need to hear me say it, I'm with you because I want to be, which is all you really need to know. Now I'm going to the ladies' room," she said and walked off.

When Gilles and Inspector Durand returned, they found me sitting alone.

"Ah, my young friend," said Monsieur de la Houssay, "have we said something to disturb your beautiful companion?"

"Oh no," I said with a shake of my muddled head. "I took care of that myself."

Before they could offer any advice, Donna came back.

"You okay?" I asked.

"I'm fine," she replied, looking directly into my eyes. "You?"

"I hope so," I said, and we all sat down.

"You have come a long way to meet your father's friend," the Inspector said.

"Yes, I have."

"There is much to be said for that," he told us, "the respect you have shown." Before I could respond, he steered our discussion to the elegance and charm of the Riviera, the reasons for its cachet, the types of foreigners who come to visit, and how some things have changed over the years while other things have remained the same. When Durand began to give us restaurant recommendations, I knew it was time to say good night.

The four of us left the restaurant together and made for the large gates of this storybook village where, to my amazement, our driver was parked not far from the stone entrance.

I asked the Inspector if there was any reason for us to be concerned about the man he thought had followed us.

"Not at all," he assured me, but when he offered no explanation I wasn't feeling all that assured.

"I've never been followed before. Is there something I should know?"

"You should know the importance of friendship," the Inspector replied. I waited for more, but it did not appear to be forthcoming, so I turned to Gilles.

"The Inspector is a wise man," Gilles said warmly. "Do not be concerned. Take this beautiful young lady to see the Riviera at night."

Gilles and I made plans to meet the next day for lunch. I thanked him for dinner, and especially his memories of my father. I could see in his eyes that our discussion was not yet at an end.

I told Inspector Durand that it was a great pleasure meeting him and asked if either of them needed a ride to wherever they were going.

The Inspector thanked me, but said he had his car and would take Monsieur de la Houssay home.

"In that case," I said, "perhaps you would be kind enough to tell our driver we'd like to take the scenic route back, and to stop at the Monte Carlo Casino. We've had a little trouble communicating with him."

The Inspector obliged by walking over and bending down to speak with our driver.

When the translation was done, I shook hands with Durand then turned to Gilles.

"I don't know what to say."

"Then say you will see me tomorrow, yes?"

"Of course."

"Good." When he took me by the shoulders and held me to him, it was as natural as if we had embraced a thousand times in the past. I was pleased that we did.

Both men kissed Donna good night, then she and I climbed into the back of our car and headed off into the darkness.

It was a warm night, and we had the windows open, the breeze swirling around us as we motored along the Grand Corniche, a road cut high into the side of the mountains that rise up from the shore. The sea was an obscure expanse below, lights from the many boats, anchored here and there, creating the impression of a dark, enormous canvas upon which so much had been painted. The hills above were dotted with houses and small buildings and thick greenery that is difficult to discern at night. The moon cast shadows around us that were pierced by the headlights as we drove on. Donna and I were quiet as we observed all of this, but she reached out and held my hand.

The silence left me to deal with several things, although the wind in my face helped me realize I had probably consumed too much wine to bother trying.

Our dissolute driver followed the instructions from Inspector Durand, but when he dropped us off at the foot of the steps leading up to the casino in Monte Carlo, I wondered if we would ever see him again.

At that point I didn't care.

I stepped out of the car and stood at his open window. Then I said in plain English, with no funny accent and no attempt to indulge him, "I don't know how long we'll be. Just wait out here somewhere and we'll see you later."

I watched as he drove off, then stood on the sidewalk beside Donna, where she was looking up at the brightly lit entrance to the casino.

"It really is grand," she said, the first words she had spoken to me in quite a while.

"Uh huh," was my snappy reply.

We watched as the uniformed doormen attended to their duties. Then I noticed Donna had turned to face me.

"What?" I asked.

"I understand, why you worried about who I am and all that."

"Thank you," I said, then began to ask her something, but she cut me off.

"No more questions right now," she said softly. "There are already too many questions."

"I agree with that."

A couple was moving slowly up the staircase toward the majestic entrance, holding hands, talking and laughing as they went. At the top, two young ladies and an older man emerged from behind the heavy brass and glass doors and began their descent to the street. They were not laughing, looking as if they had a rough night at the roulette table. Or maybe that was just the kind of people they were.

"Are we going in?" Donna inquired patiently. She had not had as much wine as I, so maybe she figured a little patience was in order.

I turned to her, noticing again how great she looked in her purple silk dress. "Why not? We're here, right?"

She laughed. It seemed like days since either of us had laughed. "We're definitely here."

I took her by the arm and said, "This is all pretty confusing for me."

"I know. Give it some time. You may sort it out."

Just as we were about to negotiate the staircase, a man walked up to us. He was nicely dressed, in a suit and tie, not as tall as I but definitely wider. He was obviously an American.

"I'm John," he said.

I thought the polite thing to do was to introduce myself, which I did.

"I know who you are," John informed me in a tone that told me I must be a dope not to have realized that. "You should come with me."

He was standing right in front of me now, so I pulled my head back as far as I could, trying to see him better. "Come with you? Why would I want to come with you? I just met you."

"I think we have some common friends."

His increasingly aggressive tone helped to sober me up a little. But only a little. I said, "Speak for yourself, pal. I don't have any common friends."

I don't think he found me amusing.

I made another effort to focus my eyes and get a good look at him. His hair was dark and cut just short enough so the waves in it couldn't run amuck. He had a swarthy complexion and blunt features. He looked Italian but spoke like a New Yorker, and I assumed he was the man Inspector Durand had spotted.

"You're, uh…" I began, then switched gears. "Who? Who do we have in common?"

"Your cousin Frank, to name one," he said, coolly as you please.

"Uh huh. You're telling me my cousin wants to see me, here in Monaco, and he sent you?"

"Not exactly, no."

"Okay," I said, raising my voice a bit, "why don't you tell me exactly what the hell it is you're saying?"

We were almost nose to nose now, except he was shorter, so it was more like nose to chin. "There's no reason to make a scene, is there?" The way he asked the question, I could tell he was trying to sound sinister. He wasn't very good at it.

"What do you mean by a scene?" He had that stale, sour-smelling breath that really drives me crazy, especially when someone moves up close, like they have this need to share it with you. I figured the wine and fish and garlic I had for dinner served him right.

"The best thing you and your lady friend can do is come with me," he said again, delivering the message with another blast of foul air. Words like "come" and "with" can involve a lot more exhaling than you might realize. I thought about offering him a mint.

"Look pal, I don't know you from a hole in the ground." Not an original line, I admit, but from champagne to sauterne, I wasn't at my best. "If my cousin wants to see me, he can give me a call." As I reached out for Donna's arm and began to turn away, he took my shoulder in a surprisingly strong grip and slowly but forcefully turned me back around.

"Your cousin isn't here, that's why he sent me. He thought you might need some help, and that's what I'm here to do. I'm going to give you some help."

I tried to shake loose from his hold, but he was strong. Reaching up and pushing his hand away, I said, "I don't need any help."

"Frank thinks you do." Then he tilted his head in the direction of a car that had pulled up alongside the curb. "Why don't we get in?"

I bent down and squinted at the sedan, getting a look inside. I didn't know the man at the wheel, but I can't say I was completely shocked to see Frank's friend Lou sitting in the back seat. You remember Lou Grigoli or Grisanti or whatever, the huge guy with the awful wig who conspired with my cousin to stick me with the tab for a lunch I didn't even want.

"Hey," I said. "How are ya?"

Lou sort of nodded, which is to say that he inclined his head forward slightly, then moved his hands a lot.

The stocky guy in front of me, who called himself John, put his hand on my shoulder again. Feeling somehow emboldened by the presence of Lou's familiar if homely face, I reached up and grabbed John's wrist, twisting it away from me.

I said, "If you touch me again, I'm gonna kick your balls up through your throat."

All he did in response was show me this thin, evil smile, and I thought, *Damn*, Blackie always told me that you should do whatever you can to avoid a fight, but if you see you can't avoid it, then there are three things you've got to do. One, make sure you hit the other sonuvabitch first. Two, make sure you hit him hard, never just give him a shove or some wimpy move like that. And three, never, and he meant never, ever, ever talk about what you're going to do before you do it.

I was thinking about that advice as the stocky guy who called himself John doubled me over with a quick right to my stomach.

For a blinding instant I thought, I'll show him, I'll throw up all over his shoes, but I was already being pulled into the back of the sedan, as Donna was abruptly yanked into the front seat by the driver.

CHAPTER NINETEEN

It all happened so fast I doubted anyone noticed us disappearing into the night, except maybe the threesome who had been slowly making their way down the regal staircase. Unfortunately, they looked like they lost so much money in the casino they would view being abducted before making your way inside as a lucky break.

There I was, stuck in the back seat between big Lou and my new friend John. I managed to catch my breath, just enough to say, "Nice sucker punch, Sluggo. I owe you one."

John offered up another one of his thin smiles, a grin he must have practiced watching old Richard Widmark movies.

Lou said, "All we wanna do is talk, that's all we wanna do."

"Sure," I agreed between gasps, "talking is good. I guess talking out there in the open air would have been against your religion."

Lou laughed, if you could call it a laugh. It was more like an asthmatic wheeze. "Your cousin always says you're a funny guy."

"That's me all right."

Donna turned toward me from the front seat, the concern visible in her beautiful blue eyes. "You all right?"

"Ducky," I told her, still working on getting a deep breath. Turning back to the big man, I said, "Lou, you don't mind if I ask where we're going, do you?"

Lou said, "I don't mind," waited a couple of seconds, then started that wheeze again. "You get it? I don't mind if you ask, you get it?"

Lou was a stitch.

We didn't drive very far—let's face it, Monaco's not big enough to drive very far, even if you go from one end to the other. We traveled up a hill to a small park, where the driver pulled the car to a stop.

"Come on," Lou said to me as he swung his door open. "You and me is gonna have a little walk talk."

"What about my friend?"

Lou was already climbing out of the car. Once outside, he shrugged his massive shoulders. "She can take a walk on her own, far as I'm concerned. She's got nothin' to do with me."

"Why'd you bring her, then?"

"What was I gonna do? Leave her there to yell for the cops."

For once, I could not argue with his logic.

"We only need a minute," Lou told me.

Donna said, "I'm not going anywhere without you."

I looked at her. "Maybe that's not such a great idea."

She opened her door, got out and slammed it shut. I got out too. The driver and Sluggo stayed in the car.

Donna said, "I'll wait right there," pointing to a bench nearby.

"Fine with me," Lou said.

I nodded. "All right. But if I'm gone more than a couple of minutes, head back down the hill to the casino. Okay?"

She didn't answer, she just gave me a worried nod, then turned and headed toward the bench.

"Come on," Lou said, and so we began to stroll into the park.

The night was late and dark, but still pleasantly warm. I loosened my tie, then reached down and felt my stomach. I sure wanted some payback from that stubby creep in the car.

After we walked about thirty or forty paces I said, "Look Lou, I've had a long day. Why don't we stop and talk right here?" From where we were standing, I still had a clear view of Donna sitting on the bench, which made it the ideal place to have our discussion.

194

Lou spun his large ugly head around, really cautious, like a wary cat or a guy who'd seen too many gangster movies. "Good enough," he agreed. He squared up his massive shoulders to face me, just in case I forgot that he was the size of SubZero.

I asked, "What the hell is this about?" As if I didn't know.

"Your cousin thinks maybe you didn't level with him. About this action, I mean. He says he has a piece of it, that he had a deal with your father."

"Is that right?"

"Yeah, that's what he says. He says he thinks you're cutting him out and he's very hurt about it."

Hurt? When he said that, I knew the big oaf was reciting a script written by Frank, something Lou probably struggled to memorize on the plane ride all the way across the Atlantic. I could picture him, jammed into a coach seat, reading from a page of notes, his lips moving as he went through it.

"Hurt? God, I really feel bad that he's hurt. You tell him that I said so, okay? Is that it?"

Lou scowled at me. "No bullshit now, huh? Where's the thing?"

"What thing?"

"The thing, you know."

"No, I don't know. And I don't think you know either, do you?"

Lou couldn't look me in the eyes now. The one thing ignorant people absolutely cannot deal with is being confronted with their ignorance.

"I'll bet Frank didn't tell you what this is about, did he?"

He still wasn't looking right at me as he said, "Hey, it's a thing, all right? What else do I gotta know?"

"What you gotta know," I told him, "is that this is bullshit, since my *cousin* has no idea what he sent you here to look for."

"Hell he doesn't," Lou protested.

I laughed in his face, which provided me immeasurable pleasure. Inebriation is not only a great fortifier of courage, it also does wonders for my sense of humor. "This whole thing is a fairy tale, and you can tell that asshole cousin of mine I said so." I laughed at him again. "I do hope you've had a nice trip to France, you and Sluggo." Then I turned away, but he grabbed me by the shoulder and spun me back around.

Lou was a whole lot bigger than I am, but goddamnit if I wasn't getting tired of people grabbing me by the shoulder. I was also full of wine, full of stories about my father and full of an overwhelming sense that it was time for me to take charge of my life. In more ways than one. As I completed the half-pirouette Lou had yanked me into, I came up with my right foot and kicked him square in the balls, hard enough to launch a punt sixty yards. Big Lou let out a groan as he began to fall to his knees, but before he could hit the ground I sent my knee up into his face, which caused some part of his nose or mouth to give way, blood spurting out all over the place. Then I tried to grab his hair with my left hand, having some idea of finishing him off with a right uppercut, but I forgot who I was dealing with and found myself holding a handful of wig as my punch grazed the side of his temple. Even so, the kick, the knee and the de-wigging created enough physical and psychic pain to cause Lou to crumple to the ground.

Then the real action began.

Sluggo and the driver saw what happened and came racing out of the car. Donna jumped to her feet and started in my direction, but the driver reached her, clutched hold of her arm and dragged her across the hill. Sluggo came directly at me with fire in his eyes, but when I saw Donna being pulled along, I ignored him and took off toward her.

I was running as fast as I could and, coming just a couple of steps from the driver, when I took a flying leap at his head, miscalculating by just a tad, and ending up with a tackle around his knees. He, Donna and I all tumbled to the ground.

The three of us wrestled around as Sluggo got there. I took a punch to the side of my face from the driver, but managed to land a couple of solid shots of my own, then scrambled to my feet. Sluggo took a wild swing, which I ducked, then I drove forward with my head into his midsection, taking the two of us down.

That was the moment when a series of searchlights went on and a booming voice with a familiar French accent spoke through a loudspeaker, ordering everyone not to move. "We are the authorities," Inspector Durand announced in clear English. "Stop where you are."

Blackie always believed in the importance of friends. He was fond of the old adage about being able to pick your friends but not your relatives, which seemed particularly apt that evening. He also liked the one about keeping your friends close and your enemies closer.

Nicky would have loved those clichés, but I don't think I need to bother with any others, at least not right now.

The point is, Gilles was my father's friend, which meant he was a friend of mine. He made sure that the Inspector arranged for my safety during our visit to the Riviera, which Durand, being a good friend of Gilles, undertook personally.

Frank, of course, was one of those relatives I never would have chosen.

We all ended up in the Inspector's headquarters, where the three men who had abducted us were placed in a holding cell while Donna and I sat with Durand in his office and talked things through. After reviewing our options, Donna and I decided not to press charges against Lou and his cohorts. On certain levels, some of which involved how this might affect Gilles and his reputation, the Inspector was relieved. Instead of pressing the criminal case, we made an agreement that, in exchange for us not prosecuting them for kidnapping, assault and whatever else they could have thrown at them, the three thugs would consent to the entry of an international protective order of non-disturbance, or something like that. They also had to immediately return to the States.

Prior to their *bon voyage*, Big Lou, Inspector Durand and I had a private discussion.

Lou didn't look so hot, what with his nose busted up, his eye turning purple and his wig an awful mess. All the same, he was grateful he would not be facing ten years or more in a French prison.

I asked him to tell us what Frank had told him.

"He told me you were after this thing, this thing that was really his, or that he had a piece of or something."

The Inspector and I shared a look of amazement at the combination of Frank's gall and Lou's stupidity.

"And this 'thing,' do you have any idea what it is?" the Inspector inquired politely.

Lou slowly shook his large head, then looked at me. "That's why I hadda come talk to you, you see? I hadda find out where you were with this thing, right?"

"Right," I said. "That's why you had to grab the girl and me and take us for a midnight walk through the park. So you could find out what the hell my cousin sent you here to find, since you didn't even know."

"Hey," Lou said with a shrug of his massive shoulders, "when you put it like that it sounds pretty bad, huh?"

"Yeah," I said, "pretty bad."

Lou told us what little else he knew from Frank. He said that my cousin told him about a large deal, claiming that my father had taken him into his confidence years ago, and how the missing piece of the puzzle might have finally been supplied by a letter I found, which was supposed to provide the clue to where the money was hidden.

I laughed.

I told Lou that there was no letter with clues to a buried treasure, that in fact there was no buried treasure, and that my cousin had lied to him, which was something he might want to take up with Frank when he returned home. Durand, still knowing nothing of my father's letter, was happy to confirm the truth of what I was saying. There was no reason to mention the legend of the Monet since big Lou had no idea about a painting and the Inspector and I weren't about to educate the big oaf.

I also warned Lou that none of them, not him or Sluggo or Frank, had better ever darken my doorstep again, unless they wanted to face an arrest warrant from Interpol. The Inspector vouched for my statement.

He told Lou, "If so much as a hair on Monsieur Rinaldi's head is mussed, every law enforcement agency in the world will be looking for you."

"Hey, loud and clear," Lou said with as much sincerity as he could muster, shaking his head and moving his hands all around. Turning back to me, he added, "I even understand you hadda kick me in the nuts when you did. It's okay. I mean bygones are bygones, right?"

I almost told him I was sorry for yanking his wig off, then thought better of it. Instead, I said, "All of this goes for Benny, too."

Lou's response was a blank look and, coming from a guy who specializes in blank looks, it was hard to tell if I was being played or not.

"Spare me the eyes of the innocent, Lou. Who visited Benny out in Las Vegas over the last couple of days?"

He looked sincerely baffled. "I thought you did."

I decided to let it go.

To this day, Lou never realized he was looking for a Monet. I wondered if he would know what a Monet was if he saw one.

Before we wrapped up the proceedings, I asked Durand if I might have an opportunity to see old Sluggo and give him a smack or two, a little payback for the sucker punch on the street, but the Inspector regretfully informed me it was not within Interpol regulations.

Instead, Durand's men escorted all three thugs to the airport in Nice. They were left there to spend the remainder of the night enjoying the hospitality of the local *gendarmes* until they were led onto the first flight home the next day. As promised by the Inspector, each of them was also treated to entry into the files of Interpol and the FBI, which can be a major inconvenience if you're ever stopped for jay-walking or want to visit anywhere outside the United States.

It was well after midnight when Donna, Durand and I returned to the Monte Carlo Casino. Gilles was waiting for us in the bar.

"I required a brief rest," he offered as an apology for not accompanying the Inspector during the evening's excitement. Then he smiled at me. "I knew you were in the best of hands."

"That's for sure," I told him.

We sat in the corner of the room, at a small, round table with a black lacquer top so shiny you could see your reflection in it.

The room was beyond ornate, with a ceiling so high you couldn't hit it if they gave you a softball and twenty throws. Each of the crystal chandeliers was the size of a truck, and they were everywhere. The walls were covered with velvet and the windows decorated with brocade fabrics that appeared to be three inches thick. There were sculptures on pedestals, small marble fountains, and oil paintings set on free standing brass easels, all of which were highlighted by directional beams that came from somewhere above. And this was just the bar.

I said I needed a drink, and Gilles suggested we order a bottle of champagne. I felt like I needed something stronger but agreed. We sat there, the same unlikely foursome waiting to see what might happen next.

Donna had cleaned up at headquarters and looked none the worse for rolling around on the ground in the park. I had tried to straighten myself out, but still felt a little disheveled. I excused myself, went into the hugest marble restroom I have ever seen, and washed up. The cold water I splashed on my face felt great, even if I did not.

When I returned to the table, Gilles looked at me inquiringly, to see if I was all right. Then he turned to Donna. "You have gotten more than you bargained for on this trip, eh?"

Donna forced a smile.

"It seems you and my young friend have some talking to do, am I right?"

Donna looked at each of us in turn, then said to Gilles, "We were sort of introduced by Benny."

Gilles nodded and said, "I know."

I felt a thousand-pound weight disappear from my shoulders. That only left about five hundred pounds to go.

"You knew?" Donna asked him.

"*Oui.* Benny told me this when we spoke a couple of days ago, when he called to say our friend's son might be visiting." Monsieur de la Houssay turned to me. "Benny told me there was a fine young woman he wanted you to meet, and I see you have."

"You are lucky in many ways," the Inspector told me.

"What am I missing?" I asked as I stared at Donna, her deep blue eyes clear and smiling now. "Am I the only one who didn't know?"

"That night you were at Caesar's," she began. "I saw you, but you never noticed me. After you left, Benny came by—he and my father are great friends and Benny got me my job at the hotel. He knew I was about to take a trip back home, to New York, and asked if I'd get on your flight if he could arrange the ticket. He has a friend at American, got me the seat across the aisle from you, and I was the one who started our conversation, if you recall."

"I do," I said.

"Benny made me promise not to tell you. He thought it would be better, without you knowing."

I shook my head. "Why?"

"He was worried you'd be upset if you thought he had me spying on you. I know I made some mistakes along the way, like mentioning the letter he told me about, but you hadn't. I saw the look in your eyes when I said it, and I wanted to tell you then, but—"

"What about this trip?"

"He just wanted me to see you in New York, have dinner, find out what you were up to. He told me you'd probably want to visit someone here, and I called him after our dinner in Manhattan, told him what was happening, that you'd invited me to come with you to France. I told him I wanted to go."

I was speechless.

Mercifully, our champagne arrived, giving me a moment to regroup. The cork was popped, glasses filled and Gilles lifted his flute for a toast.

He said, "To friendships, old and new. To adventures, real and imagined. And to love, eh?"

Who could argue with any of that? We all touched glasses and drank. Then I decided it was time to tell Donna the legend of the Monet.

"Have I explained it accurately?" I asked Gilles.

"*Parfaitement*," he replied.

Donna turned to the Inspector. "I heard you say earlier that this was all some sort of myth, what we might call an urban legend. Now that I understand the story, I'm not sure why you don't believe it. If so many other paintings were stolen and moved around during the war—and the ownership papers were changed—I mean, why not this particular painting?"

Durand placed his glass on the shiny black top of the round table. "As I have said, there are so many reasons. First, I have come to know Gilles over these many years. There are certain judgments we make about our fellow men. In his case, the pursuit of great wealth was never important."

"But you never knew my father," I pointed out. "Or Benny, for that matter."

"Ah, *oui*. But if they were in possession of such an artifact, why has it been kept secret for so long? What benefit did they derive? This was more than thirty years ago. There is what they call a statute of limitations, I am sure you understand."

Statute of limitations? That had not occurred to me. "You're saying that enough time passed to make them immune from prosecution?"

"Not necessarily. War crimes are a special matter. As you know, artifacts are still being recovered and returned to their rightful owners. But let us say the painting was passed to another, a dealer let us say, who claimed to have bought the Monet at some art fair or whatever you like, and there is no *provenance*, no one claiming a right to it, then what would anyone be able to do? You see?"

"I think so."

"You hear stories all the time of valuable paintings being found in attics and sold for a mere pittance. If the Monet were real, something like that might have been done to cover up the theft."

Donna and I looked at each other, then at Gilles, but none of us spoke.

The old man smiled. "As it happens, Benny and I have no children. You are the only heir to the legend."

"Legend is right," I said.

Inspector Frederique Durand studied me with an amused look in his eyes. "Belief is a matter of the soul, as are friendship and love. Each is a rare and beautiful thing."

* * *

THERE'S JUST ONE MORE STORY about Blackie I need you to know. It happened a couple of years before he died, after he had his first heart attack.

The doctor said it wasn't a bad coronary. The bad ones kill you. But it was serious enough for him to spend a few days in the hospital.

It was summer, and I was involved in a weekend baseball league with a bunch of high school and college kids who played hard ball at Van Cortland Park in the Bronx. My father, who had been released from the hospital the week before, came by to see us play.

The team I played on was pretty good. Our pitcher was left-handed, a cocky guy who had just finished his first year at Farleigh Dickinson as the number two pitcher in their junior varsity rotation.

We had other solid players, including my cousin Nicky. He didn't run well because of a bum knee, but he could crush the ball from the left side of the plate. I was an all-field no-hit shortstop, as I may have mentioned already, but my dedication to the game earned me the role as captain.

Our team expected to be competitive in our division, at least until our pitcher broke his ankle in a freak accident as we began warming up that day. He twisted his leg shagging a fly ball, and ended up on the ground, writhing in pain.

After his mother helped him in the car and drove off to the hospital, we had no idea we were about to lose him for the season. Our concerns were more immediate. First, we had lost our pitcher for that day's game. Second, we only had eight players.

In softball, anyone can pitch the ball underhand. In hardball, the pitcher is the key player on the field. In softball you can also make adjustments and field eight guys, but in a hardball game you need all nine positions covered.

We had a problem.

As I stood on the sideline facing the possibly of a forfeit, Blackie saw what was going on and walked over to me, saying he had an idea.

"I'll pitch," he said.

Nicky and a couple of the other guys were nearby. I didn't want to embarrass my father, so I said nothing. My cousin, who knew that Blackie just had a heart attack, said, "Hey Unc, you're still on the mend. I don't think it's such a good idea."

The rest of my teammates weren't as kind. After a look at my father's stocky frame and flabby stomach, one of them even laughed. "Come on, Mr. Rinaldi," another one of them said, "knock it off."

My father wasn't insulted. "Tell you what," he said, "how about I pitch batting practice? You're short a man anyway. I'll throw a few, then you decide. Meantime, maybe one of your other friends will show up." He reached out and took the ball Nicky was holding. "I think the old man's got a few innings left in him," he told us.

I'd heard stories about what a great ballplayer Blackie was in his youth, most of which were told by Blackie himself. That day he was determined to show us.

My cousin and I looked at each other, then turned to my father. "I agree with Nicky. I don't think this is such a good idea."

Blackie slapped himself on the chest, hard. "Fit as a fiddle," he said, then started walking to the mound.

Blackie threw pretty well in batting practice. At least he was getting the ball over the plate, and his basic pitching motion looked like he knew what he was doing.

A little while later the umpire arrived and told us to start the game. As my team finished practice and left the field, we were still short a man.

My father strolled toward the bench and gave me a wink.

"I was just warming up," he assured me. "The fastball's still got some zip to it, you'll see."

My teammates did not want to forfeit, we were there to play, and we were out of options. I went to speak with the captain of the other team, to see if it would be all right with them if my father replaced our injured pitcher. For Blackie's sake, I was hoping they would say no, which would have ended the debate. Once my father got an idea like this, I was never going to be the one to change his mind.

As you can imagine, after the other team looked over at our paunchy, middle-aged replacement player, they said sure, go for it.

I trudged back across the field and told my team it was a go.

We were home team for this game, so the other side was up first. Someone from their team loaned Blackie a glove. Obviously we had no uniform for him. He played in his gray slacks and black short sleeved knit shirt. He didn't even change shoes, wearing his signature Lloyd & Haig black tassel loafers. It was clear he didn't intend to do a lot of running. We took the field and, as I stood at the shortstop position and watched him take his final warm-up tosses, I could see he was beginning to throw harder. I trotted over to the mound.

"You sure you want to do this?" I asked one last time.

He offered a grin in response. "Take your position, fella," he told me. Then he went to work.

He threw mostly fastballs, best as I could tell, with an occasional curve or change-up. He set their team down in order in the first.

As we came off the field, my teammates were slapping him on the back.

"Good job, Mr. Rinaldi."

"Nice throwing, Mr. Rinaldi."

He tossed the glove to the player on the other team, then turned back to us. "Hey guys," he told them, "just call me Blackie."

It was a hot, humid, summer day, and I was more worried about my father collapsing in a heap than about winning the game. He was already sweating quite a bit, and we were only in the bottom of the first. Nicky came over and put his arm around my shoulder.

"Don't worry. He's okay."

I nodded. Then I watched our team go down, one, two, three.

Back on the mound, Blackie began to look vulnerable. He walked the first batter on five pitches, then went behind two and nothing on the next guy. But he bore down, and his fastball seemed to have a little extra pop. The hitter fouled off the next two pitches, then took a called strike three, a curveball on the outside corner. The next guy popped out to second. Blackie struck out the last batter of the inning, stranding the baserunner at first.

In the third he struck out the side.

I led off our bottom half of the third, fearing I would have trouble concentrating, but to everyone's surprise I lined a single to center. I batted eighth, so that brought my father to the plate.

I called time out, which I could do as captain, then ran toward home plate to have a chat with Blackie.

"We need the run," I said, "so bunt me over to second."

I was sure he'd ignore me. How many more chances was he going to have to drive a ball over an outfielder's head? But he laid it down the third base line on the first pitch, they threw him out easily when he only trotted halfway to first, and I advanced to second. Our leadoff man struck out, but the next batter singled me home.

We were up one zip.

Blackie continued to mow them down, even though this was their second time through the line-up and they had each had a look at his pitches. In the fifth, when he came to bat again, he took a couple of rips before grounding out to second. By the time he shut them down in the top of the sixth inning, it seemed everyone was rooting for him, even the parents of the players on the other team.

The field was mostly dry dirt, especially the infield, and a lot of it was sticking to my father's damp shirt and slacks. The sweat was really pouring off him, which I mentioned to Nicky, but my cousin told me to find a mirror because I was looking a little soggy myself. I went up to my father as we headed to the bench for the bottom of the seventh and asked him how he felt.

He took a couple of deep breaths, then said, "Old, son. Really old." Then he paused. "But kind of young too." Then he managed a smile.

"Let me move you to first, Vinny can cover right and Nicky'll finish pitching the game. What do you say?"

He didn't answer at first. We moved me off to the side, where the others couldn't hear us. "I'm pitching a no hitter," he confessed in a whisper.

"I know, Dad."

"If they get a hit I'll move to first."

I stood there staring at him. He was huffing and puffing and perspiring, and I was scared. But I knew he would rather die right there than have me take him out. "Sit down," I told him. "Catch your breath. When you get up to hit this inning, just swing through the ball, like a real pitcher. Strike out, for Chrissakes, will you please?"

Blackie smiled. "It's not in my blood," he told me.

207

I turned away, but he called my name. When I looked back at him, he was about to tell me something, then thought better of it. Instead he asked, "Anybody have a towel around here?"

When he got up to bat, he cut and slashed and wound up popping out to short, which was a blessing as far as I was concerned, since he didn't have to run out a ground ball or anything.

Then he took the mound for the eighth inning.

He got the first batter on a weak grounder to first. He struck out the second guy. Then, after several foul tips, he gave up a base on balls. I started toward the mound, but he gave me look that stopped me in my tracks. I backed up to my position and hollered out, "Let's get 'em."

Two pitches later I got a sharp bounder to my left, gloved it and flipped to second for the third out.

Our team was positively jubilant as we headed in from the field. It was the bottom of the eighth, we were up three nothing by then, and Blackie was throwing a no hitter.

He walked slowly to the end of the wooden rail that served as our bench and sat there, not speaking with anyone. I let him be.

Nicky came up to me and said, "He'll be fine. He's doing great."

"Sure," I said. "Just order up the oxygen."

The top of the ninth came and no one anywhere near the field was sitting down. The foul lines were crowded with players and spectators who'd finished their own games on the other diamonds. The word was out that some old guy was tossing a no-hitter, and everyone wanted to see it. Blackie finished his warmup quickly, then went to work. He reared back and threw one fastball after another. I was amazed at the strength in his arm as pitches whizzed by or were barely tipped. He struck out the first two players, needing one more out to finish it off.

Blackie started with a curve ball that the batter fanned at badly, then followed with heat on the inside for a ball, one and one. He came back with a change up, but the guy didn't bite as the ball bounced in the dirt in front of the plate, two and one.

The catcher threw him the ball and, as Blackie took off his glove to rub it up in his bare hands, he turned to look at me. He drew a deep breath and managed a weak smile. He must have seen the worried look on my face, so I nodded at him. He nodded back.

"Let's get him," I called out above the noise of the cheering and shouting all around the field.

He turned to the plate, set his black tassel loafer on the rubber, wound up and let it fly. The batter guessed fastball and he was right. He swung early enough to get good wood on the ball, sending a screaming one hopper into the hole to my right. The third baseman dove and missed it, but I extended as far as I could on the dead run. The ball skipped into my glove on the backhand side, I spun around to my left and then, getting everything I could on the throw, pegged it to first.

The guy was out by a full step.

Everyone went kind of nuts at that point. Our team was whooping and yelling, the outfielders raced in toward the mound, and people were cheering from the baselines. But Blackie was spent. Our catcher, Eddie, ran out to congratulate him, and for a few moments my father mustered the energy to celebrate. He was all smiles as he shook hands and exchanged high fives. Then I put my arm around him and said, "That was amazing Dad, really. Now let's go home."

He nodded, as weary and submissive as I had ever seen him. He got in the car and I drove him home, where he wound up in bed for four days. When his doctor heard the story, he said my father was insane. He wasn't interested in hearing about the no-hitter. He said Blackie was lucky he survived the day.

I wanted you to know that last story about Blackie and me because, if there was only one moment between the two of us that I could share with you, that would be the one. Not at the end of the game, when everyone was celebrating. Not when he was zipping fastballs by the opposing batters, I don't mean any of that. I mean that moment in the ninth inning, when he turned to me and nodded, as if he knew his no-hitter was going to depend on me, that the last play in the game was going to come my way, and that somehow he knew I would take care of it for him.

CHAPTER TWENTY

The next day I sat with Gilles de la Houssay one more time.

It was just the two of us, which was Donna's suggestion. We met outdoors, at a small cafe in Antibes overlooking the sea. He entertained me with more stories about Blackie, about their time together at the end of the war, and about the years since. Then he asked if there was anything else I wanted to know.

"Well, there is the obvious."

"Ah yes, of course."

"I still don't understand why you believe I have the painting."

He pursed his lips in that way that people do when they have to tell you something they may not want to say. "For some time the Monet was here. Then we all thought it best that it be elsewhere. Frederique Durand had become my friend and I was not pleased to deceive him. If it had ever been discovered here, Frederique would have been compromised. Not to mention what it would have done to me. It was your father who made the arrangement. I never saw the Monet again."

"When was that?"

"Oh my friend, it was years ago."

"You actually sent him the painting?"

"I did. It was complicated, but it was done. I was pleased to bid it farewell."

"And you believe my father knew where it was when he died? Or that Benny knew?"

"Your father, most definitely. Benny said he does not know, and I believe him."

I nodded my understanding. "I need to tell you something about Benny. I'm sorry I didn't say anything before, but I don't have any details." Then I related my discussion with Selma. "I'm afraid someone went to see him after I did. Since I can't get through to him on the phone, I'm not sure what to do."

Gilles reached across the table and patted my hand. "I know," he told me. "I spoke with Benny last night when I got home. He is fine."

Benny did have visitors, Gilles said. Two men stopped by his place the day after I left Las Vegas, asking the same questions I was asked by those two thugs who came to my apartment. Since Benny knew the group that sent them, there was no rough stuff. As Benny described it to Gilles, they showed him the professional courtesy to which he was due. "He and his visitors, how do you say, spoke the same language. Benny convinced them it was all nonsense, and sent them on their way, but after they were gone, his angina acted up. When his wife got back, she took him to the hospital. He is home already, and doing fine."

"I feel a lot better knowing that," I told him.

Monsieur de la Houssay took a sip of his espresso and I looked beyond him, at the blue green sea, the large boats that swayed gently on the tide, all of it a painting itself. In a few hours I would be gone from here, and it would all seem a strange dream.

"Your father was the only one of us who knew where the painting was," he said, returning to the subject at hand. "I also know he did not sell it. He did not enjoy any, how would you say, economic benefit from it."

I thought about what little Blackie left my mother when he died. "That seems pretty clear."

"He would have told Benny and me if he sold it. It would have been a matter of honor. Which means you are the only one who could have it. If not," he shrugged, "it is lost to us forever."

"Honestly, I don't think there's any way I have it. Unless I'm missing something."

He shrugged again. "It is no matter now. I have met you, and so the circle of friendship is complete, eh?" He smiled.

"I appreciate that, I truly do. But I'm still confused. Why would my father have written the letter? It's not as if he knew he was going to have a car accident and die. Why did he write it when he did?"

Gilles blinked.

I stared at him, recalling what Gerry Egidio had said in his pastry shop a few days ago when I mentioned my father's death. I felt myself go cold again, the same way I did that morning.

"My father has been dead for several years now," I said, speaking very slowly. "I've never asked much about how it happened. But I think I always knew it wasn't an accident. I know it now, from that look in your eyes, and I know it because it's the same look I saw in the eyes of another of my father's friends, just a couple of days ago."

The old man's expression turned sad. "Benny?" he asked.

"No, someone else." I sighed. "I realize my father made choices about his life. They were his to make. But I'm his son, and I think this is something I'm entitled to know, don't you?"

Gilles nodded his head slowly.

"All I'm asking for is the truth. I think it's time."

"Ah yes. But what is the truth?"

"I don't know," I admitted. "But I believe you do."

"Yes," he conceded. "I do."

And then he told me.

It had to do with my father past-posting in his bookmaking operation. I always assumed he found a way to pay the money back, and that was that.

It was not.

213

Monsieur de la Houssay did not know, until it was too late, that my father was in serious trouble. He learned afterward, as I did, that Blackie went to his brother for help, and that Uncle Vincent turned him down. He took a deep breath. "You are right, of course, there never was a car accident."

His words sent another chill through me, the warm sun offering no help as I shuddered at the memory of Blackie lying in the hospital near death as I spoke to him, hoping he could hear me.

"Your father bargained for as much time as he could, trying to find a way to pay them back. He was too proud to ask Benny for help. Or me. We never knew of this problem." Gilles gazed out at the Mediterranean, remembering. "Not even when he called and asked if I knew of a safe way to sell the painting. As I have explained, I told him I could not be involved, and Benny wanted no part of it. It was just a few months before his death. All he said was that it was time to move it. To sell it, you understand?"

I nodded.

"He never told me why it was the right time, and I did not ask. But it takes a great deal of, how you say, arranging to make such a transaction. This was not something you can take to a, uh, *maison de prêt*, a, uh, pawn shop."

I nodded again.

"The people to whom this money was owed, he would never tell these men about the Monet or give it to them. He owned it with Benny and me, you see?"

"I do," I said.

"I have no way of knowing if he tried to sell the painting. I only know that he did not sell it. There was simply not enough time. I learned what I know from Benny, after, uh, you understand."

I nodded.

His shoulders slumped as he said, "They killed him before he could make the sale."

Killed him. The words, finally spoken aloud by my father's friend.

"Killed him?" I could hear my voice shake and so, obviously, did he.

Gilles regarded me with his moist hazel eyes. "I am so sorry to be the one to cause you this sorrow. Benny warned me that you might ask these questions. We agreed it is only fair that you know."

"It's all right," I assured him, making an effort to steady myself. "I needed to know."

"Yes," he said as he took out his Gauloises. I picked up the matches on the table and struck one. He reached for my hand and held it as I lighted his cigarette. "*Merci*," he said, then paused to take a long drag. "Benny knows many people in your father's world. He learned afterward that three men located your father in a bar in the Bronx. Without any warning they beat him, the details are not important. They left him there to die. Your father survived for a few days, then passed on. Benny tried to find out who was responsible, but never discovered who they were."

"My family was told it was a car accident." I felt my face go hot and red and tasted the anger as it rose up in my throat. "A car accident."

"Yes. You and your sisters were told this."

"And my mother?"

"I am sorry I never had the privilege to meet your mother. She is a strong woman, from what I am told by Benny. She never asked any questions. Whatever she knew from your father's last days, or suspected from what others told her, she kept the faith in order to protect her children. Especially you. I believe you should do the same for her."

I pressed my lips together and blinked several times. Then I nodded slowly.

"There is nothing to be gained by trying to do anything about this now. As you say, Blackie made choices in his life. He made a mistake and paid the ultimate price. We must all respect that."

I leaned back in my chair, realizing that I had been sitting forward with every muscle in my body stretched taut. "That's why Benny wants nothing to do with the Monet. My father guessed that if he couldn't get it sold, then Benny—"

I didn't need to finish the thought. Gilles simply nodded. "Like me, Benny wanted to put it behind him."

We sat in silence for a few moments as he smoked his cigarette. "What now?" I asked.

"I wish I knew. Perhaps you follow the advice Benny gave, which is to let it be. Perhaps you find the painting and create great wealth or great difficulty for yourself." His eyes narrowed. "Perhaps you do what your mother has feared all these years."

"With all his contacts, Benny couldn't find out anything six years ago. What could I do now?" I considered that for a few moments. "My father's death was the saddest event in my life. And I admit, right now it feels as if he's died all over again."

"Ah, *oui*. He paid the price for the mistakes he made. I don't believe he would want you to compound the error, do you?"

"I suppose not."

"No," Gilles agreed with obvious relief.

I gritted my teeth and said, "Even so, I sure would be pleased to find those three gorillas and whack them around with a baseball bat."

"A natural reaction," he replied calmly. "But an impossible quest. Benny told me that the man who was your father's boss has also passed on. Who is left to account for any of this? No one."

I took a deep breath and spent some more time looking out at the sea.

"So," Gilles interrupted my meditation, "I must now ask you. What do you do next?"

Still gazing out at the water, I said, "I guess I get on a plane and go back to my real life."

"*Bon.*"

"And as to the Monet, you think my father may have tried to sell it. Which means there may be others who knew about it."

"I doubt it. If there were, you would have heard from someone in all these years."

"True." Frank certainly knew nothing about a painting. Likewise the two goons who came to my apartment and the men who visited Benny. "I guess you're right" I said, "but there is one more thing I should tell you." I felt a little foolish for not mentioning it up to now, but I described the painting of a landscape my father had given me years ago.

Gilles was intrigued, even if my description of the painting didn't sound familiar to him. I assured him it was no Monet.

Then he said he had a thought and asked to see my father's letter one more time.

* * *

I WENT TO THE PHONE IN THE LOBBY of my hotel in Antibes and, after going through two operators and three disconnects, I listened to Benny's phone ringing in Las Vegas. It was pretty early there, and he didn't sound too thrilled to hear from me at that hour, but I was glad to find he was back home, and at least Selma didn't answer.

The first thing I told him was how sorry I felt about getting him mixed up in something he obviously wasn't keen about being mixed up in all over again.

"Forget it, kid. Hey, if I don't know how to take care of myself by now, what the hell." He told me he was feeling fine, that Selma over-reacted when he started huffing and puffing just because he was so damn angry at those punks showing up.

I told him about the visit I had, and about someone going through my apartment.

"I don't like to hear that, but I think they'll go away now, since they talked to me and after what happened in Monaco."

I said I hoped he was right. Then I asked if he wanted to know what his old friend Gilles had told me, but Benny still wasn't having any of that conversation over the phone. "How is he?" he asked.

I told him how terrific it was to meet Gilles, that he was a great guy, but that he really wasn't doing all that well.

"Sorry to hear that. I really am."

"Yeah," I said. Then I asked about Donna.

He told me that she was the daughter of a friend. Yes, he had gotten her a job in the hotel. Yes, she was a fine young woman who'd done him a tremendous favor by keeping an eye on me in New York. No, he never asked her to go with me to France. "She ain't some broad from an escort service, kid, she's a nice girl who did me a favor. What'd you think?"

I didn't answer.

"I get it." I heard him let out a full breath. "Well, you may have been a chump about her, but it's understandable, with all this going on."

"I hope she understands," I said.

"We'll see, you may need to give it some time. She's a good lady, I can tell you that."

I thanked him. Then I said, "I know about Blackie, too."

I didn't need to say more, he knew what I meant. He said, "I'm sorry, kid."

"You don't need to be. You've been a good friend to me all these years, I just never knew how good."

I heard Selma start yelling in the background, demanding to know who was on the phone. Benny told her to shut up.

"I guess maybe you should go," I told him.

Benny said, "Don't worry about Selma. She just worries, is all."

I told him that wasn't a bad thing.

"You're right," Benny agreed, then changed the subject, saying something about how he'd like to see Gilles again, how he'd been meaning to grab a flight over there, just to pay a visit. But I knew Benny. I knew he never would.

* * *

BACK IN THE HOTEL ROOM, Donna had her bag packed and was ready to take the train to Paris.

"How was Gilles?" she asked.

"Tired," I told her. "And I think a little sad to see us go."

"Me too."

She was standing in front of the open window, the blues and greens of the sky and sea providing her a worthy background.

"Before we leave, I've got something to say. About you. About how spectacular you've been through all this."

She laughed her melodic laugh. "A few hours ago you were worried I was a call girl, or some kind of gun moll working for your cousin."

"I'm not saying any of that is true, but you did tell me you understood why I had doubts about you."

"Oh, I understood all right, but to be thinking the things you were thinking about me." She shook her head. "Just hideous."

"Gun moll?" I asked, the look on my face getting her to laugh again.

"That's exactly what you believed."

"If I did, then you are the most beautiful gun moll of all time."

"How far do you think you're going to get with a line like that?"

"I don't know," I admitted, "but what if I add something like, Donna I've fallen in love with you?"

I stepped forward and took her in my arms and she reached up and held me to her.

CHAPTER TWENTY-ONE

Donna and I spent two days in Paris. We went sightseeing, strolled along the *rive gauche,* had dinners at *Taillevent* and *Chez Andre,* all of which was wonderful to experience, but boring as hell to have someone tell you about.

Especially since you want to know about the Monet.

* * *

WHEN WE GOT BACK TO NEW YORK we headed straight for my apartment, dropped our bags in the foyer, grabbed a screwdriver and made for my bedroom. Donna sat on the edge of my bed as I took my father's painting off the wall, that oil of a French countryside he'd given me years ago. I held it in my hands, looking it over front and back, then laid it face down on the floor and began carefully prying the canvas from the frame with the screwdriver.

It came apart easily, so I put the gilded frame aside, which left only the painting, stretched on its wooden struts. I had a close look at the edges of the canvas, just as Gilles had instructed. And just as he had instructed, I removed the heavy duty staples that held the canvas to the wood.

I peeled the canvas away, expecting to find the Monet underneath. It wasn't there.

* * *

THE NEXT DAY I HAD TO RETURN to my real life. I left Donna sleeping in my apartment and went to work.

My boss, Harry, was positively thrilled to see me, especially when I told him I hadn't done a thing on his new automobile account.

"Let me get this straight," he said, his corpulent frame vibrating in his chair, his cigarette hand extended toward me in a vague attempt at a menacing gesture, "all your promises about what you would be doing while you pulled your little disappearing act, you did none of it. Have I got this right?"

"Not exactly. I did sort of think about the campaign."

"I see. You *sort of* thought about it. Well then, what else is there to say?" He stood up which, as I have mentioned, was a major physical activity for Harry. "I'll just call the client and tell him that my cracker jack account exec has *sort of* been thinking about him and his car dealership, and that pretty soon we may *sort of* put together an ad campaign for him. How's that?"

After everything I had been through over the past week, the predictability of Harry's tirade came as a familiar relief.

"When have I ever let you down, Harry?"

"Let me down?" he bellowed, though there wasn't much fire behind it.

"That's right. When have I ever said I was going to do something I haven't done?"

"Don't play games with me," he demanded, making an effort to raise his voice with each word. "I need that workup, and I need it pronto."

In the past, I would have said "Yessir," gone back to my small office, and set out to do whatever he was asking. This time, however, I just stood there and smiled.

"What the hell are you grinning at?" he wanted to know.

I had no answer for him.

"What is it?" he asked again, this time a little less gruffly.

"I don't know, Harry. I was just thinking, that's all. I mean, how worked up are we going to get about a guy on Long Island who wants to sell a few more cars? I'm not saying I won't do it, you know I will. And you know why I will? Because we're just a couple of working stiffs, you and me. Perspective, Harry. That's what I'm smiling at."

"Perspective?"

"That's all," I said. Then I left Harry standing there, having no idea what the hell I was talking about.

* * *

DONNA HAD TO LEAVE NEW YORK that afternoon, and saying goodbye was not easy. I took her to the airport, helped her check in and stood by the security entrance.

She said, "I hope it all works out for you."

"Thanks."

She laughed. "Thanks? That's it?"

"I don't know what else to say. I'm caught between sad and confused and feeling just awful to see you go. I miss you already."

"Me too."

"Which part? I mean, 'me too' to which part?"

"How about, all of the above."

I took her in my arms and we kissed, and for a fleeting moment I considered holding onto her, not letting her get on the plane. Instead, I asked how soon I could come out to see her.

"How about tomorrow?"

"I'll see what I can do," I told her.

She was about to walk away, when I called her back. "Did I mention how great you were? Through everything."

She didn't answer. She just looked at me, gave me a little wave, and I watched her until she disappeared down the long corridor to her gate.

* * *

I DECIDED, SINCE I WAS AT THE AIRPORT on Long Island already, to stop by the car dealership and say hello to the owner, just to show how interested I was in his Cadillacs and to make Harry happy.

I was walking through the terminal toward the parking lot exit when a familiar looking, middle-aged man came up beside me. On my other flank appeared a younger guy I had never seen before.

I didn't wait for them to speak. I said, "I was wondering when I would see you again."

The man who had come to my apartment a few days before, claiming he was my father's old friend only to have his sidekick rough me up, gave a slight shrug of his shoulders in reply.

I looked from him to his new companion, then asked, "Where's Silvio? Attending an anger management seminar?"

They didn't answer so I stopped walking and so did they. We formed a cozy little circle with a steady flow of travelers hurrying to and from their flights all around us.

"Look," the older man said, "let's siddown and have a talk, nice nice, eh?"

"What are we supposed to be talking about this time?"

"We still think you got something belongs to our friend. We think you should give it to us."

I laughed, I mean genuinely laughed out loud. "God," I said, "You guys are something."

They glanced at each other, then went back to watching me.

"All right," I said, "there's a bar right over there. We'll talk."

We sat on tall chairs around a small table in one of those Formica airport lounges where you can buy a second hit of booze in your cocktail for an extra dollar. I asked for a double Bloody Mary. Tweedledee and Tweedledum each ordered a beer.

"Okay, so what is this thing I supposedly have?"

The older man said, "Look, I don't know exactly how to explain this, but, uh—"

"But you don't know what it is, right?"

He shrugged his shoulders again.

"But you figure it belongs to you, whatever it is."

"That's right, that's exactly it." He was happy we were suddenly on the same page.

"I've been running into that a lot lately."

He gave me a look that convinced me he was just as moronic as I had guessed.

"My father's been dead for six years. You guys run a rather inefficient collection service."

He stuck his lower lip out at me. "Hey, nobody never said nothing to you before, because you was not an involved guy, you see? But now you been askin' questions, seein' people. Our boss says it's got something to do with this something that you gotta give us. Like I said, your father owed it, right?"

That was the moment, when he mentioned what my father owed to his boss, that I thought about what Gilles told me about Blackie's death, how Benny never found out who the three men were, and how maybe, just maybe, this creep had something to do with it. My head started to pound.

"So," I said, after taking a long pull of my Bloody Mary, "you guys must know a lot of people in your business."

"What?"

"I mean, with all this talking you say that I'm doing, you two must get around and meet a lot of people."

"We get around, sure."

I took another swallow of my drink. "So how well did you know Blackie?"

The older man said, "Blackie? Tell you the absolute truth, I didn't really know him that good. He was part of the Arthur Avenue crowd. I'm kinda downtown myself."

I nodded, draining off a little more liquid courage. "The other day you told me you were an old friend of his."

"We met, but not really friends. I hadda say somethin', right?"

"I guess you did," I said.

"Never knew him," the younger man said, obviously deciding it was time to enter the conversation. "Heard he was a fun guy though." He looked at his cohort for agreement.

"Funny?" the older man asked.

"No, not funny," the younger man said. "Fun. You know, like a good guy."

"Oh, yeah, yeah, I hear he was."

I studied each of them without speaking. They had neither the intelligence nor the motive to lie to me, and neither of them was that good an actor. I puffed out my cheeks and let out a long breath, but my head and chest kept a strong and steady pulse. "Too bad," I said, meaning that in more ways than one. "You would have liked Blackie. He would have liked you too, I bet."

"Look kid, let's get on with this. We know you're a straight guy. Don't make no trouble for yourself, all right?"

"It's all right with me, except I still don't know what you're talking about."

They looked at each other again before the older man said, "You gonna work with us or not?"

I leaned forward a bit, so I was right in his face. "Now pay attention, because I want to be really clear about this. I have no idea what you're after, but I can guess that your boss probably heard some bullshit from my cousin Frank who, I don't mind telling you, is a certified scumbag of the first order, so take that into account when he's feeding you his stories. You can tell your boss that I'll sit and talk with him any time about my father, if that's what he wants, but he better check out Frank first. I'm sure he'll discover he was sold a load of crap. You can also tell your boss that my father's slate was wiped clean six years ago—the hard way, as I hear the story—and you can tell him I said that too. Tell him exactly that, the slate got wiped clean the hard way. All of which, I understand, has already been conveyed to your friends out in Vegas." I drank off some more of the cocktail, never taking my eyes off him. "Now, I think it's time for us to say goodbye."

The younger guy didn't seem all that impressed with my speech. "You play it smart or you play it stupid, that's up to you."

I stood up, ignoring him and turning back to the older man. "Last time, you barged into my apartment, telling me you were some old friend of my father. This time I know who I'm dealing with, which happens to be a couple of guys who have no fucking idea what they're talking about or why they got sent on this little errand in the first place. Am I right?"

The younger man lowered his voice. "You're talkin' pretty tough today, for a guy I hear can't take a punch."

I took a step toward his seat, so we were almost up against each other as I stood over him. "I've had a few interesting days of training on that score, so you do what you're big enough to do."

The older man stood up. "That goes for you too, kid. We tell the man what you're up to, then it's whatever. You understand?"

Without taking my eyes off the younger man, I said, "I understand perfectly."

Since there wasn't anything left for them to do, they each took a swig of their beers, as if it were some sort of team event.

"It's not important to us," the older man finally said, "not one way or another."

"Me either," I told him, "so tell your boss everything I said, because if he thinks this is my way of playing it tough, he's got it all wrong. The guy you should be talking to is my cousin Frank. Let him tell you what he thinks I've got, which he found out is nothing. Then you won't have to bother me again."

The older man started to say something, then stopped.

I lifted my glass and finished off the drink. "Now I'm going back to my world and you can go back to yours, and if you want to talk to me again, call and make a fucking appointment and I'll be sure to have the FBI with me." With that, I pulled a business card out of my jacket and threw it on the table. "And thanks for the drink," I said. Then I turned and walked away, feeling like I had checked off one more item on a very old list.

* * *

THE NEXT DAY I FIGURED IT OUT.

It happened, as these things tend to happen, in the dead of night. I woke up thinking about my father, realizing that I knew him well enough to guess what he would have done in those weeks before they came for him, in those final days when he wrote me the letter, when he was trying to arrange for something he'd never done before, the fencing of a multi-million dollar painting. I realized all I had to do was think about it the way he would have.

For starters, Blackie never intended to put me at risk, so he certainly wouldn't have stuck me with a stolen painting, not without telling me I had it.

He also wouldn't take the chance of losing the Monet by leaving it storage or some other such place.

He knew that Benny didn't want any part of it, and I believed Benny when he said he didn't have the painting and didn't know where it was.

Which meant there was only one other person he would trust enough to hold the Monet.

That afternoon I made the phone call, then left the office, got in my car and made the drive alone, my memory bank spinning into overtime all the way up the highway and across the Tappan Zee Bridge.

When I pulled into the driveway I sat there, staring out the windshield at the familiar house. It struck me how the place looked smaller than I remembered it. Odd, how when you're a kid things seem so much bigger and more important.

After a minute or so, I got out and walked up to the front door. He opened it before I could ring the bell.

I said, "Hello Uncle Vincent."

"I heard you pull in."

I had not seen him since my Aunt Mary's funeral. He looked frail and even a little shorter than he used to be. His hair was combed straight back, just as he'd always worn it, but it was whiter and thinner now. He reminded me of my grandfather.

"We need to talk," I told him.

"I know," he said.

I followed him inside. The house looked the same as it always did, except it was older and worn and it had that stuffy smell of old people, as if all the doors and windows ought to be thrown wide open for about a week.

He led me into the living room, and before we sat down he asked if I'd like a drink. I said I would.

He left me there, standing in the room where I'd spent so many weekends and holidays, so many birthdays and weddings and wakes. I watched the ghosts milling around the room, none of whom seemed any more surprised to find me there than my Uncle Vincent did.

When he came back he was carrying a bottle of Johnnie Walker Black in one hand and two shot glasses in the other. "You gonna need water?" he asked.

I shook my head.

"Good boy," he said with a wan smile. Then we sat down, opposite each other across the well-worn oak cocktail table, and he poured us each a full jigger of scotch. "Here's to your father," he said, hoisting his glass.

I held mine up and touched it to his, then we threw back the drinks. He filled the glasses again before we spoke.

"I know everything now," I told him. "Everything."

He nodded slightly. "I'm sorry you had to find out."

"Why?"

"So many reasons, son. So many reasons." He didn't wait for me as he drank down the second shot. "Can't fly on one wing," he said.

"Guess not," I agreed, and lifted my glass. "To truth," I said, and drank it off just the way he'd shown me years before, when we got drunk together, a few weeks after Blackie died.

"I loved your father, you know. I loved him very much."

"I know you did. For whatever that's worth."

He eyed me expectantly, as if there was something else to say about it.

"So," I asked again, "why are you sorry I know?"

His posture was very straight, as it always was because of his stiff back. He placed his palms flat on his thighs, as if he were in the military, sitting at attention in the presence of a commanding officer. "Your father loved you more than you can know. He wouldn't want you to think badly of him."

"Why should I?" I asked. "We all make mistakes. He paid for his."

Uncle Vincent couldn't look at me now. He said, "We all pay for our mistakes, one way or another. Some of us just have to live with them longer than others." Then he leaned forward and lifted the bottle to fill our glasses.

I told him I'd like to talk a little more before I had another drink.

"All right," he said, setting the bottle back on the table.

I looked around the room, watching as the ghosts gathered close around us. I said, "You've always known the truth, haven't you?"

He didn't move, didn't look at me. "Whatever we think that truth is, yes, I've known since a short time after."

"A short time after my father died?"

He inclined his head forward as if he was nodding, then seemed to have trouble sitting back. When he did, I could see he was crying.

"You should have told me," I said.

He was silent for what seemed a long time. "How could I?" he finally replied.

I reached out and poured us each that next drink. I lifted my glass and waited for him to do the same. "I miss him," I said, my voice giving way to my feelings.

"So do I," my uncle said. "Every day of my life. Every single day." Then we drank again.

I put down my shot glass, feeling the warmth of the scotch course through me. Then I said simply, "I think you have something for me. That's why I'm here."

He didn't say anything in response. He got slowly to his feet and walked out of the room. When I heard him going down into the basement, I stood up again, having another look around the room. That's when I heard the front door to the house open and close. I turned, not completely shocked to see my cousin Frank.

"Well," I said, "the gang's all here."

Frank showed me his pearly whites. "Yeah cuz, 'bout time we settled this thing, don't you think."

"Oh yes," I agreed.

We stood there in silence for a moment, until we heard my uncle coming back up the stairs from the basement. He was holding a green metal cylinder, a couple of feet long and a few inches in diameter.

When he saw his son in the entryway he said, "Frank," somewhere between surprise and relief.

Before anyone spoke again, I walked over and took the container from my uncle's hand. The metal was cold. The ends of the cylinder were crudely sealed with wax, a Blackie move if ever there was one, like something from a gothic novel. Whatever was inside had been locked in there for a long time.

"You've had this for all these years?" I asked.

"Since a couple of weeks before…before he died."

"Why didn't you give it to me?"

My uncle uttered a long, uneven sigh. "He told me never to open it and never to give it to anyone except you. But only if you asked for it."

I nodded. "And you've kept it for all these years, without opening it, without ever telling anyone about it."

"No one," he said. When he looked at me, his eyes moist and sunken and sad. "I never told anyone. It was the least I could do. Once I knew what happened, it was the least I could do, to keep that promise."

"So," Frank asked, "what the hell is this thing?"

I ignored my cousin, for a moment trying to imagine what it must be like for my uncle, knowing that his brother had come to him for money, that he turned him down, and then living with how that ended up. I told Frank, "It doesn't matter what it is. It's over."

My Uncle Vincent took a deep, halting breath. "I feel like I killed him," he said. "You understand that? I might as well have beaten him to death myself." He was sobbing now, and I watched him cry without saying anything. He steadied himself, then said, "Frank, you're my son, but he's right, this has nothing to do with you."

But Frank didn't care about what happened to Blackie, what his own father had to do with that, or anything other than what I was holding in my hand. "This has everything to do with me," my cousin said, giving me a look that was supposed to worry me.

Not feeling particularly worried, I said, "Too bad you feel that way, because you're wrong." Then to my uncle, I said, "I'm glad you never told anyone. I know my father would have been glad."

He nodded slowly. "I never opened it, still don't know what's in it." He tried to smile, but it didn't work. "You need to believe that. It was like a matter of faith for me. I couldn't bring myself to look."

Frank took a couple of steps forward. "I think I'll take a look," he said. Then he held out his hand. "Let's have it cuz."

I stared at him. "You must be kidding."

"Don't make any more trouble for yourself. Just hand that over and we'll figure out what we're going to do with it, right here, right now."

I thought of a lot of clever things to say, which would be my usual reaction to a situation like this, but I let them all pass because I also thought of Blackie, and how I hadn't followed his advice when Sluggo got the drop on me in front of the casino in Monte Carlo. Determined not to make that mistake again, I didn't say anything at all, waiting until Frank took one step closer. Then I swung the metal canister like a baseball bat, hitting him across the side of the head with a shot that would have been a double in any ballpark in the country.

He staggered back and I moved forward, driving the end of the container up under his chin, knocking him off his feet and onto the ground, flat on his back.

I stood over him, watching the blood begin to run from the side of his mouth. "Look out," I said, "you're going to stain your fancy white shirt, *cuz*."

He muttered something like, "What the fuck," then appeared to be on the brink of losing consciousness. His father hurried to his side and kneeled down. Then he looked up at me.

"What are you doing?" my uncle moaned.

I looked at the two of them, figuring fathers and sons get what they deserve in the end. "He's lucky I don't kill him," I said, then walked past them and out the door.

I have to admit, I kept looking in my rearview mirror on the ride home, imagining guys pulling up alongside me, or worrying about what might happen later, if they came crashing through the door of my apartment in the middle of the night to take the painting and slit my throat. But I remembered what Inspector Durand had told Frank's pals and decided my days of worrying were over.

I got home, parked the car in the basement garage and went upstairs, locked myself in, pulled the window shades closed and sat in the living room where I had first opened my father's box of memories, just a week before.

I broke the wax seal of the canister with a pocket knife and slowly pulled out the rolled up canvas. I flattened it out on the table, then stood over it, gaping at the most beautiful painting I had ever held, a Monet sunset on the water.

* * *

It was too late to call France, so I telephoned Gilles the next morning.

He asked how I was getting on with Donna. I told him I'd arranged a business trip to Las Vegas the following week, and that she would be coming back to New York for a long weekend after that. He was pleased, saying that the connection between us, having been made through Benny, gave the entire romance a special quality, particularly for him. He said I should never forget that she was a special lady.

I promised never to forget.

I did not tell him about the visit with the two men in the airport, not wanting him to worry about me any more than he already did. As far as I was concerned, all of that was over and done.

Then I explained, in the most cryptic terms, that I had located the item. He said he was happy, but sounded concerned about the trouble I might cause myself. I told him I had a plan, and that I had already deposited the article in a safe place.

"It has no rightful owner," I said to him. "Not even you and me. But there has to be a certain order to things, don't you think?"

He agreed.

When I told him my plan he said he was proud of me.

I thanked him.

He said my father would be proud too.

I told him I wasn't too sure about that.

* * *

A MONTH AFTER THAT CONVERSATION, just a couple of weeks before Christmas, I received a package from Nice. Frederique Durand wrote to say that the cancer Monsieur de la Houssay struggled against for the past few years had finally won its grim victory, and our friend was no more.

The package Durand sent with his note contained a medal for valor that Monsieur de la Houssay had received in the war, and a sealed envelope. Inside was a letter from Gilles, telling me how much our coming to know each other had meant to him, and how he wanted me to keep this medal, his most prized possession, because I could now appreciate the significance it had for him. He also said again how pleased he was that I had found our mythical treasure and how happy it made him to know that I, as Blackie would say, was doing the right thing.

* * *

REMEMBER THAT RALLY I PASSED outside the United Nations? Well I started thinking about it as soon as I took the painting from my uncle's house. I also thought about everything Gilles told me about their mission in France at the end of the war. He and my father and Benny had left it to me to figure out what to do with the Monet, so I did.

I knew someone involved with plans to raise funds for a new museum that was being constructed—as it was explained to me, it was a memorial being built so the world would never forget. I shouldn't say more than that, for reasons that should be apparent. The important thing was that the painting was going to be given a real purpose when it surfaced. The day after I got it from my uncle I placed it in a safe deposit box at a bank near my office. Then I did all the background checking I could about the museum project, making sure it was the right choice.

It was.

At my request, my contact arranged a meeting for us at the most prestigious auction house in New York. I collected the metal tube and headed uptown.

The art appraiser and my friend were pretty knocked out when I showed them the painting, which is understandable given how beautiful it is, so I allowed them a minute to catch their breath. Then I explained the conditions of the sale. The proceeds would be paid as an anonymous donation to the memorial fund. My identity would remain a secret, never to be revealed. And I had nothing more to say.

The appraiser obviously had about a thousand questions, especially about the painting's *provenance*, but I assured him there would be no dispute over the ownership.

"Do what you need to," I told him. "Whatever research, whatever background checking that has to be done." I knew what he would ultimately find—there was no one around to contest the ownership.

My friend and the representative from the auction house assured me that the entire thing would be handled with both the utmost discretion and—in response to a little something that I also demanded—total security. After all, I am Blackie's son, and I did not want to hear about the Monet getting itself stolen all over again. In fact, I had taken photos of the painting in my apartment, placing it beside a couple of daily newspapers, just in case it happened to turn up missing, or in someone's private collection, without the money going where it should.

After all those arrangements were made, I called Benny.

It was a tough conversation for many reasons, the first being that I had to tell him about Gilles's passing. Then, of course, was the fact that I was giving the painting away but, as Benny and I both knew, it was my decision, which was how all three of them wanted it. As the survivor of their threesome, I just wanted to be sure that Benny was all right with what I was doing.

He was.

* * *

THE PAINTING CAUSED QUITE A STIR in the art world, since it was a Monet that had not been seen by anyone for more than forty years. The evening of the auction I was offered a seat in the front row, but chose to sit in the back of the large room. I had already seen the painting close-up enough times, so I was fine there, waiting anxiously for the lot number to be called. As we approached the sale of my painting—which is how I will always feel about it—a sinister looking man in a dark suit sat down beside me. I glanced at his profile a couple of times and, when I turned toward him for a third glimpse, he was the one who spoke.

"Do I know you?" he asked.

"I don't think so," I said.

He opened his catalogue to the page that featured the main event of the evening, my Monet. "Some painting," he said as he showed me the picture.

"It is," I agreed.

"I read about it in the paper. Missing since before World War Two or something."

I nodded, my head bobbing up and down like it was on a spring. "That right?"

"Wonder where it's been."

I didn't respond. I just looked at him, waiting for more.

But that was it. He never said another thing to me.

It got me wondering again what Frank and his cronies thought. They had taken their run against me and Benny, but came up empty, never realizing what they were after. Neither my cousin Frank nor my Uncle Vincent knew there was a Monet in the metal canister I used to break my cousin's jaw, and they would never know how close they came to owning that prize. After all these years, I have never seen or spoken with either of them again.

The auction of the Monet was pretty wild and I won't make you sick by telling you how much some wealthy art collector paid just to have the right to have it put on display in a museum with his name on a plaque beside it. It truly is beautiful, and you'll probably see it some day in a Monet exhibition somewhere. The important thing, as far as I was concerned, was that the money went to good use.

Oh sure, I had some second thoughts, like maybe I should have gotten a finder's fee, or a commission, or even some sort of charitable tax write-off for the next fifty years. But it was like Blackie said, straight shooters always win, and I think that's the one piece of advice he'd really want me to hold onto. I've decided to stay with that and let the rest of it go—I figure I've already spent enough time wrestling with so many other lessons from the past.

ABOUT THE AUTHOR

Jeffrey S. Stephens is the author of the Jordan Sandor thrillers, *Targets of Deception*, *Targets of Opportunity*, *Targets of Revenge*, and *Rogue Mission*, as well as the murder mystery *Crimes and Passion*. A native of the Bronx, Stephens now lives in Greenwich, Connecticut, with his wife, Nancy, where they raised their two sons.